Praise for Zara Rahee[...]

The Marriag[...]

Named one of PopSugar's Best Books to Put in Your
Beachbag this summer and one of the best books of July

A Booktrib "Romance to get you in the swing for
Wedding Season" of 2019

A Book Riot "Five New Diverse Romantic Comedies"

Bustle's "21 new summer novels to spice up your summer
reading"

"An intimate and entertaining glimpse into the life of a
young Muslim American woman whose family wants her
married. Now! You'll want to read this in one sitting."
—Susan Elizabeth Phillips, *New York Times* bestselling author

"Please cancel your weekend plans, because once you dive
into *The Marriage Clock*, it'll be impossible to tear yourself
away. This romantic and insightful book introduces us to
Leila Abid, who's torn between her traditional parents trying to arrange her marriage and her own desire for agency."
—*Cosmopolitan*

"*The Marriage Clock* is a warm, funny debut novel about
love, how we find it, and how we can keep it."

—PopSugar

"Zara Raheem's *The Marriage Clock*, however, takes a unique and charming look at the beliefs we hold in regard to love and marriage. And that's precisely why readers should be adding this novel to their August TBR piles."

—Culturess

"Raheem's debut uses chick-lit tropes to smartly skewer modern ways of dating and to bring humor to more traditional South Asian ones."

—*Booklist*

"So fresh and charming and fun! I adored being in Leila's world, from her girls' nights with her friends to her conversations with her loving, pressuring parents to her many first dates. What a joy to read."

—Julia Phillips, author of *Disappearing Earth*

"Zara Raheem's *The Marriage Clock* is a unique, beautiful story about a woman coming to accept herself—and the notion that maybe marriage isn't everything."

—All About Romance

"Raheem dedicates the book to every woman who has ever been told she wasn't enough. In the face of ubiquitous cultural traditions that measure a woman's worth by her marriageability, Leila's journey shows us that the true measure of a woman's worth is that she values herself."

—Booktrib

The Retreat

ALSO BY ZARA RAHEEM

The Marriage Clock

The Retreat

A Novel

ZARA RAHEEM

WILLIAM MORROW

An Imprint of HarperCollins*Publishers*

THE RETREAT. Copyright © 2023 by Zara Raheem. All rights reserved. Printed in the United Kingdom. No part of this book may be used or reproduced in any manner whatsoever without written permission except in the case of brief quotations embodied in critical articles and reviews. For information, address Harper-Collins Publishers, 195 Broadway, New York, NY 10007.

HarperCollins books may be purchased for educational, business, or sales promotional use. For information, please email the Special Markets Department at SPsales@harpercollins.com.

FIRST EDITION

Designed by Diahann Sturge

Library of Congress Cataloging-in-Publication Data has been applied for.

ISBN 978-0-06-303500-3

23 24 25 26 CPI 10 9 8 7 6 5 4 3 2

For those we call sister.

Prologue

The moment she hears the dense thud against the glass, Nadia rushes into the parking lot to examine her car. If it weren't for the stiff quills of feathers strewn on the pavement near her front tire, she would've guessed it was just some piece of litter chucked from one of the passing vehicles on the busy thoroughfare fronting Tuttle's 19-Minute Photo Lab.

"Shit," she utters when she sees the tiny sparrow crumpled into a ball, its brown-speckled feathers ruffled into sharp spikes. Despite her typically composed demeanor, she's upset; mangled vertebrates are likely to unsettle anyone that early in the morning. Sliding the envelope into the pocket of her blazer, she kneels. "Please don't be dead," she mutters, lowering her face to the ground. The bird stares at her from beneath the front grille, its polished eyes blinking rapidly. After a few moments, it smooths its plumage, gives a quick shake of its wings, and hops into the parking lot, darting its tiny head with a stunned expression.

Nadia stands up, dusting the knees of her slacks. She looks up into the sky, cupping her right hand over her brows to shield her eyes from the sun. "Seriously?" she calls out, throwing her other arm up. "This is the best you can come up with?"

Ever since her mom died of cancer last summer, Nadia has had reason to believe she has been trying to communicate with her via nature, of all things. Though she's never confessed this belief to anyone, for fear of sounding ridiculous, how else can she explain the stray cat that suddenly appeared whenever she hid empty fast-food containers at the bottom of the recycling bin before her husband, Aman, came home? Or the vociferous owl who fitted itself in a cozy nook in the branches of the ficus tree right outside her bedroom window? She isn't intuitive enough to dig deeply into the meanings behind these encounters; however, the last twelve months have transformed her from someone who wittingly spent her life disconnected from the natural world into some aberrant Disney princess attracting forest fauna and winged creatures, much to her chagrin.

Dropping her right hand, she notices an elderly man parked directly behind her holding his car door open as he looks up at the patch of blue into which she was just shouting.

"Looks like rain," she says, pointing at the unclouded sky as he stares at her with furrowed brows. "Climate change, am I right?" She unlocks her car and slides into the driver's seat.

She waits until the man shuffles into the photo lab before removing the envelope from her blazer pocket. Lifting the flap, she pulls out the prints, expecting snaps of her and Aman from the past weekend; however, a sinking realization shocks her into silence the moment she sees the first photo. One by one she flips through the images, her thoughts racing in disbelief, as a startled cry escapes from her lips.

1

Two hours earlier, the only thing on Nadia's mind is breakfast as she sifts through the small stack of photographs left for her on the kitchen counter with the note: *Tell me what you think.*

The photographs were taken two days ago, on the morning of her thirty-fifth birthday. Aman pulled Nadia out of bed while the sky was still smudged in darkness, and the two of them drove to Abalone Cove, an ecological preserve just south of Los Angeles, and climbed the trails traversing the snaking bluff side. At first, Nadia was not thrilled. She would've preferred sleeping in, followed by a late brunch downtown, anything besides rigorous outdoor activity; however, seeing Aman behind the lens of his Pentax K1000 again almost made the early wake-up worth it. Almost.

"I can't believe we made it in time," Aman said as they stood atop Inspiration Point watching the upper dome of the sun bloom on the horizon—the golden rays fading into delicate pinks, creating a hue Nadia was convinced she had never seen before.

"Aren't you glad I stopped griping long enough for us to get up here?" she said, prodding for his reaction.

"Your words, not mine." Aman half grinned.

There was something about witnessing the first sunrise in her new year of life that made Nadia feel alive. In that moment, she craved Aman's touch; for him to wrap his arms around her, enclosing the intimacy that once occupied the space between them. But after ten years of marriage, she reminded herself that it was normal for outward forms of affection to fade over time and be replaced with something quieter—less obvious. While this reminder allowed her to avoid dwelling on the changes in their relationship, her desire for physical closeness still often consumed her, especially in moments like these.

As Aman stood a few feet beside her, absorbing the colors from behind his camera, she watched him snap photo after photo of the sun rising over the escarpment. He zoomed out to the west to catch a glimpse of the ocean peeking between the cliffs. Then he turned the camera toward her and took candid shots of her sun-kissed smiles, her face framed by wayward curls floating in the morning breeze. Though the glossy images in Nadia's hand now don't quite reflect the vibrancy of that morning as she remembers it, she is impressed nonetheless that Aman was able to capture its beauty to some degree.

AMAN'S LOVE FOR photography began long before he met Nadia, in his sophomore year of high school, when he signed up for an Intro to Black-and-White Photography class. The rest of his schedule crammed only with advanced placements, he desperately needed an extracurricular to round out his college application. Between home economics, theater, and photography, the latter was the only elective that his parents didn't outright oppose for their only son to take. Assuming it would be an easy class and nothing more, Aman did not expect to get swept up in the creative freedom the course offered. From behind the lens, he witnessed the world in its most raw and honest form—a perspective unshaped by external judgment and cultural expectations; an outlook to which he was instantly drawn and one he was unwilling to give up once exposed to its rarity.

During the first years of their marriage, Aman's camera was on hand to capture every birthday, anniversary, and moment in between. When they initially toured their future home, a 1930s Tudor in the heart of Cedar Heights, the deciding factor for them both was a large storage closet attached to the study.

"This would make an excellent darkroom," Aman exclaimed, admiring the oak-paneled walls and peg flooring.

"I was thinking more of a downstairs nursery," Nadia said. Newly graduated from optometry school, and with Aman finishing his final year of a cardiology fellowship, she felt certain their dreams of starting a family would come to fruition sooner than anticipated.

"What about the upstairs bedroom with the arched doorway?"

"That one too. Can't we have more than one?"

"It depends," Aman said, eyes flickering with amusement. "How many babies are we planning on having?"

"Enough to fill this entire house!" Nadia grinned, pirouetting into his arms, dizzy with delight.

While Aman eventually staked his claim on the darkroom, neither of them could have predicted that all these years later, the bedroom with the arched doorway would remain unoccupied. Each of them dealt with this reality by plunging deeper into their work, leaving hardly any time for much outside of that. But now and then, there were glimpses—like the morning of her birthday—that reminded Nadia of the Aman from years ago.

BACK IN THE kitchen, Nadia sorts through the photos, her eyes lingering on one. It is a picture Aman took of her unwrapping her birthday present soon after they returned from their hike. There was a large package sitting on their front porch, and Nadia immediately knew it belonged to her from the eagerness on Aman's face.

"Happy birthday, Nadi," he said, bringing it inside and setting it down on the dining table. He watched with bated breath as she ripped open the packaging with first her hands, and then a pair of kitchen shears. "I meant to wrap it, but they didn't ship it in time."

Nadia knew all too well that Aman had likely placed his order too late, but she smiled and played along, lifting the gadget from the box. "You got me a *Roomba!*" she said through pressed teeth, trying to contain the disappointment in her voice.

"Not just any Roomba; it's the s10. This one has an automatic disposal bin and a self-adjusting cleaner head—"

Nadia feigned interest as Aman ardently explained all the features to her in excruciating detail. His lack of awareness was endearing, and she couldn't help but smile when looking back at the photograph.

Like any married couple, she and Aman had experienced their share of growing pains over the course of their relationship, and she had long since accepted that romantic gestures would never be Aman's strong suit. Particularly when it came to gift-giving, his selections were influenced more by utility than by romance. Last year, Aman surprised Nadia with a food processor. The birthday before, it was a high-end mist humidifier. After a decade of birthdays like this, Nadia often teased Aman about how he at least always stuck to a theme. But deep down, she wished he were not so practical *all the time*. Though she had learned to temper her expectations over the years, she sometimes found herself wondering what it would be like to receive a bouquet of roses or an expensive bottle of perfume—the kinds of gifts her girlfriends flaunted on their social media. Captioning #husbandgoals under an ergonomically designed ironing board didn't quite get the same number of likes. But hashtags were not a part of Aman's domain, nor was social media. Gadgets and gizmos were the only love language he spoke.

Flipping to the final photo, she immediately notices something missing. The selfie she had begged Aman to take of the two of them atop Inspiration Point is not in the stack. Wanting to post the image for her #throwbackthursday, she spreads the photos out across the countertop and counts as she lines them up in rows of six.

Eighteen.

The film Aman uses is a twenty-four exposure. She knows this because he orders it online, like everything else, and she remembers seeing *24* in a bold blue font on empty boxes in his study just a few weeks back. She counts the photos again but arrives at the same number. Eighteen candid snapshots of just her or the sunrise—six photos are missing from the ones he left for her.

Upstairs, the shower door squeaks open, prompting Nadia to abandon the photographs and get back to her morning routine. In approximately twelve minutes, Aman will be downstairs dressed in a dark suit, a dab of cologne behind each ear, his thick hair neatly combed back. She places the teakettle on the stove, ignoring the high-pitched screeches from the water and her stomach as both boil to a bubble. Next, she places two slices of sprouted whole-grain bread in the toaster oven and rotates the knob until the coils turn orange. From the fridge, she gathers a few stalks of celery, kale, dandelion greens, and fresh ginger. As they mix in the blender, she carefully adds a few apple slices, half a lemon, and a sprinkle of turmeric. Lifting the lid, she samples the liquid with the tip of her finger, pleased by its consistency but repulsed by its taste. Why Aman insists on drinking this grassy muck every morning is beyond her.

"Something smells good," Aman says, walking into the kitchen just as she tops the toast with ripe avocado and a drizzle of agave. He smells of Brylcreem and aftershave, and she breathes in his familiar scent as she hands him his smoothie. Pressing her fingertip against the white porcelain, she lifts a stray bread crumb from the surface of the plate and sets it down where he sits.

"How have you not grown tired of drinking the same green drink for breakfast each morning?" she asks.

"Hmm?" Aman says, distracted by his phone.

Nadia sighs. For the last few months, Aman has been fixated on getting back into shape. Aside from frequenting the gym after work, he's also cut back on refined sugars and taken up meal prepping. At first, Nadia was all in; she too had developed some destructive eating habits since her mom's passing that she was ready to shed. However, she quickly realized that replacing two meals a day with barely digestible "smoothies" was not on par with her level of commitment.

"I'm just wondering when we can have donuts again."

"Donuts?" Aman asks, a slight disappointment coating his voice. "Eating clean isn't that bad once you get used to it." He takes a sip of the green sludge to prove his point.

"But we've been eating clean for months! Don't we get a cheat day at least?"

Aman raises his head.

"Okay, maybe not a whole day, but at least a cheat meal? Otherwise, what's the point?"

Aman sets his smoothie down and sighs. Once Nadia gets locked into a topic, it's difficult to pull her away. "Did you see the photos I printed?" he asks, changing the focus. "I think they came out good, although some of the images are a bit too warm."

She squeezes a few squirts of honey into her teacup and sits down on the stool beside him. The hot steam tickles her nose as she lifts the cup to her lips.

"I might have to go back and adjust the temperatures," he continues, biting into his toast.

"Are those all of them?" she asks of the photos lined up on the counter. "I think there might be some missing."

"That was everything on the film." His cell phone suddenly vibrates, and he stops midbite to check it. She glances at the screen but cannot make out the text. *Just work stuff*, he'll say if she asks what it's about, so she doesn't bother.

"What about the one we took of us on top of the cliff? I couldn't find it in the stack."

"It's probably in there, Nadi," Aman says as he types out a message with his thumb. "You just have to look through them."

"It's not," she says. She senses his impatience but feels compelled to ask again. "I counted only eighteen. I'm pretty sure there should be six more—"

"Nadia," Aman says, glancing at his watch. "Let's talk about it later. I have to get going." When she doesn't immediately respond, he pauses for a moment and softens his tone. "I'll review the film again tonight. Okay?"

"Sure." She takes a sip of her tea, but the liquid tastes bitter as it passes down her throat.

"I'm gonna head out, then," Aman says, taking a final

bite of his breakfast before getting up. He lifts his napkin and shakes the crumbs onto the floor.

"Aman! You're making a mess!"

"Relax," he says, walking over to the Roomba plugged in behind him. "That's why we got this guy. Why don't you give it a go?"

"Later," she says. "That thing might get all the crumbs from the floor, but there's no robot to clear away these dishes."

"*Yet.*" He arches his brow as Nadia suppresses a smile.

"What time will you be home?" she asks, using a towel to wipe away the leftovers.

"One of the interns is still out sick, so I might have to stay past my shift again," Aman says, pouring the dregs of his smoothie into the sink.

"But we have that dinner planned with Sheila and Damien."

"That's *tonight*?"

Nadia heaves a sigh. Her friend Sheila has been dating her new beau for four months now, and they have yet to meet him.

"Can't you reschedule it? Just tell them I have a thing."

"That's the excuse I gave the last time we canceled on them."

"I'm sorry, Nadi," Aman says, raking his fingers through his hair. "The hospital's been so busy lately. You know we've been short-staffed ever since Dr. Cole left."

"I know," Nadia cuts him short. They've had this conversation multiple times over the past few months. "I'll . . . figure something out."

Aman hesitates, as if deliberating how best to respond.

"It's okay. Really." She turns to him. "Now go, otherwise you'll be late. I have to get to work too."

"Okay." Aman nods, looking slightly relieved. He grabs his briefcase and heads toward the door. "I'll try my best to get home when I can. Don't wait up, though, if it gets too late."

As the grind of the garage door vibrates through the walls, Nadia turns her attention back to the kitchen. Before the low hum of Aman's Tesla fades into the street, Nadia finishes loading the dishwasher and wiping down the countertops. From her secret stash in the lower cupboard, she pulls out a Pop-Tart and leans against the countertop. Her stomach grumbles as she unwraps the aluminum foil, pressing it down into silver ripples. Reveling in the pasty sweetness, she thumbs through her newsfeed, scrolling aimlessly through a never-ending highlight reel. Amid the perfectly curated photos of her friends' lives, it is always the baby posts or pregnancy announcements that strike her the sharpest. "Allahumma barik," she whispers out of habit.

"YOU WANT ME to say a prayer for someone else?" was Nadia's exact reaction the first time her mom told her to repeat those words. She couldn't believe her mom would even suggest such a thing after she had just expressed how unfair it was that Monica Rinaldi had won first prize—a coveted handheld electronic dictionary—for collecting the most canned goods in their grade for the schoolwide food drive.

"But both her parents are pastors! They know practically everyone in town. Of course she brought in the most cans. That dictionary should've been mine!"

Unlike Monica, who had an entire congregation at her disposal, Nadia and her sister, Zeba, had spent weeks trudging door-to-door, collecting an impressive 263 cans, just to be eclipsed by her fourth-grade rival.

"Jealousy leads to nazr, Nadia, and that's not something you should sully someone else's happiness with."

"But what about *my* happiness?"

Her mom sighed. Evil eye was something her mom had always been very cautious of. She believed any bad luck was a direct result of someone's envy or dislike, so all good things—no matter how small or big—were to be closely guarded, almost to the point of paranoia. Although Nadia regarded her mom's advice, she didn't think her mom fully comprehended the value of what had been lost.

"You know how much I wanted that electronic dictionary. It has a hundred and fifty thousand words in its data bank with an eight-line display screen!"

"Asking for protection over someone else's blessings indirectly opens the door for those same blessings to come to you."

Her mom's insistence forced Nadia into reluctantly praying for Monica's blessing, but she felt doubtful at the time that a similar fortune would come into her life. It was far too expensive a device to even make that thought plausible. However, when less than a month later, her mom hauled in an almost complete set of the *Encyclopedia Britannica* that she had haggled down to ten dollars at a neighbor's garage sale, Nadia wondered if that blessing—albeit less cutting-edge—had been returned in its own way.

SINCE THAT EXPERIENCE, Nadia often recited "Allahumma barik" to deter any unwanted feelings of envy; however, those words didn't always protect against the sadness that sometimes lingered beneath. Despite all the babies and pregnancies she's prayed blessings upon, here she is, still waiting to be granted that same stroke of luck.

A sudden chime of notifications pulls Nadia from her thoughts, and she looks down at the screen of flashing messages. The first is a text from Sheila with the location of the restaurant where Nadia and Aman are supposed to meet them for dinner. She clicks on the message bar and begins typing.

Don't be mad, but Aman's working late. I promise I'll make it up to you. So sorry!

She hits "send" and sighs, placing the phone on the counter. She stares at the Roomba plugged into the outlet stationed across from her. The six buttons curved along the circular front panel glow white, reminding her that the crumbs on the floor still need to be cleared. Regretting not asking Aman for a quick tutorial before he left, she goes into his study to try to find the instruction manual.

Of all the rooms in the house, the study is the one that gives Nadia the most anxiety. *Organized chaos* is how Aman describes it, but all she sees are dust-coated bookshelves, thick piles of paperwork, and layers of rings around half-filled coffee mugs littering every surface. Unsure where to begin, she checks the filing cabinets first, but the drawers are all locked, even though she sees papers poking out of the edges. Pushing aside reams of clutter, she rummages through Aman's desk next and even skims the bookcases along the wall, but with no luck. Feeling impatient, she decides to figure it out without the manual. *How hard can it be?* she thinks. But as she is about to exit, she notices the door of the attached storage closet slightly ajar.

Though Aman doesn't typically allow anyone in his darkroom without him, her mind drifts back to the missing photographs from earlier and wonders if she might succeed in finding the ones she is looking for. Knowing Aman, he'll likely be too tired to look for them by the time he arrives home anyway. She pushes open the door the rest of the way and flips on the light switch, blinking as her eyes adjust to the red glow. Immediately, she scrunches her nose as a heady blend of chemicals inundates her senses, greeting her with the tartness of vinegar and sweetness of gasoline. Holding her breath, she walks around the room, fingers grazing the plastic trays along the center worktable, each with its own set of tongs. On a small shelf sit a handful of tube bottles with handwritten labels that read: DEV. FIX. STOP. Next to it, in a far corner, hangs a string of photographs that she recognizes on closer look as duplicates from the ones in her stack. Unlike Aman's study, every inch of his darkroom is tidy and organized, causing her to feel less at ease about poking around.

When she turns to switch off the light, her eyes are drawn to the open wastebasket near the door. Leaning down, she pushes aside some crumpled photo paper to find a single strip of negatives peeking out from beneath. Touching only the edges, she lifts the film, holding it against the light streaming from the doorway. She narrows her eyes to squint at the black-and-white images but cannot make out what is on them. They are too small and shadowy. It is clear, however, that the film bears a sequence of six images—the exact number of photos missing from the stack.

Bingo. She smiles. She considers texting Aman to show

him what she found—as proof of her rightness—but then she'll have to confess to him about going into his darkroom. She changes her mind, placing the strip of negatives into a white envelope that she finds on Aman's desk and carrying it upstairs. It is almost eight by the time she's showered and finishes dressing.

"Call the clinic," she tells her phone while swiping on a second coat of mascara. It takes a few rings before Julie, her front desk receptionist, finally picks up.

"Nadia's Optometry Clinic, how can I assist you?"

A shiver of pride still passes through Nadia whenever she hears that greeting. Financing her way through college was no easy feat, so to become an optometrist—one with her own practice—is more than she ever imagined for herself. "Julie, hi. It's me, Nadia. What does my morning look like?"

"Your appointment with Mr. Sedonis got canceled, so your first patient doesn't come in until ten."

"Can you see if you can push that appointment back another half hour? I have to make a quick stop before I come in."

She places the envelope into the pocket of her blazer and tucks in her camisole. She has a little over an hour left, which is just enough time to locate a photo lab and see if they can print out the negatives. She twists her hair into a low bun and secures it with a tortoiseshell clip, pulling out a few loose strands to frame her face. There might even be time, if she plans it out right, to pick up a fruit bowl to balance out the Pop-Tart from earlier. *Aman would be proud,* she thinks as she fishes her car keys from the bottom of her purse and steps out of the house.

2

TUTTLE'S 19-MINUTE PHOTO LAB read the letters on the window.

A quick Google search brought Nadia to a small, unimposing storefront on the other side of town—the only place within a fifteen-mile radius that still develops 35mm film. If it weren't for the sign and the specific directions on her GPS, she never would have spotted the tiny lab squished between a dog groomer and a shuttered nail salon. The wiry man behind the counter, Todd—according to the name tag pinned to his wrinkled shirt—tells Nadia that her prints will be ready in approximately twenty minutes.

Turning to her phone, she bides her time by checking to see if there are any fruit stands or juice bars open nearby. A few options come up. As she glances over their menus, she fights back her cravings for a breakfast burrito over an açai bowl. Undecided, she switches back to her notifications and scrolls through the birthday posts she received over the weekend.

Happy birthday, Nadia!

Many happy returns!

Wishing you all the best.

For a fleeting moment, she is touched by the messages, even though aside from Sheila and a handful of others, most are from people whom she barely interacts with and won't likely hear from again until next year. The one message that surprises her the most, however, is from her sister, Zeba.

Happy birthday, Nadi . . . we miss you.

Nadia's finger hovers over the "like" button as she reads it again.

. . . we miss you.

An image of her nephews pops into her mind, and she feels a rush of sadness course through her.

WHEN SHE AND Zeba were children, the two were inseparable and constantly mistaken for twins, despite there being a two-year difference between them. Nadia ungrudgingly lived in Zeba's shadow for the first third of her life, holding her in the highest esteem. There was no one who possessed a more extensive Nancy Drew collection, could obtain all six Chaos Emeralds in *Sonic the Hedgehog*, and knew how to weave the perfect fishtail braid. Beneath that admiration, though, she wished Zeba feared less, conformed less. Whereas duty and responsibility were qualities Nadia worked actively to mind, with Zeba, they came intuitively—the threat of opposition never even arising as an option.

It wasn't until Nadia moved away for college that she finally started shedding layers of Zeba's identity to make room for her own. Though Zeba often voiced her disapproval of Nadia's decision to live independently while Zeba commuted from home for years, they still maintained their bond even through the distance. If a day went by without hearing her sister's voice, Nadia felt the absence. It was their mom's illness, however, that put the heaviest strain on their relationship.

As Zeba became the primary caretaker, the one her mom

relied on for doctor's appointments, radiation sessions, and emotional support, an unspoken resentment wedged between them. With their mom requiring more around-the-clock assistance, Nadia's standing in the family, which was shaky to start with, felt even less significant. Her presence became superfluous. So, she did what she thought best: she retreated, causing a rift between them that they never quite recovered from. Daily calls dwindled to weekly calls, which soon turned into emergency-only calls—and when their mom eventually passed, all communication ceased indefinitely. It was not that Nadia had stopped caring. In fact, she thought of Zeba often, wondering if there was a way to bridge the divide. But without an easy answer to explain her withdrawal, she saw no point in trying . . .

REREADING HER SISTER'S message triggers old feelings. As she presses the "like" button, her phone chimes with another message from Sheila.

No excuses! Still come! It'll give us a chance to celebrate your birthday too. Damien won't mind.

While Nadia appreciates Sheila's offer, an evening of third-wheeling sounds less than fun.

I don't want to impose . . . she types, to which Sheila responds immediately.

Better yet, what if we ditch the boys altogether and just make it a girls' night? I can call Maryam to see if she's available.

Suddenly the offer sounds a lot more enticing. Nadia hesitates a moment, considering the idea. It has been ages since she went out for a proper girls' night. What used to be regular occurrences in her twenties have been rare and uncommon in this current decade—unless they included the added company of significant others. As she wonders how to respond to Sheila's new proposition, Todd emerges with an envelope.

"Your prints are ready," he says, handing it to her. While she waits for him to process the service fee, she messages Sheila back.

I'm in. Keep me posted.

She exits the store just as the sparrow makes its crash landing into her windshield. Troubled and dismayed by yet another one of her mom's "surprise" visits, she is even less prepared for the shock of what follows.

NADIA FEELS STILL, in a strange trance almost, as she fastens her seat belt. Even her heartbeat is steady, beating in silence along with the start press of the engine. She backs out of the parking spot carefully just in case the sparrow is still puttering about underneath.

The envelope sits in the back seat, as far from her as possible. Struggling to keep her focus, her mind keeps drifting back to what she saw on the film.

A romantic candlelit dinner.

A silk tablecloth covered in rose petals.

A rooftop terrace with a city-lights view.

Nadia turns the radio up to drown out the interference and concentrates on the traffic signal ahead, beckoning her with its bright emerald hue.

A shadowy photo of Aman's fingers wrapped in someone else's hand and another of three long-stemmed roses beside a card that reads *Happy Anniversary, baby.*

Though the selfie she and Aman took on Inspiration Point is also on the film, the other five photos are what capture her attention, lodging themselves into the dark recesses of her mind. She tries to make sense of what she is feeling. *Confused?* Partly. But it's heavier than that. *Maybe angry?* But not like last week when Aman left a stray navy-colored sock in her load of whites and turned her new organic hemmed bedsheets a drab shade of blue. No, this feeling is different. Unfamiliar.

After ten years together, could Aman actually—Nadia shakes the thought from her mind and stares at the road in front of her. However, that strange ache continues to tug at her. It is a feeling she has not felt since the early days of their marriage. It's doubt.

She cuts across the street to make a U-turn, zooming past the intersection while keeping an eye out for the nearest freeway ramp. As unsettled as she feels, *This is Aman*, she reminds herself. Aman, who relies on his Google calendar to schedule all their dates because he can never remember otherwise. Aman, who can't watch more than one TV show at a time because he has trouble keeping track of all the story lines. Aman, who thinks nothing of tossing a film strip into an open wastebasket without even bothering to properly conceal it. The Aman she knows isn't capable of being duplicitous; he doesn't have the finesse. Still, she can't ignore that feeling of doubt constricting every muscle in her chest. Pressing her foot to the pedal, she picks up speed, passing another light just as it turns yellow and hurtling down the street as her mind continues to wander.

"AT LEAST YOU two can consider yourselves above average," Dr. Soufan said to her and Aman in his office last January. His eyes shrank beneath his overgrown brows as he offered an apologetic smile. Three is the number of IVF cycles it takes on average to achieve pregnancy, she and Aman were told. Three was the number for which they had been emotionally prepared. For almost two years, they had followed every rule. They went to all the appointments; they set alarms making sure the twice daily cocktail of injections was being taken at its respective times; they did their best to relax and keep a positive mindset. But when on the fourth attempt they learned that their efforts had failed yet again, it was one blow too many.

"So, what can we do?" Nadia remembers Aman asking. His voice was small, the disappointment in his face impossible to conceal. Dr. Soufan outlined the next steps, speaking slowly and methodically as Nadia stared at the bookcase behind his desk. Failure pressed down on her as she glanced at the photographs scattered on the shelves—of his wife and three children. Of their completed family and unmitigated access to a world to which neither she nor Aman could seem to gain entry.

On the drive back home, she finally broke down. "I don't think we should try again. I can't go through another failed cycle. It's not working. Nothing we're doing is working." The pain of her admission was immense; the only person capable of easing it was Aman. But unlike in the past, Aman's reaction was silence. He did not reach across the console and take her by the hand. He did not tell her he understood or remind her that the devastation she carried was shared. Instead, when they reached home, he went into his study and closed the door, leaving her on the other side to process the grief on her own.

FINDING HERSELF ON the outside again, Nadia feels that same desperation resurfacing. With a shaky finger, she taps the first number listed in her favorites, but it goes straight to voice mail.

"You've reached Aman's phone. Leave a message or send a text, unless it's an emergency, in which case, dial 911!"

She ends the call without waiting for the beep. Although it's not uncommon for Aman to not pick up these days, the missed connection introduces a new set of anxieties—ones she had never considered before. If the photos are evidence of an affair, then Aman's lack of availability suddenly takes on a different meaning. All the late nights at work. The overtime shifts. Her head reels with unanswered questions as she goes back and forth, trying to untangle the truth from past conversations. Nauseated, she taps on the next number listed in her favorites. She glances at the clock on her dashboard. It reads a quarter to ten. There is not much time left before her first appointment.

"Hey, Julie," she says as soon as it connects. Drawing a deep inhale, she steadies the tremor in her voice. "Listen, I'm actually not feeling well . . . No, nothing serious, but I think I'm going to take the day off to rest." She pauses as Julie reads out the appointment cards, feeling thankful that Mondays are not their busiest. "Sure, do the best you can. I'll be back in tomorrow."

Confident in Julie's ability to get it all sorted, Nadia drops her phone on the passenger seat and merges onto the freeway, heading this time in the opposite direction. For miles, she drives down a route that she's avoided for months but can still recall by memory. Crossing over the bridge, the six-lane freeway narrows; the dense greenery bordering the other side of the river faces boxlike factories sprouting plumes of black smoke into the smoggy air. Maneuvering through the streets, she drives past the eight-screen Metro-plex and the Ridge Park Library, where she used to ride her bike after school. On her left, she sees the empty parking lot of South Village Mall, where Zeba taught her how to paral-lel park. Every so often, she releases the accelerator to dip around misshapen craters that blemish the road. When she reaches the end of Junipero Street, she presses up against the steering wheel in anticipation of the stuccoed half-moon signage marking the entrance of Casa Del Rey—a compact subdivision of older ranch-style homes not far from the neighborhood where she grew up.

When she sees it, she slows down and turns into the tract. The landscape of the neighborhood is sparse, brown lawns flanked by cracked sidewalks—each street named after the trees that have been razed to make room for more houses. Careening past a few kids playing basketball in the street, Nadia drives to the end of the cul-de-sac, circling around until she is parked in front of a cantaloupe-colored house with overgrown hostas lining the graveled walkway. The front door is shut, but behind the pulled curtains, the glow of a television screen flickers from the front windows of the living room. She picks up her phone and scrolls to the bottom of her contacts, tapping on the final name on the list.

"Hello?" a dulcet voice answers on the second ring.

"Salaams . . . hi. It's me, Nadia," she replies. From the other end, she hears Zeba take in a sharp breath. It's been almost a year since she and her sister have spoken; the last time was the morning of their mom's janazah. She imagines Zeba leaning against the kitchen table, phone wedged between her ear and shoulder, contemplating how to respond.

"I was driving through the neighborhood . . . and I just thought I might stop by for a bit."

Apart from the sound of her breathing, Zeba is silent on the other end.

Nadia shrinks into the seat, her cheeks feeling hot. Even through the phone, she knows her sister can tell she is lying. "I'm actually parked outside your house now." She hears shuffling from the other end and pictures Zeba peeking through the blinds to see if she's there. "But if now is not a good time, I can always come back—"

The front door swings open, and Zeba stands in the rectangular frame: black leggings, an oversize T-shirt, and a checkered scarf chicly twisted into a turban atop her head. She holds the phone against her ear with one hand, the other akimbo at her waist.

"Are you just going to sit there or are you planning on coming in?" Her tone is impatient but not unfriendly.

Nadia shuts off the engine and feels her shoulders release from her ears. It is the first sense of relief she has felt all morning.

3

___

Short bursts of laughter cut through the small kitchen. Nadia and Zeba sit on opposite ends of the table, listening to Noman and his baby brother, Alim, on the other side of the pass-through window. Neither of the boys notices Nadia walk into the house; they sit in a glassy-eyed stupor, fixated on the animated puppies dancing on the screen. She knows they are too young to know any better, only five and three, but still their nonacknowledgment stings as she realizes the *"we miss you"* from her sister's message was more figurative than literal.

Sitting across from Zeba, Nadia is reminded of the long stretch of time that has passed since her last visit. The conversation that used to flow with ease between them now feels taxing, charged with whatever guilt and resentments each has been harboring since their mom's death.

"How have you been?"

Zeba stares back, responding only with a shrug.

"Shit, doggo. Shit down!" they hear Alim shout at the screen. The floorboards creak under his heels as he bounces excitedly off the couch.

"It's *sit*, Alim. You're saying it wrong," Noman corrects his little brother.

Nadia clears her throat. "The boys have gotten so big, masha'Allah. Alim was barely talking the last time I saw him."

"That's because the last time you saw him was a year ago." Zeba looks toward the other room. "He turned three last month."

"I saw the photos you posted of his party." Nadia feels the heat rise to her face. "I'm sorry we couldn't make it. Aman had a thing . . ."

Her sister looks at her, unconvinced. Nadia swallows, realizing she's been caught in another lie. Although it was true Aman was working the day of Alim's party, Nadia had every intention of attending on her own. She had ordered balloons and even picked up a Farm Animals Lego set for him. But just as she was about to leave, the anxiety of seeing Zeba again—this time without their mom present— was too intense. Rather than deal with it, she fell back on an excuse to not show up.

From the other room, they hear Noman bellow over his brother. "Alim, *shush*! Be quiet or else I'm going to *shit* on you!"

"Sounds like they're getting along," Nadia says as Zeba rushes to the pass-through window.

"Stop that, Noman," she calls out. "Be nice to your brother." She leans against the counter and pinches the space between her brows. Nadia walks up to her, recognizing the exhaustion in her slumped shoulders.

"They're just boys," she reassures her. "Remember all the fights we had as kids? It's normal."

"Normal?" Zeba remarks. "The other day I caught Noman staring at the microwave. When I asked him what he was doing, he said, 'Mummy, how long do you think it would take to cook Alim?'"

"Fuck," Nadia mutters as she watches the older boy mount the couch and belly-flop onto his brother's face.

"He's an Abbasi," Zeba says. "How normal can he be?"

Before Nadia can respond, Alim runs into the kitchen— his cheeks as red as the Superman logo on the rump of his pants. "Noman hip me," he cries, tears trickling down his chin.

"Aw, aloo, come here," Zeba says, reaching down to pick him up. She uses the cuff of her T-shirt to wipe the snot from his nose as he rattles off his complaints in choppy, mispronounced words. A sharp pang twists at Nadia's side as she watches the child cradle Zeba's face with his small hands, making sure her attention remains only on him. While Zeba coaxes him with small kisses, Nadia is struck by the emptiness in her own life.

NADIA WAS ONLY five, around Noman's age, when her and Zeba's father first disappeared. One day he went out to buy some milk from the grocery store, and he simply didn't return. For months afterward, his clothes still hung in the closet. His shoes stayed lined up at the door. Even his toothbrush, with its frayed bristles and black molded base, sat in the holder untouched. His remnants remained visible from every corner of their home, almost to the point of suffocation, as if they were just holding their breath waiting for him to reappear.

When he finally did, he'd stay for only a weekend or so every few months, but each time their mom would make a big show of it. She'd clean the house from surface to ceiling. She'd prepare pots of food—lamb pulao and goat biryani and mutton korma—all the meats that were too expensive to buy when it was just the three of them. She'd put on a sari and apply kohl around her eyes—the only makeup she owned.

Nadia noticed how their father too made small changes to his appearance. He started combing his hair straight back instead of parting it to the side. Even the convex curves around his middle flattened until he looked trimmer than he did in the wedding albums kept inside their mom's bedside table. One day he arrived, and his thick mustache had been completely shaven off. It was the shock in her mom's face that she remembered most, the way she reached out to touch the space above his upper lip but then jerked her fingers back like they had just grazed a heated surface.

On those weekends, her mom went to great lengths to make things appear normal. The four of them sat around the table for every meal. After dinner, they'd watch movies past the girls' bedtime, and their father would carry her and Zeba to their beds once they had fallen asleep. But even in those moments when their family began to feel complete again, normalcy never lasted long. As suddenly as their father would reenter their lives, he'd disappear. Where he went and why he never stayed longer than a few days was not discussed, so she and Zeba learned to accept it. And they accepted it for years. Until finally one weekend, he was supposed to come, and he never did. No explanation was ever given.

Nadia remembers being awoken one morning by her mom's voice on the hallway phone. She was speaking in Urdu, but Nadia could tell it was their father on the other end because she kept saying "jaan." Her voice rose higher, and she kept referring to an "aurat." Nadia wondered who that woman might be. Peeking through the crack of her bedroom door, she glimpsed the expression on her mom's face—the line between her brows as she pled her grievances; the anger and pain flashing in her eyes when she spoke—all of which frightened Nadia for reasons she did not yet understand. She crawled back into bed, feeling anxious and guilty over the little she had overheard.

Though Nadia never mentioned the phone call to her mom, she grew aware of what followed—largely the stretch of time that passed since their father's last visit. As weeks dragged into months and eventually into years, Nadia stopped wondering when he would come. Intrinsically she knew he was gone, though small traces of him still surrounded her. His yellow-toed socks in the bottom drawer of her mom's dresser. His deodorant and half-full bottles of Polo in the medicine cabinet collecting dust. *Your father will need them when he comes*, their mom would say when asked about them, as if she still believed he would. As if the keeping of those items would conjure him into existence, and he might walk through the door at any given moment.

While Nadia silently accepted these delusions—making space for her mom to cope in her own way—she resented the emptiness their father's absence carved into their lives, the time and energy wasted in preserving his memory when it was clear he had moved on. Though she did not have the power to change the relationship between her parents, she could, however, shape her own future to make it look

the way she wanted. And what she wanted more than anything was a life different from her mom's. A life centered in
love and happiness and, most importantly, truth.

HER EFFORTS TO create this, however, came at a cost—a
cost she is reminded of as she stands in Zeba's kitchen,
watching her with Alim. The innumerable pregnancy
tests; the recurrent miscarriages; the final decision to
forgo another cycle of IVF; it's been one heartbreak after another, and though she only recently reached a point
of resignation, what she didn't expect was for everything
else to fall apart as a result. The last few years have certainly taken a toll on her and Aman's relationship, but
Nadia never fathomed it would challenge their commitment to each other.

She diverts her attention to the flashes on her phone
screen. Sheila has left another half dozen texts suggesting possible locations for their girls' night. The thought of
spending the evening with her girlfriends no longer sounds
exciting. As Nadia skims through the messages, she tries to
gauge how disappointed Sheila will be if she bails on their
plans—again.

"Here, take this"—Zeba hands Alim a pack of fruit
snacks from the pantry—"and give one to your brother,
but only if he promises to be nice, okay?" Nadia looks up as
Alim gives Zeba a kiss and totters back to the couch.

"Chai?" Zeba asks, pulling out a pot from the cabinet.

Instinctively, Nadia nods as she places her cell phone on the countertop and hoists herself up beside it. As Zeba spoons three tablespoons of black tea into the boiling liquid, her phone buzzes with another message from Sheila.

Maryam just confirmed a sitter for the night! Let's do Sufra's at 8?

Zeba peers at her but doesn't say anything. Noticing, Nadia flips the phone over and watches her sister collect cinnamon sticks, dried cardamom pods, and sprigs of mint to put into the chai. From where she stands, Zeba reminds her exactly of their mom: hip jutted against the stove, slightly hunched as she grates fresh ginger into the pot. For a moment, she gets lost in the aromas surrounding her. She can't remember the last time she had a proper cup of chai and has forgotten how much she misses it.

"Hand me the milk, will you?" Zeba says to her.

Nadia hops down from the counter to grab the carton from the fridge. She waits for Zeba to pour it in before returning it.

"How have you been?"

"Good," Nadia replies automatically. "Work has been busy . . . for both of us . . . but you know how it is."

"No, I can't say that I do," Zeba says as she turns to face

her. Nadia tucks some loose curls behind her ear. Beside her, the cell phone continues to vibrate.

Zeba turns off the stove and pulls two teacups from the cupboard. Using a strainer, she fills both and hands one to Nadia.

"How are you able to make it taste just like hers?" Nadia asks, taking a sip. "I can never seem to get it right."

"Well, you didn't have a year's worth of practice like I did."

Nadia's jaw stiffens. When their mom got ill, Zeba took on the bulk of responsibility. It wasn't something the two sisters had discussed, but it seemed to make the most sense, Nadia rationalized. Zeba was the eldest. She was the favored one. Still, Nadia was aware of the sacrifices her sister made in order for the arrangement to work, ultimately quitting her job to stay home full-time. But because Zeba never contested it, Nadia thought she was fine with it. With Zeba, one never could tell. Her sister rarely said what she thought because any form of opposition would require confrontation and that was something she'd never accede to.

"Ammi used to get so upset if I didn't put in just the right amount of masala," Zeba says. "'Chi! Are you trying to kill me with this pani wali chai?'" she mimics in their mom's voice.

Nadia smiles. She remembers how particular their mom was about certain things.

"It bothered her so much whenever she was not in control. I'll never forget how angry she got when her hair started to fall out. Did you know she refused to let anyone see her for weeks? I mean, except Noman and Alim, and that's only because she couldn't bear to stay away from them."

Zeba continues chattering as Nadia is reminded of better days. But listening to her reminisce causes another rush of guilt. Nadia knows she could've done more to be there for their mom in that final year, but she was also going through her own fertility treatments at the time. Perhaps it was her selfishness. Or her determination to prove something, to show her mom that she and Aman could create the type of family that she'd never had. But she also never expected her to die. Their mom was not one to give up easily. She was too stubborn. Nadia figured cancer was just one more obstacle for her to overcome. How could she have known that it would take her so quickly?

THE FIRST TIME Nadia brought Aman home to meet her mom, *unyielding* was the word he used to describe her. "Your mom is unyielding," he said to her afterward. "Once her mind is made up, there's not much that can change it."

Seeing Aman's car pull into the cracked driveway of their two-bedroom home made her so self-conscious on that first visit. Aman's parents were both doctors. They had been married for almost forty years and lived in a neighborhood where homes were modeled after European manors and glimpsed through the bars of wrought iron fences. The intersection of their lives could not have been more unlikely.

When she met Aman in her second year of optometry school at Berkeley, Nadia was shocked that he had noticed her at all. They were at a mutual friend's house and all the girls were elbowing each other just to get at him. He was a few years older and a total catch. Smart. Charismatic. Ambitious. Although she and Aman didn't speak at all that night, a week later he came into the coffee shop where Nadia worked between classes, and for some unknown reason, he took a liking to her. His parents, on the other hand, were not so keen on the idea. They felt Aman needed someone more refined and like-minded. So, when Aman asked Nadia's mom for her hand in marriage upon first meeting her, Nadia too was taken by surprise.

It was her mom's flat refusal, however, that surprised her the most. "I don't think you are right for Nadia" was her exact response.

Nadia was mortified. "How could you say that to him?" she rebuked her mom after Aman had left. "He wants to be with me. Why is that so hard for you to accept? Is it because you can't stand the idea of my having something you never did?"

Her mom stared, fire raging in her eyes. But she didn't

fight back; the only explanation she offered was: "Think of me what you will. But I stand by what I said."

And she did, for several months. However, when Aman's mother unexpectedly rang her up to convince her mom to reconsider the proposal, she hesitantly accepted. Even Zeba, who as the eldest daughter was meant to marry first, put aside that tradition and gave Nadia her blessing. Her mom never explained the reasons behind her changed decision. Nadia assumed it was simply that she'd recognized the error of her judgment. What she did often wonder about, however, was what caused Aman's parents to change their minds—especially since they had strongly opposed the union at the start. As the years went on, those doubts and uncertainties faded . . . only now to be replaced by new ones.

"SHE DEFINITELY HAD her own way of doing things," Nadia agrees.

Zeba looks at her, whatever had prompted her to warm up a moment ago quickly forgotten. "Why are you here?"

"What do you mean?"

"At my house. In the middle of the day." She arches her brows, searching Nadia's face for an answer. "You don't expect me to believe you just stopped by for some chai and a chat?"

"I was in the neighborhood—" Her sister lets out an exasperated sigh. "What? I thought we could catch up."

Zeba scoffs. "You haven't been around here in *a year*. Why now?"

Nadia sets the teacup down. From her periphery the phone screen flashes, but this time, she doesn't check it. She's not trying to be disingenuous. If only she could confide in Zeba and tell her about the photos, about her troubled suspicions over Aman's possible indiscretions, but given how long it's been since the two of them have spoken, she questions how appropriate it would be to dump all of that on her sister.

"Fine. I guess we're just going to pretend like everything is normal."

"Who said anything about normal?" Nadia says. "We're Abbasis, remember?"

Zeba pushes back her seat and walks her teacup to the sink. "This is just like you, Nadi. Only doing things when it's convenient for you."

"This is far from convenient—"

"Do you know how many times I reached out to you since Ammi died? All the phone calls. The messages. You just up and vanished without even the slightest courtesy to tell me why."

Nadia's face burns. She's not accustomed to seeing Zeba so upset. Though she owes her an explanation, she doesn't have one to give—at least not one that would satisfy her. "I can leave if you want," Nadia says, standing up.

"Is that your go-to move, now? Like father, like daughter?"

Nadia flinches.

"Ammi is dead, Nadi." Zeba's voice cracks. "In case you haven't noticed, there's no one else left. It's just me and you. Do you really think this is what she would've wanted?"

"Sorry to disappoint you, Zeba, but not all of us live our lives according to what Ammi would've wanted."

The room, for a moment, is swollen with silence.

"How brave of you, Nadia, to live like you want. But some of us don't have that luxury. Some of us have to be responsible . . . even if it means doing things that are hard."

Nadia doesn't respond. She sees how her actions seem selfish to her sister, but the truth is, they stem from a feeling of inadequacy. While Zeba can grieve their mom's death with the comfort of knowing she did everything that was expected of her, Nadia cannot. She retreated when she should've stepped up, and though she knows Zeba is not to blame for that choice, she feels slighted by a competition that was never hers to win.

"Seriously, Nadi," Zeba mutters under her breath. She returns to the dishes, mouth turned back in disgust. "And can you answer your freaking phone already? It hasn't stopped buzzing since the moment you walked in."

Nadia looks at the screen; the messages blur together. She wishes she could go back and rewind the day. On the other side of the wall, she hears Noman barking at Alim while he laughs uncontrollably. "I should go," she says, grabbing her phone. Zeba dries her hands on a dish rag and follows her into the living room. She waits by the door as Nadia leans down and kisses each boy on the forehead. They twist toward her, smelling like Play-Doh and graham crackers as she pulls them in tight. On the front porch, she finally turns to face Zeba.

"I shouldn't have turned up like this. I'm sorry."

"It's fine," Zeba says, the expression on her face conveying otherwise.

"For what it's worth, it was good seeing you," Nadia says, hoping her sister knows how much she means it.

Zeba stares into Nadia's face before finally letting out a sigh. "Any chance you'll be in the neighborhood again?"

"Why, so you can lock your doors and shut the blinds?"

"That's not fair," her sister says, her mouth set in a hard line.

"It was just a joke, Zeba."

"To *you*. But while you've been dodging phone calls and making excuses, I've been here all along. *I'm* not the one who went anywhere."

Nadia looks away. As she walks back to her car, her heels sink into the gravel, feeling heavy with each step. Unsettled by how much is still left unsaid between them, she wonders if she and Zeba can ever go back to the way they were before their mom got sick. Not wanting to wait another year to find out, she turns back. "You're right, Zeba. I know I can't make up for the time that's passed, but . . . are you doing anything tonight?"

Zeba scrunches her face, confused by the question.

"I'm supposed to meet up with some girlfriends for dinner," she explains. "Do you want to come with?"

"Why would I want to come with—"

"Because a night out could be fun. Plus, it's also my birthday."

"Your birthday was Saturday."

"I just thought it might be nice to celebrate together . . . the way we used to. Like old times."

Zeba sighs, annoyed by Nadia's attempts to guilt her.

"Besides, what else do you have going on?"

Zeba looks behind her as Noman and Alim's high-pitched voices carry through the open front door.

"I'm sure Shoaib will be happy to watch them," Nadia quickly says, sensing her sister's dithering. "It's just for one night."

Zeba leans forward, her body slumping against the porch railing. "I don't know, Nadi—"

"Don't say no yet. I'll text you the address, okay?" Taking Zeba's nonresponse as a positive, Nadia climbs into the front seat of her car. As she circles around the cul-de-sac, the image of her sister standing on the front stoop sticks, and she continues to think of her even after crossing the bridge over to the other side.

4

Almost every table at Sufra's is occupied when Nadia and Zeba arrive. Heavy doses of clove and cardamom linger in the stagnant air, mixing with the sweet smoke of hookah saturating every corner. The pockmarked walls buzz beneath the melodic trills of Nancy Ajram's voice and the sounds of silverware clinking against plates loaded with much-too-large portions.

"Do you serve halal here?" Nadia hears her sister ask the hostess who ushers them through the restaurant past clusters of Arab uncles who leer at them between sips of arak and Middle Eastern politics.

Nadia wraps her cashmere shawl around her shoulders and folds her arms across her chest. On the way to the restaurant, she tried calling Aman again. He hadn't responded to her missed call from earlier, not even with a text like he normally did. Before this morning, she would hardly fret over something so small, but now she can't help but see every action through a screen of doubt. She still hasn't processed what to do with the photographs but feels a desperate need to reach him, to hear the familiar sound of his voice in some irrational hope that it might soften the sharp edges of her worry into something recognizable. Her call was sent straight to voice mail on the very first ring.

It strikes her how oblivious she has been to the signs in front of her. All she did was press slightly and every crack in their relationship came straight to the surface. In a matter of eight hours, everything she always believed to be true had suddenly transformed into something strange and unknown. If she hadn't gone into Aman's darkroom, if she hadn't found the strip of negatives, if she hadn't developed those images, she and Aman would've continued to exist as if all was fine. She wouldn't be obsessing over every loose thread of her marriage as if it were a precious garment being authenticated for consignment.

Near the patio, she quickly spots Sheila, all made up in pink painted lips and a sparkly gold jumpsuit cinched tightly at the waist, her figure mimicking a perfect hourglass. As soon as their eyes meet, Sheila rises from the table at which she's seated and motions them over with great élan. "Hi!" she says in a high, girlish voice. Despite being a few years older than Nadia, she possesses a vigor matching that of her three adolescent children. "I'm so happy you made it!" She lifts onto her toes to give Nadia a kiss on both cheeks.

"Sheila, this is Zeba, my sister." Nadia makes a quick introduction. Zeba holds out her hand with a stiff-lipped smile, as if unsure what to do with the bottom half of her face. Of the two sisters, Zeba has always been more socially timid, adopting her reserved nature from their mom. Hardly venturing beyond her small circle of friends, Zeba is out of her element. Her social skills are clearly a bit rusty; however, this makes Nadia all the gladder that she agreed to come along in the first place.

"Your sister? What a surprise!" Sheila exclaims, unfazed by Zeba's awkwardness. She cups her hand against the side of Zeba's chin and kisses her as well. "Nadia talks about you *all the time!*"

Nadia blushes, hoping her sister might be moved by the fact.

"It's lovely to *finally* meet you!" She pulls back, gently tapping the black studded hoops that peek out beneath Zeba's hijab. "Such gorgeous earrings."

"Thank you," Zeba says, taken aback by the compliment. As she tries to recall the website she bought them from upon Sheila's insistence, Nadia is relieved to see Zeba start to relax, her initial nerves eased by Sheila's graciousness. As the two of them talk, Nadia sits down at the table, admiring the Moroccan lanterns that hang neatly overhead across the ivy-covered pergola. A soft light filters through colored glass, creating a starry canopy that blankets the entire patio with an orangish glow.

"How is Damien?" Nadia asks.

"Wonderful." Sheila swoons at the mention of his name.

"Please tell him we hope to meet him soon," Nadia says sincerely. She pours herself a glass of ice-cold water and listens with interest as Sheila shares with Zeba the details of how she and Damien first met—how "fate interceded" by matching the two of them on a dating app that her twelve-year-old daughter encouraged her to download. It warms Nadia to see her friend basking in the glow of this new relationship—the first since the loss of her husband two years ago.

Sheila's experiences as a young widow have been trying, particularly in this past year. Her conflicted desires to seek love again while simultaneously mourning the death of her spouse have been met with callous judgment by those closest to her. As she dipped her toes back into the dating world, many faulted her for moving on "too quickly," as if an appropriate grieving period were universally demarcated. There were some who even blamed her for desecrating the memory of her children's father. But the voices of these critics faded the moment Damien entered her life. She was able to move past the guilt she had been bearing and ease into this fraught territory with less worry, more self-assurance.

Though Nadia has yet to meet Damien, she acknowledges the void he has filled in Sheila's life—a space that had been vacant for some time.

As the waiter brings a few bottles of laban for the table, the last member of their party, Maryam, walks onto the patio with an unmistakable irritation across her face.

"You're here!" Sheila exclaims, jumping up to greet her.

"Sorry to keep you ladies waiting," Maryam says. Her voice is rushed and breathy, coming out in short spurts as if struggling to keep up. "My nanny showed up late, and just as I was about to leave, Kubo threw up on the rug. And as I'm showing this poor girl how to clean it up properly, Samara insists that I read her one more bedtime story." She moves hastily as she speaks, floating from one end of the table to the other, acknowledging them each with a quick peck. "Anyways, I almost canceled the whole night, so it's a miracle I'm even here."

"When does Rafiq get back from Austin?" Sheila asks.

"Not soon enough." Maryam rolls her eyes. "He's meeting a few more investors, so if all goes well, he'll be back by the end of the week. Insha'Allah." She stands for a moment, making sure her crushed-silk dress gets its due appreciation before sitting down next to Nadia. Unzipping her handbag, she gropes around until she fishes out a compact and clicks it open with her polished fingernail.

"This is my sister, Zeba, by the way," Nadia says, but

Maryam is much too consumed by her preening to take note. Not in the slightest disconcerted by the other eyes on her, she almost seems to savor the attention she garners, a personality trait that Nadia has always found off-putting. She first met Maryam through Sheila, and though they've been orbiting the same social circles for years, Nadia wouldn't consider them to be close by any means. Her friendship with Maryam has always been forged by mutual acquaintances more than common interests. But even so, she hopes Maryam might take a liking to Zeba in the same way that Sheila has.

"Do you have kids, Zeba?" Maryam asks. Though she addresses her directly, Maryam's gaze remains fixated on her own reflection in the tiny mirror.

"Two," Zeba says, surprised by Maryam's sudden interest. She eyes Maryam with curious fascination as she carefully lifts the upper folds of her coral hijab to powder the shine across her forehead.

"Names?"

"Noman and Alim."

"Ages?"

"Five and three—" Zeba looks at Nadia, visibly perplexed by the volley of questions.

"Aww," Sheila says. "*Such* fun ages!"

"They drive me up a wall sometimes, but they are a lot of fun," Zeba admits.

"Do you have photos?" Sheila asks, passing the bottles of laban around the table as Zeba pulls up some images on her camera roll. When she holds out the phone to Maryam, instead of cooing over their cuteness, Maryam returns to her interrogation.

"Have you considered sending them to a dual-language school? They are very good. Very rigorous. My Samara is already speaking French along with Latin."

"I actually homeschool them myself."

Maryam blinks, looking at Zeba from beneath the metallic shimmer of her eyeshadow. There is a quiet judgment in her astonishment that feels almost palpable against the clamoring voices surrounding them. "How intrepid of you," she finally says. "If only we all had that type of free time."

Zeba's face burns at Maryam's not-so-subtle gibe.

"Zeba used to be a schoolteacher," Nadia interrupts, her voice taking on a slightly protective tone. Though she owes Maryam no explanation on her sister's behalf, she feels compelled to offer it. "So she's more than qualified with her background and expertise."

"Sure sounds like it!" Sheila says, proffering a smile to offset Maryam's rudeness. "I can't imagine homeschooling two boys under the age of six." She releases a soft whistle. "You must have your hands full!"

"As do all moms," Maryam says.

"As do *all of us*—parents or otherwise," Zeba clarifies, her irritation edging. For a moment, the table is silent. Maryam glares back while Sheila takes a sip of laban, the sweat from the bottle dripping onto the table.

"What I meant was, take Nadia and Aman, for example." Maryam shifts her gaze. "You two are still living like newlyweds." She extends her freshly blotted lips into a smile so saccharine that it makes Nadia's stomach turn. "But who needs to rush it, right? Consider yourselves lucky. Between Samara and Rafiq, most days I don't even know where the time goes."

"I wish I could say it gets easier," Sheila says. "But as they get older, the bedtime stories and play dates just get swapped for soccer games and trips to the mall." She shakes her head, her gold jhumka earrings jangling with the movement. "Thank goodness for Damien. Seeing him and nights out like these are the only breaks I get!"

While Sheila and Maryam resume their requiem over their loss of "me time," Nadia checks in with Zeba to make sure she isn't too shaken over Maryam's earlier quip.

"I'm fine," Zeba says, her voice chafed. "But that underhanded comment about you and Aman . . . are *you* okay?"

Of course her sister would be more concerned over Nadia's feelings than her own. She's always been selfless in that way. "I don't think anything was meant by it." Nadia shrugs, lowering her voice. Even though Sheila and Maryam are fully immersed in their own conversation at the other end of the table, she still wants to be certain they don't overhear. "I've never mentioned anything to them about all the *infertility stuff.*"

Her sister's dissatisfaction with Nadia's explanation is evident from the tiny frown between her brows. "What difference does that make? Isn't it just common decency to not comment on those sorts of things?"

While Nadia is no fan of Maryam's, she also can't fault her insensitivity when it was she who chose not to disclose the messy details of her and Aman's struggles—partly out of shame and partly to avoid any pitying remarks. "Trust me, Zeba. I'm not bothered by it. *Andheri,*" Nadia emphasizes. It's the final word, the name of their mom's ancestral hometown, that gives Zeba reassurance—though her expression remains indignant, making clear her disagreement. She leans back against her chair, not saying anything more.

As the night progresses and the mood lightens with the arrival of the food, Nadia's mind drifts back to Aman. She wonders what he is doing, if he is at work . . . or someplace else. But each glance at the phone yields no further clarity. Hating how deeply her doubts have burrowed into her mind, she places her phone facedown on her lap. She refuses to let Aman preoccupy all her thoughts, especially when he's clearly not thinking of her. Bypassing the salad, she goes straight for the lamb mandi.

"So how did you and Nadia meet?" Zeba asks Sheila in between mouthfuls of kibbeh.

"Our husbands worked together at the hospital," Sheila replies. She thinks for a moment before turning to Nadia. "Do you remember that couples' karaoke contest we got roped into—"

Nadia groans. "The hospital Christmas party. Three . . . no, maybe four years ago?"

"What was that song we sang? Love . . . something. Love getaway?"

"'Love Shack,'" Nadia says, cringing at the recollection.

While Sheila continues sharing more memories of that night, Nadia's phone vibrates. She turns to the screen, seeing that it is just a check-in from earlier that Sheila has tagged her in.

Nothing cures Monday Blues like a girls' night with my ladies!

<3

As she masks her disappointment with a "like," it doesn't escape Nadia that it is a quarter to nine and Aman still hasn't bothered to return her missed calls.

"Everything okay?" Maryam asks, leaning over to glance at her phone screen.

"Fine." Nadia smiles, quickly closing out her messages. But Maryam continues to peer at her with a prying interest.

"How are you and Aman, by the way?"

"Alhamdulillah. Thanks for asking."

"Sheila was telling me this impromptu girls' night was courtesy of his last-minute cancellation?"

Nadia's cheeks burn. Maryam's personality she realizes is more of an acquired taste, palatable enough among larger groups, but verging on unappetizing up close and personal. "Yeah . . . he had to work late," she admits, cautioning herself against sharing too much.

"Rafiq used to be the same way. Work, work, work. But once we had Samara, he's become so much more available."

"Didn't you say he's in Austin right now?"

Maryam looks away and fans herself with a menu. Nadia hides a smirk, unable to help herself. She hates being petty, but sometimes it feels good.

"Oh, Aruna called the other day," Sheila says, turning to them. "She sends her love and says she's settling nicely in New York."

"I mean, how settled can she *really* be?" Maryam mutters.

"Who's Aruna?" Zeba asks.

"Just an old friend," Nadia explains.

"Such a shame what happened." Maryam clucks her tongue against the roof of her mouth.

"If you mean Sajid cheating on her, then yes, it was a shame," Nadia responds. It was no secret among their circle that Aruna had moved out after discovering emails on her husband's work computer from a woman from out of state. After Aruna's departure, whispers continued for months surrounding the dissolution of their marriage—many even blaming Aruna for refusing to work through it.

"Let's not pretend it was all black and white." Maryam rolls her eyes. "We all know there were things that could've been done to prevent . . . *you know.*"

"The *divorce*? Besides Sajid not cheating, what else?"

"You're married, so you should know," Maryam quips.

"Clearly you have additional insight." Nadia notices the discomfort on her sister's face but proceeds nonetheless. "Please, enlighten us."

"I think what's important is Aruna is doing well," Sheila says to relieve some of the tension. Though Nadia agrees, Aruna's situation has also struck a nerve that drives her curiosity.

"Of course, I don't agree with what Sajid did." Maryam sighs, as if inconvenienced by having to explain the obvious. "But my mother always said 'A man away from home is like a ship without an anchor. It's only a matter of time before he drifts away.'" She glances at Nadia. "Everybody knew Sajid was gone *a lot*. Always working late and whatnot. As wives, it's our job to give our husbands a reason to come home. That's what I do with Rafiq. I cook his favorite meals. I make sure to put on makeup and slip into something nice before he arrives home." She takes a puff from the hookah and exhales, a cloud of smoke billowing in front of her. "Call me old-fashioned, but I'm certain nothing makes a man rush home faster than a hot wife and a hot plate of food."

"Oh, please," Zeba voices under her breath.

"Excuse me?"

Zeba looks around the table, not wanting to cause a stir. "I just . . ." She clears her throat. "That just sounds like advice you'd get from a fifties handbook." She laughs nervously, but Maryam stares back, less than amused.

"To be fair, they were both busy with their careers," Nadia interjects. "I'm sure whatever issues they had went deeper than just a lack of time together." Even as she says it, though, she realizes Maryam is not the only one she's trying to convince. She tries to recall the last time she and Aman planned a date night for just the two of them—not because they were celebrating something but just because—yet nothing comes to mind. If their lack of time together is what's driven Aman to find someone else, as she suspects, what are the chances her situation will fare any better than Aruna's?

"Careers are important, but no relationship succeeds without sacrifices," Maryam says matter-of-factly. "And if women aren't willing to prioritize their marriage above all else, can we really be that surprised when the relationship falls apart?"

Nadia looks across at Zeba, thinking of their mom. If

anything, the woman overprioritized her marriage to their father and it still fell apart.

"I disagree," Sheila cuts in. "All marriages have their rough spots. Even Naveen and I had our issues, but not every problem can be resolved by one thing or another. The fact is, some marriages are made to survive, and others are not."

Nadia remains quiet, wondering which category hers falls into. She and Aman have endured several rough spots in their ten years together, but in the past, she never doubted they would get through it. She always knew they would. This time, however, feels different. This time, it goes beyond just the two of them. If those five photos in the back seat of her car are proof of someone else's involvement, it adds a layer of complication that she may be unequipped to handle.

When the night is cut short by a phone call from Maryam's nanny, Nadia is relieved. Although the news is not great—Maryam's cat, Kubo, has thrown up for a third time that evening—her announcement that she's leaving early allows the others to follow suit. The women exchange half-hearted promises to "meet up again soon," and after divvying up the bill, Nadia and Zeba walk into the parking lot, feeling tired and worn but for totally different reasons.

"I'm so sorry," Nadia says when they reach the corner where both of their cars are parked. "I had no idea there'd be so much gossip surrounding the evening. This is probably not what you had in mind."

"Are you kidding? This is *exactly* what I expected when you said a night out with your girlfriends. Why do you think I was hesitant to come?"

"Since when did a simple dinner turn into one of Ammi's kitty parties?" Nadia groans, covering her face.

"At least there was no money jar or rishta hunting involved."

"*Phew.* I was afraid we had crossed over entirely."

Zeba lets out a small laugh.

Her sister searches for her keys as Nadia collects the words to express what she's been wanting to say to her all night. "Thank you for coming tonight, Zeba. It was nice just being together again."

Zeba looks up, her brown eyes peering into Nadia's. For a moment, it appears as if the iciness between them is finally starting to thaw. "Good night, Nadi," she says, getting into her car.

Disappointed, Nadia walks back to her own. Unlocking the door, she notices a message from Aman on her phone.

Sorry missed your calls. Still at work. Don't wait up.

She contemplates responding, but instead decides to leave it on read. She waits until the reds of her sister's taillights fade into the darkened street before she pulls out of the lot and heads home in the opposite direction.

5

Nadia is already on her second cup of tea when Aman walks into the kitchen the next morning. He is dressed in a gabardine suit with his signature scent trailing like a shadow.

"Good morning," he says, sitting down beside her. Nadia offers him a smoothie and a bowl of steel-cut oats topped with blueberries and a drizzle of agave syrup. Although she has not quite worked out the best way to broach the conversation that's been on her mind, she emotionally readies herself for when the moment arrives.

"Sorry about last night," Aman says, taking a bite of his oats. Though he is speaking to her, his eyes stay fixed on his phone screen. "I don't even remember what time I came in."

1:47. Nadia knows this because her eyes were on the clock when she heard the garage door open last night. Not wanting Aman to know she was still awake, though, she buried her face beneath the covers when she heard him walking up the stairs. "Why didn't you return my phone calls?" she asks.

"I thought we'd just talk when I got home, but you were already asleep, and I didn't want to wake you."

This too is untrue. From the small opening she had shaped into the covers, Nadia could see Aman barely take a glance at her before crashing onto his pillow. He hadn't even bothered to remove his socks or change out of his work clothes.

"You wouldn't believe the night I had," Aman continues, scrolling through his messages. Although it's irritating to have to compete with his phone for attention, Nadia's curiosity prevents her from calling him out. Instead, she listens to him share details of his night, while at the same time she figures out how to bring up what she really wants to talk about. As she waits for the perfect pause to jump in, his story turns unexpectedly. "One of the patients went into cardiac arrest while I was checking him for chest pains."

"Oh," Nadia says, noticing the creases beneath his eyes. "What happened?"

"Luckily, there was an **ENT** on call to handle the other patients, so I was able to run the code and defibrillate him multiple times. It was a bit of touch-and-go, but we finally got him stabilized."

The somberness in Aman's voice convinces her he's telling the truth. Seeing how wearied he looks suddenly makes her feel guilty for doubting him. She reaches out to touch his arm, wanting him to know that she believes him.

"How was dinner last night?" he asks.

"Good," Nadia replies. She can hear her phone buzzing from all the photos Sheila tagged her in, but she ignores the notifications. "Since you weren't able to make it, we invited Maryam and Zeba along and turned it into a girls' night."

"You invited your sister?" Aman asks, surprised. His face is plastered with questions, but he settles on the most obvious one. "How was that?"

"Fine," Nadia says. Over the past couple of years, Aman often inquired about her and Zeba's relationship, particularly their dwindling communication from multiple times a day to barely at all, but because his style was always more passive, he never pushed Nadia to reach out, recognizing that whatever reasons for the fallout were beyond his understanding. Still, she sees how unexpected their reconciliation must seem to him after all this time. "It was nice seeing her again," she adds.

"I think that's great."

"That's it?" Nadia says when he doesn't follow up. "You don't have anything more to say?"

"I mean, I'm glad you two are spending more time together."

Nadia is quiet, reminded of the reason she drove to her sister's house in the first place. She draws in a breath and blurts out the question she's been meaning to ask.

"Speaking of time, do you think *we* spend enough time together?"

Aman furrows his brows. "What do you mean?" he asks, confused by the sudden shift in conversation.

"I don't know." Nadia shrugs. "Do you feel like things have been different between us lately? Like maybe we're sort of drifting apart?"

Aman sets his phone down and chews on her question for a moment. "Do you?" he asks, looking closely at her.

Nadia clears her throat. She doesn't want to say anything until she knows how he feels.

"I think things have been busier lately," he says cautiously. "But no, I wouldn't say we're drifting apart."

"When was the last time we did something together, just the two of us?"

"This past weekend," he exclaims. "We went hiking for your birthday, remember?"

"That's different. Excluding special occasions, when was the last time we planned something just for the sake of it?"

Aman is quiet as he tries to recall the past several months, the lines between his eyes deepening as he thinks.

"Can you even remember the last time we sat down at the dinner table together?"

Aman doesn't answer.

She waits for him to tell her she's overreacting. That he can't help that the hospital is short-staffed and how unfair she's being by making him feel bad about working long hours when she knows he has no choice. These are all the excuses she's heard in the past, so it would be no surprise if he reverted to them again. But what she doesn't expect is for him to concede to her concerns.

"You're right," he says. "Tonight. Let's sit down for dinner, just the two of us."

Nadia is shocked into silence. After all their years together, astonishment is an emotion that rarely occurs; however, she is genuinely taken aback.

"Unless you have other plans?"

"I don't . . ."

"It's a date, then," he says, getting up. He reaches out and wraps his fingers around hers, giving her hand two squeezes—his code to tell her he loves her.

She feels herself soften, temporarily comforted by his touch. "Promise?" she asks.

"Promise."

She squeezes his hand back three times, letting him know she loves him too.

"Eight o'clock," he says, standing up to grab his briefcase. "I'll see you tonight," he calls from the doorway just before he leaves.

As the front door shuts, Nadia feels hopeful. If Aman is going to make the effort to work on things, the least she can do is the same. As she wipes down the remaining countertops, her anxiety settles in. Less than twelve hours remain to plan a dinner for tonight. Though typically she'd just pick something up on her way home from work, Maryam's opinion about a "hot wife and a hot plate of food" echoes in her mind. She shakes her head to remove the voice, but it continues to repeat, demanding to be heard.

Takeout won't cut it for tonight, she realizes. As much as she hates to admit it, she finds herself rethinking Maryam's words. Antiquated as the advice may be, if this is her chance to save her marriage from heading down the same path as Aruna's, she'd be a fool not to take it.

JULIE, HER RECEPTIONIST, thumbs through the filing cabinets, trying to locate the records for the day's patients. She hums a little melody as she pulls out some folders and adds them to the growing stack on her desk.

"Dr. Abbasi." Julie looks up when she sees Nadia. "Your next appointment is running a bit late. Mrs. Mejuri called to say there's some geese blocking traffic on Michelson Road, but she's on her way and should be here soon."

"That's fine," Nadia says as she leans against the desk. "Just don't schedule any late walk-ins, because I have to be out of here by four today."

"Duly noted," Julie says, pressing her index finger against the bridge of her nose to push back the red-framed glasses that are intentionally too large for her face.

"New pair?" Nadia says, pointing to the round frames.

"Ordered them online," Julie says proudly. "I think they make me look dignified. What do you think?"

"Total Sally Jessy Raphael vibes."

"Who?"

"Never mind." Nadia admires Julie's dedication to the job. Ever since she hired her almost three years ago, Nadia has seen Julie accumulate more pairs of frames than most women own shoes. For someone with perfect vision—Nadia has routinely examined Julie's eyesight over the years and knows she possesses the visual acuity of an eagle—she puts an impressive amount of care and attention into making sure each frame perfectly accessorizes her ensemble for the day.

"Big date with the mister tonight?"

"Something like that."

"Ohhh." Julie places her chin in the cups of her hands. "What are we celebrating?"

"Why do we have to be celebrating anything?"

"I just figured it must be something special if you're leaving early on a weeknight."

"Nothing special. Just a quiet dinner at home."

Julie scrunches her face, thinking for a moment. "Is 'dinner' code for something else?"

Nadia has no idea what date nights entail for early twentysomethings these days, but considering Julie's reaction to her lame, normal "dinner," she's not sure she wants to find out. "It's been a while since the two of us spent an entire evening together. Consider it nothing more than a nice gesture."

Julie leans back, pressing her palms together as if assessing a problem. "Are you sure you don't want to supplement your dinner with a few other *nice* gestures?"

Nadia swats Julie on the arm with one of the files on the desk. "Would your glasses approve of that type of *un*dignified talk?"

"I'm just trying to help."

"What I need help with is the menu," Nadia mutters. The pressure to cook the perfect meal has been mounting since this morning, and she has yet to pin down an idea that seems appropriate for the occasion.

"You're *cooking*?"

"Yes. Why?"

"I just took you for more of a takeout person."

"I might not be as confident around the kitchen as I am around a phoropter, but I can do some things."

"*O*kay. You do your thing, then."

Nadia smiles as Mrs. Mejuri, a smallish woman with ruddy cheeks and a permanent smile, enters through the doors. "Hello, Mrs. Mejuri. So nice to see you."

"Those new glasses look great on you," Julie adds.

Mrs. Mejuri bows her head to express her thanks.

"Come, follow me," Nadia says, grabbing the manila folder Julie hands to her and walking her patient back into her office. "So how are the new bifocals working out for you? I remember you were concerned about adjusting to the two focal points."

"Oh, they give small trouble at first, but now it's okay."

"And how would you describe your vision?"

"Perfect. Everything much clearer now."

"So glad to hear that." Happy the glasses have given Mrs. Mejuri the vision she was seeking, Nadia scribbles down notes in her file while at the same time wondering if her own search for clarity will prove to be just as successful.

6

Nadia wanders the aisles, empty cart in tow, thinking for a moment. Baked chicken breast and cauliflower rice has been on heavy rotation these past few months; however, before Aman went on his green juice health kick, his favorites used to be traditional dishes—meats, curries, meals that required more extensive preparation; the types of recipes beyond her current skill set.

When she and Aman first married, Nadia dedicated herself to trying to learn his favorite meals. At the time, he was also working long hours completing his residency and studying for his licensing exam. Eager to show off her domestic prowess, she experimented with different recipes, sometimes succeeding and other times failing miserably. Her most triumphant efforts, however, were always achieved with a little help from her mom. Cooking was the one topic she and her mom could discuss without argument.

When it came to food, Nadia knew better than to question her mom's expertise. She had no problem deferring in that area, and she sensed her mom, too, enjoyed feeling needed.

She recalls when she dialed her mom in a panic from the halal butcher shop because she didn't know which cut of goat she should get for the biryani. Her mom stayed on the phone with her for hours, walking her through the steps, from handling the pressure cooker to preparing the meat to seasoning the curry with fresh herbs and masalas. Nadia was surprised by how calm and patient her mom was in that moment, even teaching her little tricks—like dropping coconut oil into boiling rice water to keep the rice moist and pressing a few grains between the fingertips to check that they were perfectly cooked.

When Aman arrived home that night, the entire apartment smelled of sweet onion and mint. The two of them sat on the kitchen floor with the pot of biryani between them, pressing their forks into fatty bits of meat and telling each other about their days. Nadia remembers looking into Aman's face as he shared a funny story about one of his patients and thinking how lucky she was that this was the person she'd spend the rest of her days with.

Over the years, these traditional dinners no longer seemed worth the effort and were gradually replaced first by quick takeout and later by low-carb options. Once her mom died, even the occasional desire to cook vanished altogether, only to rematerialize now. Desperate to re-create the magic of those early meals, Nadia fills her cart with the ingredients that come to mind. The uncertainty, however, lies in whether she can shoulder the task on her own.

"AT THE TONE, please record your message. When you've finished recording, you may hang up or press one for more options."

Nadia sighs and presses the "end call" button. She is parked outside Zeba's house, trying to muster the courage to face her again. After yesterday's impromptu reunion, she doesn't want to press her luck. However, she also realizes that if she wants to put her mind at ease and work on her marriage, she needs to first come to terms with her sister. Taking a deep breath, Nadia steps out, hoping the reception might be a little warmer this second time around.

ZEBA OPENS THE door to find Nadia standing on her front stoop with bags of groceries dangling from each wrist. Thick, unruly curls peek out from beneath Zeba's wrapped turban; her unwashed face drawing attention to the dark shadows outlining the bottom rims of her eyes. "I didn't realize this was going to be an everyday occurrence," she says, her frazzled expression a mixture of surprise and panic.

"I tried calling, but it went straight to voice mail. Can I come in?"

Zeba steps back as Nadia pushes through the door frame, hauling her bags past the messy living room and into the kitchen, where she drops everything onto the linoleum floor.

"I don't know where my phone is," Zeba says, following behind. She watches as Nadia massages her wrists, trying to soothe the jagged red lines that have carved into her skin. "I think Noman might've hid it again."

"'Again'?"

"Yeah. It's something he does when he's upset with me. Anyways, I looked in all his usual hiding spots—the toilet, the garbage disposal. I even checked if there were newly dug holes in the backyard where he might've buried it."

Nadia stares at Zeba, bewildered by how casually she speaks. "Are you *okay*?" She looks around, taking another peek into the living room. "Is everything good here?" Despite the toys strewn across the carpet in a haphazardly formed obstacle course, the room appears to be empty.

"It's just one of those days." Zeba sighs, staring at the bags lying on the floor. "What is all of this?"

"Groceries."

"I can see they're groceries. What I mean is, why are they here?" Zeba asks, watching her sister empty the contents onto the countertop and place the bags of mutton and beef shank into the sink.

"Where are the boys?" Nadia asks, skirting her sister's

question. The eerie quiet of the house makes her uneasy, and she wonders if her sister's current state combined with the absence of her nephews should be cause for concern.

"Shoaib came home early, so I told him to take them to the park—"

"So, you're home alone?"

"For now . . . what are you doing?" Zeba's impatience grows as Nadia separates the ingredients near the stove to create a neat pile of yellow onions, lemons, fresh garlic bulbs, ginger, and green chili peppers.

"Do you know if they'll be back soon?"

"They just left. For fuck's sake, Nadi, can you tell me what this is all for?"

Nadia swallows, trying to piece together the words for her request. From the final bag, she pulls out two boxes of Shan masala and stacks them beside the onions before turning to her sister. "I thought maybe you could show me how to make Ammi's nihari."

"Now?" Zeba asks, grabbing one of the Shan boxes from the counter. "First of all, Ammi would have congestive heart failure if she saw you walk in here with this. Secondly, it's past five o'clock." She points to the clock on the microwave. "If you wanted to make nihari, you should've come here two hours ago."

"Aman won't be home until eight. I have plenty of time. I'm not worried."

"That makes *one* of us."

"Zeba, c'mon," Nadia says, trying to lighten the mood. "Teach me your ways, will you?"

Zeba mutters something inaudible as she rummages through the contents spread out on the counter. "Is this everything?" She rechecks the bags, tossing the empty ones to the side. "How are you planning on seasoning the meat? Just onions?"

"I don't know. I figured you'd have all the masalas and stuff."

"You don't actually know what goes into a nihari, do you?"

"I mean . . ." Nadia hesitates. "Only one of us really needs to know how to make it, right?"

Zeba narrows her eyes.

"But I want to learn! That's why I came to you." Nadia holds up her phone, screen side out. "I'm going to write down every single step. Just think of me as one of your students."

"What makes you think I have time to teach you? Not everything runs on your schedule, Nadia. Believe it or not, some of us have actual things we're dealing with. We don't all have the luxury to just drop everything because we're craving nihari."

Nadia bites her bottom lip, her face burning. "I'm sorry." She walks to the dry ingredients and starts placing them back into the bag.

Zeba is quiet.

"It's just Ammi used to be the one to help me with this stuff, and I didn't know who else to ask—"

Zeba sighs. From inside the oven, she removes a large Indian-style pressure cooker with the black seeti attached. "Open that cabinet and grab me some cinnamon sticks, laung, elaichi, haldi, kali mirch, laal mirch, hari mirch," she says, counting the ingredients on her fingers.

Nadia looks up, surprised by her sister's change of heart.

"I'm also going to need the roasted jeera, fennel seeds, a few bay leaves, mace, and the chana ki dal bottle."

Nadia drops the bag and scrambles from cabinet to cabinet, trying to locate everything her sister names but struggling to remember all the meanings of the words. "When you say elaichi, do you mean the green cardamoms or the black?" she says, holding up two separate bottles. "Also, what's the difference between bay leaves and curry leaves? They look the same."

"Nadia, if we're going to do this, you have to be quicker," Zeba says, her words wrapped in an impatience that keeps Nadia on her toes. She plugs in an old Black + Decker coffee grinder and motions for Nadia to hand her each item. Carefully, Zeba spoons the whole spices into her palms for measure before dumping them into the metal cup. Using just her fingers, she grabs pinches of laung, elaichi, kali mirch, and jeera mix and adds them in next. Finally, she places a few cinnamon sticks and bay leaves on top and sets the lid before pressing the button.

"How do you know how much of each thing to add?" Nadia asks over the sound of the grinder. Though the Notes app on her phone is open, she is too busy watching and forgets to type in the instructions. Zeba lifts the lid and shakes the excess powder from the edges of the metal cup. She holds it out for Nadia to see.

"Once it looks and smells like this."

Nadia leans in and closes her eyes. The sharp fragrance fills her nostrils, the familiar scent stirring memories of her childhood. She awkwardly motions to the boxed spices still on the counter. "Should I just toss these out?" she asks.

"No, they're still packed. The receipt is in that bag; you can just return them."

"I think they were only a few dollars." Nadia shrugs, but when Zeba looks at her with a raised brow as if to say, "*And?*" she quickly places the unopened boxes back in the bag. "What can I do to help?" she asks, wanting to feel useful. She wrings her hands, waiting for Zeba to give her some direction.

"You can rinse off the meat and put it in this." Zeba hands her a stainless-steel bowl and points her to the sink. "In the meantime, I'll get the oil in the pressure cooker warmed up."

Nadia removes her blazer and folds it over the back of a

chair. Cuffing the sleeves of her blouse up to her elbows, she lifts the tap so the water remains at a slow, steady stream and runs each piece of mutton and beef shank under it. When she hears the sizzle of the oil in the pressure cooker, she gently adds the cubes of meat into the pot, creating an even layer on the bottom surface. She then waits for Zeba to add in the chopped garlic, ginger, and dry spices before lowering the heat. For the next twenty minutes, the sisters take turns stirring, making sure the meat is fried and evenly browned on each side.

"So, why the sudden craving for nihari?" Zeba asks when they finally sit down. By this point, the lid of the pressure cooker is secured, so the only thing left to do is wait until the meat softens and becomes tender.

"Aman's coming home early tonight."

"*Okay*," Zeba says, thinking. ". . . And how does nihari fit into that?"

Nadia runs her fingernails over the surface of the table. "I just thought it would be nice if dinner was homemade. Like the meals I used to cook for him when we first got married."

Zeba narrows her eyes and rubs the bottom of her chin with her thumb. "So, this has nothing to do with wanting him to come home to a 'hot wife and a hot plate of food'?"

"Stop that, Zeba."

"The bigger question is: What are you going to wear? Because this"—she gestures to Nadia's polka-dotted blouse—"doesn't exactly scream *hot wife*."

"I was just trying to make it special . . ."

"In that case, call up Maryam! I'm sure she'll have *plenty* of advice for how to spruce yourself up."

"*IthinkAmanishavinganaffair*," Nadia blurts out.

Zeba exhales. "What?"

Nadia leans back, looking directly at her sister. "I found these in his study." She pulls out the photos from her purse and hands them to Zeba, one by one, watching her carefully as she sifts through each image. The expression on her sister's face reveals nothing, though, and Nadia cannot tell what she's thinking.

After a few moments, Zeba simply says, "Have you asked Aman about these?"

"Not yet."

Zeba hands the photos back to her, her lips pressed tightly together. After what feels like an eternity, she finally takes a deep breath. "Do you remember what Ammi used to say about giving seventy excuses?"

Nadia remembers. Their mom was big on giving others the benefit of the doubt, seeking excuses for poor behavior rather than assuming the worst. Nadia doesn't mention, however, that she always thought this practice required too much generosity. It was, after all, her mom's willingness to make such excuses for their father's absence and cover his faults with undeserved platitudes that allowed him to get away with so much. It also prevented her from accepting the reality of her marriage—causing them all to suffer as a result.

"How can I make excuses for what's right here in these images?" Nadia says, flipping through the photos. "The roses. The anniversary card." She holds up the photo of Aman's hand enclosed in someone else's. "What am I supposed to think?"

Zeba reaches out and takes the photo. "Are you sure this is even Aman's hand?" she asks, peering closely at the shadowy image.

Nadia knows the photo is dark, but whose hand could it be if not Aman's?

"You said you found these in Aman's study. Where?"

"In the wastebasket."

"There's a million reasons he could've tossed them out. Maybe they don't belong to him? Or he took them of someone else? All I'm saying is, be completely sure before you jump off the deep end. It's Aman, after all . . . Give him the benefit of the doubt . . . for your own sake."

Behind her, the seeti pops on the pressure cooker and a high-pitched whistle echoes through the air. As Zeba gets up to check on the meat, Nadia thinks over her words. Although there's a chance her sister might be wrong, who's to say she isn't right? After everything she and Aman have endured over the past ten years, doesn't she at least owe him the generosity of these excuses?

7

_____

After carefully packing the nihari and garnishes into separate Tupperware containers, Zeba helps Nadia carry the food and leftover groceries to her car while rattling off a list of instructions. "Don't add the fried onion and chilis until right before Aman gets home, otherwise they'll start to wilt. And make sure to stir the nihari gently, so the oil redistributes."

"Thank you again for this," Nadia says as she double-checks the pot sitting snugly in the passenger seat. "I couldn't have done this without you."

"I know," Zeba snaps back, though the annoyance in her tone has softened considerably.

As they walk to the driver's side, they see Shoaib pull into the driveway. From the back seat, Noman comes bounding out the sliding door.

"Mummy, Mummy! I climbed across the monkey bars!"

he shouts, running straight into Zeba's arms. "And Baba didn't even help me! I did it all by myself!" Zeba bends forward, grabbing Noman's face with the palms of her hands, and gives him a kiss.

Shoaib follows behind with Alim perched atop his shoulders. The small boy laughs gleefully as they approach. "Hey, salaams!" Shoaib exclaims when he sees Nadia. A friendly grin spreads across his face. "If I knew we were having company, I would have dressed up more." He pinches the front of his white Star Wars T-shirt and gives her a sheepish smile.

"By 'dressed up,' do you mean swapping out your cargo shorts for joggers?" Zeba teases.

"Yes, my *nice* joggers." Shoaib laughs. Though he is a big guy, he has this gentle way about him that is impossible to not find endearing. "How's Aman doing?" he asks, handing Alim to Zeba as she ushers both boys into the house.

"Good," Nadia says with a thin smile.

"It's been so long since I last saw him." He runs his hand across the top of his shaved head, and the stubble of stiff hairs makes a bristling sound against the soft part of his palm. "And how are things at the clinic?"

"Growing steadily. Business is good. We just finished the remodel of the front waiting space." She pauses as Zeba rejoins them. "Zeba tells me you're now tenure-track. Congratulations!"

"Thank you, thank you," Shoaib says, wrapping his arms around Zeba's waist and pulling her in close. "The stability is nice, but really I'm just glad to be home more with this beauty and those two beasts back there." He glances toward the open front door, where the boys are shrieking in either glee or pain—their perfectly imperfect family causing a slight ache in Nadia's chest. "It was great seeing you again, bhabi. Don't be such a stranger around here."

"Trust me, she hasn't been," Zeba says, the corners of her mouth slightly lifting.

"Give Aman my salaams. Hopefully we'll be seeing more of you guys."

"Insha'Allah," Nadia replies, unsure of how much Zeba has told him about their falling-out this past year. The invitation alone, however, makes her relieved things are slowly moving back to a comfortable place between them. As she slides into the driver's seat and fastens her seat belt, Zeba waits at the curb.

"Listen, Nadi, you and Aman are going to be fine," she says when Nadia rolls down the window. "But if you need someone to talk to . . . I'm here."

ALTHOUGH TRAFFIC HAS already died down, the drive home is still challenging. Nadia's stomach grumbles as she tries to ignore the mouthwatering smells wafting through her car. Her sister's final words linger in her mind, as does her brief interaction with Shoaib. Seeing the two of them together rekindles past resentments she has not thought of in some time . . .

"WHAT DO YOU mean Ammi gave you her blessing just like that?" Nadia blurted when Zeba first broke the news of her engagement. She stood in Zeba's bedroom, in total shock, as sharp stabs of jealousy bubbled beneath every pore of her skin. After all the trouble her mom had given Aman about wanting to marry her, she couldn't believe how easily she had granted Shoaib permission to do the same with Zeba, especially given their differences. Shoaib was the stark opposite of Aman. Intellectually, they shared the same wavelength, but they contrasted in every other way. Marriage to Aman offered Nadia a chance to scale the social ladder, to gain access to a life she had always felt excluded from, whereas Zeba's life with Shoaib would not look much different from the one they grew up with. Even his career path, teaching introductory economics to undergrads at a community college, was not nearly as prestigious as what Aman had to offer. This was not to say Nadia disliked Shoaib; she just worried Zeba might be settling for something familiar rather than aiming for more.

"I can't believe it," Nadia scoffed, unable to conceal her frustration. "She didn't even try to talk you out of it?"

"No." Zeba shook her head. She knew Nadia was upset,

but there were other worries weighing on her mind. "Do you think I'm making the right choice, Nadi? I care about Shoaib, but how do I know I'm making the right decision?"

"What did Ammi say?"

"She said what she always says about loving too much. That it's dangerous for us, but not when it's the other way around."

Nadia rolled her eyes. She remembered her mom offering similar advice about Aman, about whether he could love her in the same way she loved him. Nadia was angered by the conversation. Love was not transactional, and she resented her mom for casting doubt on their relationship, a relationship she felt so certain of at the time. So, she had brushed off these warnings, chalking them up to a scorned worldview and her mom's own cynicism when it came to love.

"She asked if I thought Shoaib loved me more than I loved him."

"Do you?" Nadia asked, curious if their mom held similar doubts about Shoaib.

Zeba thought for a moment. "Yes. And she said if that's true, then I should marry him because it's the only way to guarantee I'll be safe."

Safe. At the time, Nadia didn't know what to make of that statement. She wondered if it was her mom's way of saying Aman didn't love her as much as Shoaib loved Zeba.

Hurtful as that was, she also questioned how "too much love" could be dangerous in a marriage, regardless of which side it came from. But, as with much of the advice given by their mom, Nadia ignored it, placing little stock in such outdated beliefs.

But now as the memory replays in her mind, she finds herself drawing another comparison—one that cannot be quantified by occupation or social status. Unlike her relationship with Aman, which has been on a steady decline, the love between Zeba and Shoaib still burns strong. It's clear in the way he looks at her, in his small gestures of affection, and she finds herself longing for the security of their relationship as she's beginning to understand what her mom meant by *safe*.

BY THE TIME she reaches home, it's almost a quarter to eight; however, one click of the remote lets her know Aman still has not returned. She pulls into the garage and parks in the empty space nearest the side door. With only fifteen minutes left, Nadia manages to carry everything inside in one trip and arranges the dining table as neatly as she can. She places the store-bought naans into a covered warmer and then rushes upstairs to change into something more alluring than the work blouse her sister gave her such a hard time about. She slips into a silk nightdress and quickly touches up her makeup in the hallway mirror. Her heart flutters as she steps back to admire her reflection—the final step of her transformation into *hot wife* complete. Taking a seat at the dining room table, she glances at the clock illuminated on her phone. All that's left to do is wait and see whether Maryam's advice will actually hold up.

THE SILENCE IN the room feels dense, compacted further by the strike of the grandfather clock standing guard in the foyer. Nadia sits at the dining table, staring at the dark grains beneath the polished casing, tracing her fingers over their circular patterns as the chimes of the clock count the passing hour. The sliced chilis that she placed on top of the nihari have shriveled into misshapen ovals, and the soggy onions float in a deluge of saffron-colored oil that has risen to the surface. Nadia's phone lies in front of her, her last message to Aman left unread. It is past nine before it finally sinks in: Aman is not coming.

Upstairs, she stares at the unmade bed from the darkness of the hallway, feeling as empty as the house. She scrubs her face clean, changes into her pajamas, and climbs into bed, her insides stinging with grief over the loss of something she can't fully articulate. It's possible another emergency came up that prevented Aman from leaving; however, to not even grant her the courtesy of a phone call . . . She is disappointed and hurt by his shift in priorities, by how, when faced with a choice, Aman will always give work precedence over their relationship.

She thinks back to Maryam's comment about men being like ships without an anchor and wonders how far Aman has already drifted. *What if it's too late?*

From the open window above her headboard, the wind rustles through the leaves. As she lies in bed listening to the faint coos of her backyard owl, its sound reminds her of the soft cries she'd often hear through the walls of her childhood bedroom after everyone was fast asleep.

IN THE YEARS after their father's last visit, Nadia's mom never disclosed to them what happened that caused him to leave. And because she didn't offer this information, neither Nadia nor her sister made the attempt to ask. They went along with the pretense that all was fine, even safeguarding the belief that he would one day return.

However, one night Nadia awoke and followed the sounds to her mom's bedroom. As she stood outside, barefoot and sweaty, listening to the soft cries that drifted beneath the closed door, the ambiguity surrounding her mom's silence lifted. There was a sadness in her cries. A longing. A deep regret. And in that moment, Nadia pitied her. She understood that her mom's silence was a futile attempt to maintain hope—one that would gradually diminish with each passing night their father didn't return. But alongside that pity, Nadia also felt gravely misled, deceived and deluded by years of feigning and the countless lies about how everything was fine when the sound of those cries made it clear it was not.

As NADIA LISTENS to the breeze outside her window, she wonders if the loss she feels now is what her mom felt. If those cries were of a woman who still missed her husband— who wished for him to return but knew it was too late. The thought of Ammi climbing into an empty bed, night after night, surrounded by her loneliness, arouses in Nadia a sympathy she has not felt before, and as she reaches across the bed to where Aman normally sleeps, she is overcome with emotion. Outside, the owl hoots louder, while inside, Nadia clenches a fistful of sheets. Encased in the dampness of her pillow, she drifts in and out of sleep, not fully waking again until right before the alarm goes off.

As THE MORNING sun slices through the blinds, she turns to face Aman lying in bed next to her. His back is across from her, the rounded shape of his body rising and falling with each breath. Last night comes rushing back to her in fragments: cooking the nihari, seeing her sister and Shoaib, waiting for Aman, the emptiness of his absence. So many questions run through her mind as she reaches out and touches his shoulder. "Aman," she whispers, wanting him to wake. He stirs slightly but does not respond. She calls his name a little louder, and for a moment, all is still as she listens to the low-pitched sounds of his deep slumber. She turns onto her back and stares at the ceiling, finding herself wondering how it's possible to miss someone who is lying right beside her.

8

_____

Breakfast that morning is tenser than usual. The conversation feels like it's wrapped in a stiff rubber band—the tautness behind each word stretching thin, threatening to break at any given moment. Although Aman is quick to apologize, his bland, worn-out excuses only further convince Nadia that he is in fact cheating, an accusation she wrestles to not blurt out. The problem is she has no way to prove it, since the photos alone are not conclusive enough, as her sister pointed out.

WHEN SHE ARRIVES at work, Julie is already there, clacking away at the keyboard. "When you get a chance, can you send out Mr. Natarus's referral, and email him a copy of his reports?" Nadia asks.

"Mm-hmm," Julie says without breaking her gaze.

Nadia leans against the desk and looks at the empty

chairs. "Can I ask you a question?" she says, clearing her throat.

Julie stops typing and peers up from behind her cat-eye glasses.

"You and your boyfriend—" Nadia screws up her face trying to recall his name.

"Trevor?"

"You two have been together for a while, haven't you?"

"Almost a year," Julie says proudly.

"Have you ever suspected . . ." Nadia halts, thinking over her words carefully. "Let's say if supposedly . . ." She pauses and starts again. "I guess I was wondering what you would do if you ever thought that Trevor, or someone you were with, might be . . ." Julie's mouth straightens into a frown, her brown eyes narrowing behind the lenses of her glasses. ". . . seeing someone else. Besides you. I mean—in theory—how do you navigate something like that?" Although her question is far from theoretical, Nadia hopes her tone is neutral enough to make it appear so.

"Is Trevor *cheating* on me, Dr. Abbasi?" The color drains from Julie's complexion.

"What? No!" Nadia exclaims, perplexed by Julie's reaction.

"Was it that brunette he was talking to on Tuesday when he came by to pick me up?"

"Mrs. Campos? Julie, she's old enough to have birthed him."

"I know a cougar when I see one."

"Mrs. Campos is not a cougar—"

"You don't think I noticed the way she kept ogling Trevor through her bifocals?" Julie scoffs as she grabs the cell phone off her desk. "And the way she's always fanning herself and talking about the heat. What a thirst trap."

"She suffers from hot flashes, Julie. There's a catalog of menopausal supplements listed in her file."

But Julie is already typing, furiously, impetuously, her nose practically touching the phone screen.

"Seriously, Julie, would you just—*give me that*." Nadia reaches out and takes the phone from her.

"Dr. Abbasi, I'm in the middle of a text!"

Nadia looks down and sees Trevor's name at the top of the chat box. She shakes her head, deleting the partially composed message that is typed in all caps. "Take a few breaths, will you?" She forces Julie back into the chair, feeling confused by how sharply their conversation turned. "My question had nothing to do with Trevor or Mrs. Campos. I was only asking *hypothetically*."

Julie's chest rises with her breath, her face dark as she cogitates whether to believe her boss.

"You know what, never mind. Forget I asked," Nadia says, walking to the flat wall-mounted panels holding the

display frames. She steps back to examine each disorga-
nized row. "Help me fix these?" She motions to Julie while
readjusting the frames on their metal pegs.

Julie walks over and quietly surveys the panels. After a
few moments, she turns to her. "Are you sure it was only
hypothetical? Your question?"

"Absolutely. It was not based on anything other than curiosity. I promise." Nadia lifts her right hand to pledge her
oath.

Julie shifts her gaze back to the panel. "I think I might've
overreacted."

"You think?"

But Julie remains deep in thought as she adjusts the
frames on the next panel. She works quietly and efficiently,
moving her way across before starting the next row. When
she finally speaks again, her voice is softer, more brittle.
"Two years ago, the guy I was dating cheated on me. I
guess I never fully recovered from it."

Nadia is suddenly sorry for bringing up the topic. "I
didn't mean to trigger you with that question." She places
her hand on Julie's shoulder. "We don't have to talk about
it—"

"They met on Snapchat," Julie continues. She stares at
Nadia, and a knowing look flashes across her eyes. "You
were asking how to navigate that situation, right?" Nadia
nods, any self-consciousness eclipsed by her desire to know.

"We were watching a movie at his place one night, and he kept checking his phone every few minutes. I didn't think much of it. But later, when I was scrolling on Snapchat, I noticed these little ongoing streaks between him and a username I didn't recognize. At first, I kept it to myself. But then a few weeks later, when I logged on, I couldn't see any activity from him, even though I knew he was on there all the time, so that's when I knew."

Nadia listens with rapt attention. "What did you do?"

"I waited until he was asleep one night and then downloaded an app onto his phone that collected all his deleted snaps."

Nadia raises her brows, completely engrossed as Julie explains how she enabled backups on her ex's phone so that new snaps would automatically be saved to a shared album to which she also had access. Her mentions of "data storage" and "cache clearing" are beyond Nadia's understanding, but Julie's detailed account allows Nadia to absorb enough bits and fragments to satisfy the questions she had been attempting to ask.

"The whole time, I felt sneaky doing it"—Julie shrugs—"but I had no choice because he never would've admitted to it on his own. If I didn't go snooping, I never would've found the vulgar exchanges between him and some woman named Alyssa James."

The lengths Julie went to in order to get the answers she

needed are no doubt impressive, but the process she under-
went sounds agonizing and overwhelming. Granted, Aman
is not tech-savvy enough to be Snapchat streaking—
whatever that means—but Nadia wonders whether she
possesses the know-how to navigate the ins and outs of
snooping as stealthily as her twentysomething receptionist.

"What did you do once you knew?" Nadia asks, leaning
against a glass display case. The queasiness returns to her
stomach as she waits for an answer she knows is obvious.

"I dumped his ass," Julie says, flipping her sleek hair behind her shoulder. "I printed out their exchanges and taped
them to a box of all his things." She looks at Nadia, her face
sullen from the memory. "We were together almost three
years. He made his choice, so I made mine to end it."

"That must've been hard," Nadia acknowledges, twisting the gold band on her finger.

"It was," Julie admits. "But it would've been a hell of a
lot harder to stay with someone who I no longer trusted."

How was dinner? Did Aman like the nihari? Zeba texts her during
lunch.

As little as she wants to retreat to her old reliance on Zeba
for every little thing, Nadia reminds herself of her sister's
last words to her: *If you need someone to talk to . . . I'm here.*

She finally texts back after deliberating how in depth she
should go. **He didn't show up.** Nadia watches the floating dots

appear and disappear on the screen multiple times. Imagining Zeba on the other end rethinking her response makes her uneasy.

Are you okay?

Nadia bites her bottom lip. **I will be**, she responds. Zeba presses further.

Did he say what happened?

Emergency at work . . . After a moment, she adds: **Seventy excuses, right?**

What if you called the hospital? Just to double check . . .

Nadia thinks for a moment, considering her sister's suggestion while at the same time grappling with the idea. In the past ten years, she never once felt the urge to check up on Aman's whereabouts. Nor had he checked up on hers, at least to her knowledge. There always existed an unspoken trust, a mutually shared faith between them, so it pains her to accept that that trust may no longer be as steadfast as it once was.

Do you think he might be lying?

I just think you'd feel a lot better if you heard his reasons confirmed.

The heat from Nadia's forehead radiates into her palms as she pushes the curls away from her face. Zeba is right: it would feel better to rid herself of the suspicions that have been percolating through her thoughts, though she isn't sure if this is the right way to do it. But with no other leads, she picks up the receiver on her desk phone and dials the number. After a lengthy recording requiring multiple number presses, she finds her way to the right desk.

"Emergency Care. How may I assist you?"

"Um, hi," Nadia says. "I was wondering if you could let me know what doctors were on call last night?"

"We can't give out that information, ma'am."

"Right. Well, can you tell me if there were any emergencies that took place between, um, seven and midnight?" She hears the nurse on staff release an impatient sigh.

"Ma'am, this is the Emergency Care unit." When Nadia doesn't reply, she continues. "Is there an emergency I can assist you with?"

Nadia clears her throat, suddenly feeling self-conscious. "No. I mean, yes. I mean—" She draws in a breath. "Could I speak with Dr. Aman Mirza?"

"Let me place you on a quick hold."

As Nadia waits, she contemplates what to say when

Aman gets on the phone. Without a good reason, she considers hanging up, but before she can, the nurse returns.

"Ma'am, Dr. Mirza is not scheduled to work today."

"What do you mean?"

"He has the day off. He won't be back in until tomorrow."

Nadia manages a hasty "thank you" as she ends the call. It feels as if the air has been knocked out of her. She turns over the information, trying to figure out why Aman lied to her. Even the suit he wore this morning gave no indication that he had the day off. *If not to work, where else could he have gone?*

BY THE TIME Nadia leaves the office, the sky is beginning to purple and the last bits of sunlight are fading into the horizon. In the distance, rows of taillights spiral along the freeway, indicating that traffic has yet to let up. As her phone vibrates on the seat beside her, Nadia inches into the middle lane, committed to taking surface streets instead. When she arrives at a stoplight, she glances at the screen to see a missed call from Zeba. She sends her a quick message.

Driving. Can I ttyl?

Distracted, her thoughts zigzag between the traffic and the phone call from earlier. She has yet to learn where Aman has been all day, but the different possibilities could very well lead her to what she hoped was not true. When she arrives home, she is surprised to see Aman's Tesla parked in the driveway. At the press of her index finger to the remote attached to her sun visor, the garage doors rise, and she pulls into the empty space.

"Aman?" she calls the moment she walks through the door. Her work bag is still slung over her shoulder and car keys dangle from the tips of her fingers. She slips off her heels and walks into the kitchen.

"Aman?" she calls again, dropping everything onto the center island. The gentle patter of the shower hums from upstairs, and for a moment, she is struck by its oddity, considering that showering is the one thing Aman does only in the mornings.

To her left, she sees his briefcase against the kitchen table, the leather shoulder straps bunched on the floor and the brass hardware clasp unlocked. Without thinking, she walks over and slowly lifts the front flap. Not sure what she is searching for, she rummages through each pocket, sifting through the rows of manila files bulging with paperwork. To get a better look, she pries open a few folders, but all she can make out is Aman's handwriting, slanted and scraggly, inked across patient reports. Disappointed, she drops the flap to re-cover the opening and heads upstairs, climbing two stairs at a time.

The door of the master bathroom is slightly ajar and steam from the shower wafts into the bedroom. "Is that you, Nadi?" Aman calls from inside.

She follows his voice, which sounds low and muffled, and peeks her head inside the bathroom. His silhouette can be seen through the reeded glass doors, and she leans her head against the door frame, inhaling the scent of tea tree and lavender. "I didn't know you were home," she says, speaking loudly over the sound of water. Biting down on her thumbnail, she thinks for a moment before continuing. "I called the hospital earlier and they said you weren't in today . . ."

Aman slides open the shower door and pushes his head through the small crack. The strands of his hair stick straight up and are covered in a sudsy froth. "You called the hospital?" he asks, creasing his eyebrows with surprise.

Nadia feels a slight panic as she wrestles to come up with an explanation. "I needed to ask you something, but your phone kept going to voice mail."

"My phone died."

"Don't you have a charger in your car?"

Aman is silent as foam from his hair drips down his neck. Nadia shifts her weight to the other leg, angered by the laziness behind his excuses. "What did you need to ask me?" he says. A concern looms in his voice that was not initially there.

"Where did you spend the day? And what happened to your charger, Aman?"

"What do you think happened, Nadi? I must've misplaced it," he says, answering the second question but not the first. He slides the shower door shut, blocking her from his view. "I thought you'd be glad that I came home early."

"How can I be glad when I didn't even know?" She can sense his irritation, but her suspicions won't allow her to let up. "Why didn't you tell me you had the day off?"

Aman lifts his arms and scrubs the top of his head. She isn't sure what he's thinking, but when he does speak again, she notices his words come out a little faster. "Because it was supposed to be a surprise. I took the day off because I felt bad about last night and wanted to make it up to you."

Nadia remains doubtful.

"I was hoping to plan something special." He peeks his head out again, the squeak of the shower door sounding almost like an apology.

"I still don't understand why you couldn't just say you took the day off—"

"Then it wouldn't be a surprise, would it?" He sighs when she doesn't respond. "Nadi, can we stop with the third degree and just have a nice evening?"

Nadia's not sure what to believe, but the seventy excuses ring in her head. "What special thing did you plan?"

"Well, I figured you'd be too tired to go out, since it's the middle of the week, so I ordered us takeout."

Takeout? She made him an entire dinner and all he did was order takeout? She reminds herself that takeout is "special" in Aman's repertoire of romance, but that doesn't quell the disappointment she feels. Fortunately, or unfortunately, Aman doesn't seem to notice.

"I got pizzas and wings from that new place on the corner of Blossom and Fourth—you know, the one you've been wanting to try?"

"That was months ago." She's surprised he still remembers and is momentarily touched by the thoughtfulness. "What about your diet?"

"I think we can make an exception. Just for one night."

Her stomach growls with approval.

"Let's have a redo of last night, okay?" he says, motioning for her.

She walks over to him, slowly nodding. Although it still doesn't explain his whereabouts all day, she puts that aside to focus on the positives. Pressing her face against his, she lets the moisture from his skin seep into hers.

"Thank you," he whispers, giving her a kiss. He draws her in closer, but she pulls back.

"Why don't you finish showering, and I'll go change into something more comfortable."

Back in the bedroom, she plucks out a pair of red satin

shorts from the hand-crafted armoire and a matching camisole edged in lace. Dragging her thumb along her spine, she presses her shoulder blades back and unclasps her bra, relaxing with its release. She doesn't want to set her expectations too high, but she hopes an evening with Aman might be exactly what is needed. Without any distractions, perhaps this time together might allow them to recalibrate the past few months and rekindle what they once shared.

As she slips into the camisole, she notices his clothes piled on the floor near the foot of the bed. Untangling his expensive dress shirt from the heap, she drapes the shirt over her left arm and smooths out the wrinkles. Lifting his pants next, she checks all the pockets and finds his cell phone and a balled-up receipt, both of which she sets down on his nightstand. The screen of his phone lights up the moment it hits the surface, illuminating a string of notification banners. Her curiosity waxing, she leans in to read.

"I think the food is on its way," she says loudly just in case Aman can't hear her over the shower. Her heartbeat pulsing, she scrolls up with her thumb, skimming each message until one catches her eye. It's from someone named L.

L?

Finding it strange that Aman would store a contact by just their initial, she holds down on the message to read it fully. It's short. It reads:

Left your charger here. Excuse to pick it up tomorrow? ;)

From the bathroom, Nadia hears the faucet turn off. A moment later, the shower door slides open, and Aman sighs as he steps onto the travertine floor. Nadia drops the phone. She walks away from the nightstand and into the closet to dump Aman's clothes into a dry-cleaning bag. Her mind races as she goes through a mental Rolodex of everyone they know whose name begins with *L*.

There's Laura, the elderly nurse at Aman's hospital whom Nadia met at last year's holiday party. But she likely wouldn't have Aman's cell phone number. There's also Brother Liaqat, one of Aman's acquaintances from the mosque he frequents on Fridays for Jummah prayers. But today is only Wednesday. And as far as she knows, it would be unusual for the two of them to encounter each other outside of the weekly prayer. The only other person she can think of is Leo, Aman's accountant. But his office is located all the way in the valley, which is quite a distance to travel, especially on a weekday . . . although not totally implausible if one had the day off . . .

A cloud of steam trails Aman as he walks out of the bathroom. The sight of him in his striped boxer briefs and fitted black T-shirt briefly distracts her, as does the sound of the doorbell. "Hope you're hungry." Aman grins, drying his wet hair with a towel.

"Starving," Nadia responds.

As they make their way to the kitchen, Aman stops at the landing to give her a quick kiss. Any concern is pushed from her mind, and in that moment, she can think of nothing other than how pleased she is to be in his arms once more.

9

Nadia stares at the ceiling, wide awake as Aman lies beside her, fast asleep. The evening went just as she had hoped, with few distractions—at least externally. The pizza Aman ordered from the new restaurant was deliciously satisfying, and after dinner, they headed into the backyard to roast marshmallows for dessert in the outdoor fireplace. Later, as the sky glinted with densely clustered stars, she and Aman curled up in the hammock, tangled together like a pair of fish caught in a net. They spent the remainder of the night talking and laughing under the moon as it hovered behind the tree branches, shining its bright blue light on everything it touched. Aman even posed for a rare selfie, which Nadia immediately posted along with the caption **Surprise date night** followed by a single red heart. But now that Aman has drifted into a languorous sleep, her mind strays back to the messages on his phone as she wonders why Leo added a winky emoji to the end of his text.

Excuse to pick it up tomorrow? ;)

She's met Leo only once, about a year ago at a mutual friend's end-of-summer party. Even in a casual setting, Leo had the look of an accountant: short and trim, with sloping shoulders and a neutral expression. Though the two of them were just briefly introduced, Nadia remembered Leo as sober—the type of man who wore tie and trousers to a backyard barbecue. The likelihood of someone with his disposition texting—let alone expressing himself through an emoticon—suddenly seems doubtful. She wants to believe it; however, something tells her that Leo is not the sender of that message. Which then opens the door to a string of other questions: If *L* isn't Leo, then who else could it be? And if not in Leo's office, then where is this place that Aman left his charger, to which he now has an excuse to return tomorrow?

Feeling unsettled, Nadia slides out of bed. Letting only the balls of her feet touch the cold hardwood beneath, she unplugs her cell phone from the nightstand, careful not to make a sound, and tiptoes out of the room. Even with the door shut behind her, she waits until she is downstairs before scrolling through her recent call list. But right before she presses Zeba's number, she glances at the clock on the screen and is reminded that it is almost midnight. On second thought, she switches to her messages and begins typing.

Are you up?

I think I might've found something on Aman's phone.

Within seconds her phone vibrates, and she accepts the call, relieved to hear her sister's voice.

"I thought you'd be sleeping," Nadia whispers.

"Alim wet the bed, so I had to change the sheets."

"Is now a bad time?"

"No, I just got him back to sleep. But now that I'm up, I thought I'd do a quick load of laundry." Nadia can hear the whir of the washing machine in the background as it starts its cycle. "What did you find on Aman's phone?"

Nadia slips into the study and quietly presses the door toward its frame. She leaves a sliver open to ease her ability to get out quietly if necessary. Leaning against the edge of Aman's desk, she cups her hand over her mouth and speaks low into the speaker. "I saw a message on his phone when he was in the shower earlier. It was from someone named L."

"L?"

"That's how he saved it. Just the initial." She pauses a

moment, waiting to see if Zeba's reaction will reveal that she too finds this suspicious.

"What did the message say?" Zeba asks instead.

"It says: 'Left your charger here—'"

"Here?" Zeba interrupts. "Where is *here*?"

"I don't know." The mahogany surface of Aman's desk feels cold under the delicate satin of her shorts, and a tiny shiver runs up her back. "But wherever *here* is, I think he might be going back to pick it up tomorrow."

"Who do you or Aman know whose name begins with an L?"

"I already did this," Nadia says. "No one I can think of who would add a winky emoji to the end of that message."

Zeba mutters something inaudible under her breath.

"Fuck, Zeba. What am I going to do?" A panic rises in her throat, but she forces it back with a swallow. Her emotions overwhelm her as she thinks back to the photos and now this message. As hard as she's tried to not assume the worst by granting him excuses, it's become increasingly difficult to explain away her growing suspicions.

"Where are you right now?" Zeba asks.

"Downstairs. In Aman's study."

"Is he asleep?"

Nadia looks up to the ceiling, listening for any sounds of movement. Aside from her heartbeat hammering against her chest, the house is quiet, as if it too is holding its breath. "I think so," she finally says. "He's a pretty sound sleeper."

Zeba releases a stiff sigh. Nadia imagines her pacing back and forth with agitated steps, brows pressed together as she comes up with a plan. "Have you poked around? Maybe he has an address book lying on his desk somewhere. Or a note-pad. Something that might tell you who this L person is."

Nadia stands up and walks to the other side of Aman's desk. She slides open the center drawer and pushes aside the items inside. There's an array of pens and paper clips. In another compartment, there's a booklet of stamps and some loose change. The side drawers are filled with out-dated bills, frayed pamphlets, and sundry objects. "I don't see anything," she whispers, pulling out a small stack of business cards held together with a green rubber band. She pulls off the elastic and sifts through each card, reading the names carefully before placing them back in the drawer. "It's useless," she says, collapsing into the chair. "There's nothing in here that's even remotely helpful."

"What about his computer?" Zeba suggests.

"It's password protected." She doesn't bother waking the monitor because she already knows it will just turn on to a locked screen. Aman always opts for computer-generated passwords—the ones with the numbers and symbols picked at random—so there's no point in her even trying to guess what it might be.

"Oh! Does he keep a journal where he writes down all his passwords? Shoaib does that—although it's more like random Post-it notes stuck together than an actual journal." Nadia can hear Zeba rolling her eyes through the phone as she walks over to the bookshelf in the corner of the room.

"Not that I know of, but I'll look around." She draws back the curtains to let the moonlight pour in through the windows. Balancing the phone against her ear, she scans the horizontal shelves from one end to the other, running her hand along the spine of each book. The hardcover bindings graze her skin as the tips of her fingers collect the dust from years of neglect. There's a collection of Ansel Adams books mixed in with old medical journals. She angles a few of the spines toward her, pulling them out just enough to glance at the titles:

Zollinger's Atlas of Surgical Operations.

Thirty-ninth edition of *Gray's Anatomy.*

The Art of Photography.

"I don't see anything," she finally says. "It looks like these books haven't been touched or dusted in years—" She stops midsentence as a white envelope, wedged between two titles, falls from the shelf and floats to the floor. "Wait, there's something here," she hisses as she leans down to pick it up. There's a small inky heart drawn on the triangular flap, which she lifts to pull out the card that's inside. It's Tiffany-blue with the word *Love* written in gold-embossed calligraphy across the center. She opens the card, instantly recognizing the three words inscribed in ink.

Happy Anniversary, baby.

The inside of her mouth goes dry. It's the same card from the photograph—the one with the three long-stemmed roses. She leans against the bookshelf, dizzy, as the dots begin to connect.

"Everything okay, Nadi?" Zeba asks. Her voice sounds thin, like it's coming from someplace far away.

"Can I call you back?" Nadia manages to answer. She stares at the written words until they fuse together to create an illegible blur; her breath goes shallow as her mind attempts to process the find. In her hand, her phone buzzes with vigor. She looks down, clicking on the row of notifications alerting her at once. They are comments on the selfie she posted of her and Aman from earlier. She scrolls through, reading each one.

#CoupleGoals

Cuties!

Have fun, lovebirds!

The card dangles from the other hand, the tips of her fingers cold in her tightened grip. The selfie of her and Aman suddenly feels like a farce; she wonders what people would say if they saw her right now, holding an anniversary card given to her husband by someone else. She shuts off the screen, sick at the thought.

"Nadi?"

The door of the study is pushed open, and Aman is standing in the frame. "What are you doing in here?" His voice is thick, still swathed in sleep.

"I-I wasn't feeling well," Nadia explains. Her heart pummels her rib cage as she loops back her hand, pressing the card against the back of her thigh to keep it hidden from his line of sight. With her other, she holds up her cell phone, and the light from the screen allows her to see more clearly his face and the tired lines framing it. He squints into the light, looking back at her with a perplexed expression.

"I think the wings may have given me some indigestion. I was looking for that stash of OTCs you keep in here, but I couldn't find them—" She keeps the light pointed at him, so he can't see the cracks in her face. "I didn't mean to wake you," she adds when he squeezes his eyes and lets out a yawn.

"You're looking in the wrong place," he says, opening the bottom drawer of his desk. "I might have something in here that will help." As he stoops forward to search the contents, Nadia swiftly tucks the card into the waistband of her shorts and pulls her camisole over it. She tugs smooth the fabric and walks up to Aman just as he holds up a bottle of Pepcid.

"Take two of these," he says, twisting the cap open and shaking the tablets into her palm. "I'll meet you back upstairs, and we can rearrange the pillows so you can sleep at an incline. That should help you feel better."

"Thanks," she says softly. Without waiting, she walks to the kitchen to grab a glass of water. When she's certain he's back upstairs, she tosses the pills into the garbage disposal and flips the switch. Back in the hallway, she notices that the door of Aman's study is now firmly shut. She stares at it for a moment, dread sinking to her feet as she climbs the stairs one by one, aware that no amount of Pepcid can fix this upset.

10

Out in the front waiting area, Julie shuffles paperwork from the filing cabinets. In her office, Nadia rubs her eyes and stares at the inbox flooded with emails. She hopes to send out a few patient reports before her next appointment; however, it's a struggle to focus on anything other than Aman.

After returning to bed last night, she could hardly fall back asleep. As Aman dozed soundly beside her, her mind itched with the anxiety of all she had discovered. The text messages, the photographs, the card—which she stuffed into her purse before coming upstairs—taunted her thoughts, forcing her to acknowledge a simple yet important truth she had spent days avoiding: Aman is cheating on her. And there are no reasons or excuses left to suggest otherwise.

So, what now?

The uncertainty of this question paralyzed her. As the sky turned from black to gray, Nadia spent a wakeful night chewing on what this might mean for her marriage while the person responsible for her upheaval slept without worry. Whether she continued to dig deeper for answers or she confronted Aman with what she knew to be true, both outcomes pointed in the same direction.

Is this the end for them? Could this really be the doleful denouement of their ten-year marriage?

WHEN HER AND Zeba's father left, their mom refused to tell anyone what had happened. She insisted that if the question ever arose, they were simply to say he was out of town or away on business. This plan, however, did not deflect the aunties from mentioning his absence every time they went to the mosque. Nor did it discourage other kids from inquiring why their abba never came to pick them up from Sunday school or teachers from asking why their father never showed up to school plays, award banquets, or graduation ceremonies. Even so, she and Zeba continued with the same response, the way they had seen their mom do on countless occasions when faced with similar questions: with a smile and a shrug. *Such a shame he couldn't make it. So sad to be missing another event. Yes, he wanted nothing more than to come, but it was a last-minute change of plans.*

For ten years they kept up this charade. It was easy. It

was rehearsed. It was a lie—one which, looking back, she realized everyone knew but pretended to accept. At first, Nadia believed their mom came up with this plan to protect her and Zeba. Divorce was not common in the South Asian Muslim community. So, to shelter them from backlash, their ammi found a lie just believable enough to work. But in truth, the lie was more for her than it was for them. Nadia was too young to grasp the stigma attached to this circumstance, but she now understands as she faces a similar predicament.

ON THE WAY home, Nadia calls Zeba from the road.

"What happened last night?" is the first thing Zeba says when she answers. "I thought you were going to call me back?"

"I'm sorry, it got late. I must've fallen asleep," Nadia lies.

"Did you end up finding anything?"

Nadia thinks about the anniversary card stashed inside her purse, likely lodged between her wallet and sunglasses. Her stomach lurches to her throat. "That's why I called. I wanted to—"

"No, Alim, Bugsy Bear is at home. Why didn't you tell me you wanted me to bring him?" Zeba sounds distracted as she negotiates with Alim in the background.

"Is this a bad time? Where are you?"

"I'm just pulling into Target."

"By the mall?"

"No, at Riverview Plaza. Why?"

Nadia swerves into the far-right lane toward the next exit and hops back onto the freeway heading in the opposite direction. "Stay there. I'm on my way."

RIVERVIEW PLAZA IS already teeming with the after-work crowd when Nadia pulls into the parking complex. She circles the lot twice before finding a spot near the Target entrance. Inside, the store is bright white and shiny; a low-level hum vibrates in the background from rows of lights stretching across the ceiling. Bodies amble through the aisles, plucking an assortment of products from shelves into red carts. Nadia walks past the clothing section, past a pair of women sporting Lululemon and bouncy ponytails, wedging their fingers between hangers of summery dresses. She feels lost in a capitalistic consumer maze festooned with faceless mannequins and crimson signs.

After walking through what feels like every aisle, she spots G47 near housewares. Sharp shrieks of a small child hurry her ahead; the moment she turns the corner, she spots Alim in the front basket of a cart, strapped at the waist with tears gushing from his eyes. His tiny face matches the color scheme of the store, and for a moment pulls at Nadia's heartstrings. A few feet ahead, Zeba leans against a shelf, flipping through a magazine.

Nadia rushes to Alim, wiping the squishy parts of his cheeks with her thumbs. "What happened?" she asks, unfastening the straps and lifting him from the basket just as a white-haired octogenarian enters the aisle in a motorized cart.

"Someone needs to quiet that kid down," she mutters in a smoke-and-whiskey croak loud enough for Zeba and Nadia to hear. Nadia sways back and forth, attempting to pacify the crying child. The woman shakes her head with disdain, backs up her cart, and whirs past the center aisle.

"Target should charge extra for the unsolicited parenting advice you get with your shopping experience," Nadia mutters, turning to her sister.

Zeba, unfazed, flips to the next page of her magazine.

"Are you going to tell me why you're wailing like a fire engine?" Nadia asks Alim, rubbing small circles into his back just as her mom did whenever she was sick.

Alim hiccups, hardly able to speak as his small body spasms in Nadia's arms. His mouth opens to release sharp, shuddering gasps in between each breath.

"He's having a meltdown because I wouldn't let him eat the candlesticks." Zeba motions to the clear boxes of skinny tapers lying in the back of the cart. "He thinks they're string cheese."

Nadia laughs, combing the curly locks from Alim's forehead with her fingers. "Beta, these are candles. You can't eat these!"

Zeba sighs. "Say it about a dozen more times, and then you'll be where I am."

Nadia places Alim back into the cart, carefully positioning his legs through the holes. From her purse, she fishes out a bag of M&M's. Tearing off the corner, she pours a handful into her mouth before passing it to Zeba. "They're no candles, but can he have some of these?"

"That's way too much sugar," Zeba protests.

"But they're peanut butter. They're healthier . . . kind of."

Zeba gives her a look as she turns over the bag to examine the nutritional information.

"Let the kid live a little, will you?" Nadia says, snatching the bag back. "You already took away his string cheese." As Alim reaches for the chocolates Nadia gives him, she clicks onto a video-sharing app on her phone. "Should we see if we can find an episode of that doggie show you like? Is it *Paw Patrol*?" she asks him.

"No doggies. *StowyBots*," Alim says, his mouth full of candy.

Zeba closes the magazine. "I'll let the candy slide, but it's not screen time, Alim," she says, walking over to him. "You already watched *StoryBots* this afternoon."

Alim's bottom lip juts forward. "I want *StowyBots*!" he says in a shaky voice. "Beep, boop, bing, bang, BO!"

"Is that code for something?"

"See, this is exactly why I said this was a bad idea . . ."

"BEEP, BOOP, BO!"

Nadia presses her hands against her ears as Alim's shouts get louder. She turns to Zeba with pleading eyes. "Is a little extra screen time really that bad?"

"Yes. It messes up his whole schedule—"

"Ten minutes," Nadia says. "I promise." She looks at Alim, who's on the verge of another meltdown. "I mean, look at him. Clearly he's had a rough day."

Zeba rolls her eyes, and Nadia translates this as the permission she needs. She clicks on an episode of *StoryBots* and hands Alim the phone just in time to halt the meltdown. Feeling pleased with herself, she shifts her attention back to Zeba. Though her sister may not approve of her methods, a distracted child means she can finally discuss the reasons she came. "Where's Noman, by the way?" she asks, just to be sure. "Don't tell me he's in the next aisle eating parchment paper."

"He's at his karate class. Thank goodness Shoaib came home early enough to take him, otherwise I would've been stuck with both." Zeba tosses the magazine into the back of the mostly empty shopping cart. "Which reminds me, let's keep going while he's occupied. I still have a million things to pick up." She hands Nadia a folded sheet of yellow legal paper that she pulls from her back pocket and pushes the cart into the next aisle.

"What's all this for?" Nadia asks, reading the numbered items on the list.

"A small dawat Shoaib and I are having next weekend. These days, unless we host something, we never get to socialize. I just always forget how much work goes into planning a dinner—even if it's a small one."

"I'm happy to help if you need. I still owe you for your last two favors."

"I was actually hoping you and Aman would come. Speaking of which—is everything okay? You never told me what happened last night."

Nadia unzips the center mouth of her purse and pulls out the white envelope that houses the card. It takes Zeba a moment, but the recognition sets in.

"Is this what I think it is?" Zeba says, turning to face her. Nadia nods as Zeba delicately lifts the front fold to read the short message penned inside. Beside them in the cart, Alim laughs loudly at the colorful robots on the screen, his light-hearted giggles juxtaposing the unease lingering between the sisters. "Where did you find this?"

"In Aman's study. It was lodged between two books. Just slipped right out when I was checking the shelves last night."

Zeba takes in a sharp breath. "And you're sure this is the same card from the photograph?"

"You tell me." She rummages the inside folds of her purse until she locates the photograph—the one she showed

Zeba at her house. She smooths out the edges, and the two of them lean in, their shoulders hunched together in the middle of the aisle as they oscillate their attention from the card to the photo with the three red roses.

Zeba lets out a low sigh and shakes her head. "There's no mistaking it. It's the same." Nadia bites her bottom lip. She isn't sure if hearing her sister's confirmation makes her feel less anxious or more. "What could this mean?"

Nadia can't bring herself to answer that question. However, she's certain her sister has reached the same conclusion by the alarm on her face.

"Why would Aman have an anniversary card that's not from you?" Zeba presses the space between her hairline and temples. "Obviously someone gave it to him," she responds before pausing to check Nadia's reaction. "Do you think it might be that L person? The one who was texting him?"

Nadia is quiet, but she is sure the two are connected. It's the only way to explain the flirtatious tone of that message, which she is even more certain now did not come from Leo.

"I'm so sorry, Nadi," Zeba says, her voice almost a whisper.

"I don't know what I'm going to do," Nadia replies. The thought of seeking out more information makes her feel ill. Between the photos, the texts, and the card, she's not sure how much more she can stomach. She barely knows what to do with the information she has now.

"You don't have to figure it out in this moment. There might still be some explanation for all of this. Something we might be overlooking."

Nadia nods, but she isn't sure she can muster that same optimism. She agrees, however, that a situation like this requires thought, careful planning. And unless she has some solid proof—like an actual name attached to Aman's mystery texter—she's not willing to risk everything over a hunch, no matter how strong it may be.

She stuffs the card and photograph back into her purse and pushes the cart, following Zeba into the next aisle. As her sister scours the shelves for table runners, Nadia waits, resting her elbows across the handlebar. Alim, upon seeing Nadia's face so close to his, holds out the phone to show her the colorful bots bouncing about the screen. She manages a feeble smile, but her mind is elsewhere, drifting to where it often does, especially as of late. What would their mom have thought of all this had she been alive? Would she have been disappointed to learn that Aman might be cheating on her? Or would she have expressed vindication in having received a confirmation of her initial disapproval? She, after all, was the one who deemed Aman unsuitable. Nadia rakes Alim's hair back and tries to suppress her conflicted feelings. It irks her to know that even in death, her mom turned out to be right.

"Is it wrong that I still feel angry at her?" she asks Zeba, who is debating between a floral lace runner and a more ornate checkered bamboo one.

"Hmm?" Zeba says, looking up. Her face softens, though, the moment she sees Nadia's and realizes to whom she's referring. "No," she answers. "I feel angry at her too sometimes."

"You do?"

Zeba stands up and dusts the knees of her slacks. "I'm angry at her for dying. For leaving us to figure out how to continue on without her." Her voice quiets as she glances at Alim. "But other times, I'm relieved. Like in some ways it's better that she's gone. In a way, I think that might be worse."

Nadia knows exactly what Zeba means; she's just surprised to hear her admit it.

"I hated how much she worried. All the time. And now, with everything happening between you and Aman . . . it would've destroyed her."

"I'm not so sure about that."

"No, really, Nadi. She wanted so much for you to be happy."

"Just not with Aman." Nadia wasn't planning on getting emotional in the middle of a Target, but she's finding it hard to keep herself contained. "We both know she never made any effort to warm up to him. Before or after we married. She never cared for him like she did for Shoaib."

"Maybe," Zeba answers honestly. "But she did care for you."

"I think that's also up for debate," Nadia says, lurching toward the thing that lingers on her tongue. "Sometimes I wonder if she might've been glad if Aman and I . . ." She stops, unable to complete the sentence.

"Nadia," Zeba says, her voice firm with dissent. "You're wrong. She loved—"

"*Being right.* It's okay to say it." She wants to tell Zeba that she doesn't need to try so hard to please their mom now that she's no longer alive. She can say what she really thinks—in fact, Nadia wishes she would.

"Look, whatever is going on between you and Aman, we'll get to the bottom of it."

"And what if it turns out to be what we think it is?" Nadia asks, her mouth weighed down in a frown. "What then?"

Zeba is quiet.

"What if I end up like her? If this is the path I was always headed on?"

"There are worse paths to be on," her sister replies. "Ammi was stronger than most people gave her credit for. I'm not saying you will, Nadi, but ending up like her isn't the worst thing."

"You mean alone? Unloved? Lying to herself and everyone around her? Even you can't possibly spin that into a positive—"

"It was the only way she could control the situation. She had to make up those stories, otherwise everyone else would take over that narrative. Was it a perfect solution? Of course not. But she dealt with it as best as she could, and she ended up fine."

"*Did she?*" Nadia scoffs. "Is that why I would hear her crying in her bedroom every single night?"

Zeba's face twists with pain.

"She might've dealt with it, Zeba, but she was far from *fine*. You can't make me believe that."

"You're right. I can't make you believe anything. Especially once you've decided you don't want to." Zeba looks as if she wants to say more, but instead she returns her attention to the table runners.

"All I know is I can't end up like her. I *refuse to*," Nadia says. "This thing between me and Aman." She searches for the exact words. "I don't know what I'll do if we end up . . ." She squeezes her eyes and inhales deep before starting again. "I don't think I can survive if my marriage falls apart. Not the way Ammi did, and maybe that makes me less strong of a person. But I love him, Zeba. I really do."

"I know," Zeba says, reaching out to clasp Nadia's hand, her disappointment replaced with a genuine concern. "Everything will be okay, *okay*?"

Nadia nods, not fully convinced.

"I know this is hard. But—"

"Zeba?"

Her offer of support is cut midsentence by a man approaching their aisle. He is tall, in his late thirties. A red basket dangles from his forearm. Nadia doesn't recognize him, but it's evident Zeba does.

"Ali?" Zeba remarks with a strained voice. She pushes her cheeks back into a forced smile and releases Nadia's hand.

"I thought that was you, but I wasn't sure." Ali shifts back onto his heels to make eye contact with them both. "I hope I'm not interrupting," he says, so directly that Nadia is certain he overheard their conversation. Her face reddens.

"Not at all. I was just picking up a few things with my sister."

Ali acknowledges Nadia with a nod. Though he's dressed quite primly—in a checkered oxford shirt and belted pants—she notices how a few stray locks of hair fall above his dark eyebrows, and a grayish stubble peppers his angular jawline. "Ali. Nice to meet you." His smile causes the dent in his chin to deepen.

Nadia slips her hand into his extended palm. "Nadia."

"What are you doing here?" Zeba asks.

"Just checking off a few errands before heading home." Ali points to the laundry detergent and toothpaste sitting in the basket on his arm.

"Ali is a colleague of Shoaib's," Zeba explains. "He teaches finance. No, accounting?" She cups her forehead, shaking her head. "Actually, I can never remember."

"Housing economics and real estate finance," Ali says, the corners of his eyes folding into soft creases. "It's a mouthful. I can barely remember myself sometimes." He glances at Nadia. She presses her lips together, struggling to come up with a humored response. Her mind is still distracted with thoughts of Aman, and unlike her sister, she cannot disguise her emotions with such ease.

"Did Shoaib invite you to the dawat next weekend?"

"He did. I'm looking forward to it. I feel like I only see him at department meetings these days." He pauses before addressing Nadia. "Perhaps we'll also meet again next weekend?"

"Insha'Allah," Zeba says, sensing Nadia's hesitation. She and Ali exchange a few more words before saying goodbye.

Nadia waits until they're alone again before disclosing her uncertainty. "About your dinner party, Zeba—"

"There's no pressure, Nadi," Zeba interrupts. "The invitation is there. If you're feeling up to it, I'd love for you to come. And Aman too."

"It's just with everything going on, I don't know if . . ."

"It's a matter of a few hours," Zeba reminds her. "Besides, it might give you guys a distraction. Something to take your mind off everything else."

"I'll think about it. I will," Nadia says. The dawat is over a week away, and more pressing issues occupy her worries now.

"I didn't get a chance to say this earlier, but you're stronger than you think, Nadi. And whatever happens, you don't have to do this alone. Maybe Ammi did, but that's the difference. You have me."

Nadia leans forward and gives her sister a hug. Regardless of how strained their relationship has been in recent years, hearing Zeba say this is exactly what she needed.

WHILE ZEBA FASTENS Alim into his car seat, Nadia unloads the shopping cart into the back of her sister's minivan. "I think that's everything," she says, transferring the last of the bags.

"Do you want me to drive you to your car?"

"That's okay. I'm just parked there," Nadia says, signaling a row over. She moves aside and blows kisses at Alim as Zeba slides into the driver's seat.

"Keep me posted about next weekend," Zeba says, turning the key in the ignition. As the engine purrs to life, she adds, "And call me. If you need anything."

Nadia nods, waving as she waits for Zeba's car to turn the corner. Walking back to her own, her steps are heavy, filled with a quiet unease. Above, the sky has slowly darkened into dusk, and a bright moon rises, bringing with it scattered stars. She fumbles for her keys as the greasy, salty smell of french fries invades her senses. At the end of the lot, there's an In-N-Out with a queue of red taillights snaking around the white structure. The smells remind her of her first summer with Aman.

ON A WHIM, they had driven to Manresa Uplands State Beach, where they rented a small cabin and spent the afternoon walking along the water's edge, collecting fragments of broken sand dollars in their palms—piecing them together to make a whole. Each time a wave would crash at their ankles, Aman would wrap his arms around Nadia's waist and pull her back toward the shore. At the time, Nadia was just ten weeks into her first pregnancy, but already a new sense of protectiveness had come over Aman, which she noticed in the small ways he watched over her.

They were young, and life had not yet shown them that even with great care, not all could be protected. Every change that occurred in those weeks was celebrated with excitement and wonder. It was in this cabin that Nadia experienced her first craving: french fries. Before the request was even out of her mouth, Aman piled her into his coupe, and they drove to the Santa Cruz boardwalk, going from booth to booth as they stuffed their faces with spiralized spuds, garlicky fries, and crisped tater tots dipped in a warm cheddar queso. In between bites, Aman would touch Nadia's stomach and ask if the baby was satisfied. Nadia swatted his hand, joking that if she ate any more, she'd give birth to a little potato.

Hours later, after returning to the cabin, Nadia awoke in the middle of the night clutching her side in pain. Imputing her discomfort to one too many fries, she hobbled to the toilet to find a bright red ring soaked through the cotton of her panties. A hurried trip to urgent care confirmed the worst of their fears.

The next morning, she and Aman emptied out the cabin and drove back home as a family of two, their hopes for an addition dashed. In the nine years that followed, Aman's sense of protectiveness gradually diminished, and she never craved a french fry again.

As the engine awakens with a start, Nadia reaches for her cell phone. The screen is blank: not a single text or missed call from Aman. Of all the challenges they have endured together, his pulling away from her is the one that cuts the deepest. It's the first time she and Aman seem to be fighting for different things, and without his reassurance to remind her that everything is okay, she is unsure she can arrive at that conclusion on her own.

As she backs out of the parking space, Nadia knows that

pretending all is fine is not going to fix her marriage. It's not going to bring Aman back to her. She must be willing to seek out the answers—regardless of how painful it might be—because the only thing separating her from the same path as her mom is how committed she is to finding out the truth.

11

The sound of Nadia's heels punctuates the silence as she and Aman walk the narrow pathway to Zeba's front door. She is dressed in a pale blue georgette kameez with a keyhole neckline, sheer quarter-length sleeves, and a front slit that begins at her waistline and ends at her knees. Beneath it, she wears white ankle-length palazzo pants bordered in the same delicate chikankari work that covers the tunic. Her curly hair is pulled back in a low chignon, revealing her pearl-studded earrings; the ivory shells match the iridescent shimmer of her eyeshadow. Beside her, Aman is equally formal in gray slacks, a taupe button-down, and a powder-blue tie. His face is clean-shaven and his thick hair combed back with the edges trimmed neatly at the nape of his neck. Nadia readjusts her dupatta, ironing the creases with her hand, before she rings the doorbell. The evening is early yet, but the hours leading up to this dinner party have already left her exhausted.

This past week has consumed Nadia, her mind struggling to accommodate the wrenching reality that has pushed its way into her marriage. Each late-night shift, every unreturned text, even Aman taking his phone with him into the bathroom sends Nadia's overworked imagination into a state of panic. She finds herself obsessing over details—looks that seem more distracted than pensive; smiles more distant than reassuring—as evidence confirming her greatest fear. Aman is pulling away from her, and there is nothing she can do to stop it. Despite this emotional tumult, Nadia is careful to appear unbothered around Aman, continuing to behave as she normally would until she figures out how to get more answers. So far, her efforts to uncover L's identity have led nowhere, the increased mystery only heightening her insecurities and making it harder to focus on much else.

By the time Saturday afternoon arrived, Nadia's feelings about Zeba's dinner party were mixed. Although Aman agreed to accompany her earlier this week, he seemed to have forgotten, as he spent the morning pacing around his study, splitting his attention between computer and phone screen—both of which she was convinced were tied in some way to his correspondence with L. Overwhelmed by suspicion, she considered calling Zeba to cancel altogether, but at the last minute, she changed her mind. She made a promise to her sister that she would come. And even if Aman backed out of that promise, she didn't want to be the one to let Zeba down—especially after it took so long to get back in her good graces.

About an hour before they were expected to leave, Nadia went upstairs to get ready. The thought of hearing another half-baked excuse from Aman prevented her from prodding him. She knew her sister would be anticipating them both, but she settled on the idea of going on her own. If nothing else, she was relieved for a chance to get out of the house and the suffocation surrounding her. As she finished getting dressed, however, Aman came into the bedroom with a freshly ironed shirt.

"I just got off the phone with Shoaib. Give me a few minutes to change, and I'll meet you downstairs?"

"Okay," Nadia said, certain Zeba had something to do with Shoaib's phone call. Unsure how to feel about it, she texted Zeba while waiting downstairs.

What did Shoaib say to Aman?

Nothing. He just told him he was looking forward to seeing him tonight.

Are you sure he didn't say anything else?

No. Andheri, Zeba added. **Some of the guests are starting to arrive. Are you on your way?**

Nadia heard Aman still scuttling around upstairs and sighed. She knew how lateness bothered her sister. **Yes**, she lied. **See you soon.**

Nadia scrolled through her social media feed as Aman finished getting ready. Although her sister's interference had warded off the whispered inquiries that a solo entrance would have garnered, Aman's sudden willingness to accompany her didn't elate her as she thought it would—partially because she knew his attendance had little to do with keeping his commitment to her, and more to do with appeasing Shoaib. As she flicked past photo after photo, Aman rushed downstairs, feet bare, his tie hanging unknotted around the collar.

"Sorry," he said, stumbling to pull on a sock. "I forgot we were going tonight; I must've lost track of time."

Without his asking, Nadia reached out to adjust his tie, wrapping one end around the other and looping it over and back to form a Windsor knot. She tightened it at the top and stepped back to check its symmetry.

"Do I look okay?" Aman asked, waiting for her approval.

Nadia nodded, smoothing out a stray lock of hair near his crown. For a moment, she was struck by how handsome he was, but the buzz of his phone vibrating through his pants pulled her back. "Would you be okay with shutting that off for tonight?" she asked.

Aman checked the phone. Nadia tried to make out

whether it was another message from L, but his expression revealed nothing. Instead, he swiped up to clear the screen and pressed the button on the side. "There. I silenced it," he said, sliding it back into his pocket. "Shall we?"

Nadia bit her lip, leading the way as they exited the house. The sky was already darkening, and she was glad he couldn't see the disappointment on her face.

On the drive to Zeba's, neither she nor Aman spoke. She kept her gaze on the road and the string of cars gliding past her window. Her resolve to remain neutral around him was beginning to weaken. She worried that her growing resentment was coming to a head and desperately hoped seeing her sister might quell some of that bitterness.

Aman seemed to sense, somehow, that things were off balance, and he reached out and touched her hand. "Is everything okay?" he asked.

"Mm-hmm," she responded, her fingers stiffening at his touch.

"Are you sure?" he pressed. "It seems like there's something on your mind—"

"Everything is fine," Nadia said quickly. The emotional energy required for this conversation was more than she currently had, and the last thing she wanted was to broach this subject right before Zeba's party. Aman glanced in her direction, but to her relief, he let it go.

As they neared the entrance of Casa Del Rey, Aman unclasped her hand to turn into the subdivision. When she spotted the orange trim of Zeba's house, she released a tightly held breath. From the number of cars parked along the driveway, it's clear they were one of the last to arrive; however, Aman nabbed a spot just a few houses down. Once parked, she grabbed the box of baklava they picked up on the way and followed Aman up the walkway. They pressed the doorbell and stood back to wait, ready with false smiles to greet their hosts.

Zeba opens the door, the apples of her cheeks the same shade of pink as her hijab. "Thank goodness you're here," she says, grabbing Nadia's elbow and motioning them inside. The living room is empty, but the sound of voices from the rear of the house carries through the kitchen and fills the space with a hum of laughter.

"As'salaamu Alaikum," Aman says, leaning in to give Zeba an awkward one-armed hug.

"Walaikum As'salaam," Zeba replies. She is dressed in a sand-colored kaftan abaya dress with a pale floral print and ruffled sleeves that cascade elegantly as she reaches back to shut the front door. Her top eyelids are lined in black kohl and her thick lashes frame her wide eyes as she turns back to face them.

"Sorry we're a little late."

"No worries. I'm just glad you made it," Zeba says, accepting the box of baklava that Nadia hands her.

"Is everyone out back?" Nadia asks as she watches her sister eyeing Aman. "Should we head out there?"

Zeba ignores her. "Aman, what have you been up to these days?" she asks, taking no notice of the sideways glance that Nadia casts her way.

"Same old, you know. Just been busy with work."

"I bet," Zeba responds knowingly. "Those late-night shifts must be taking a lot out of you, huh?"

A small crease forms between Aman's brows. "I suppose. How did you—"

"Oh." Zeba waves her hand. "Busy with work usually translates into late nights. At least it does for Shoaib."

"Speaking of Shoaib, is he around?" Nadia asks, hoping his presence might lighten the mood.

"That's tough, though." Zeba plows forward. "It's all about finding the right balance between work and fun. Have you found something *fun to do* to take your mind off work, Aman?"

Confusion furrows Aman's forehead as he tries to figure out what Zeba might be getting at.

"He's here tonight, isn't he?" Nadia laughs nervously.

"We're so glad for that," Zeba remarks, patting Aman on the back—a little harder than necessary, Nadia notes.

"Aren't there other guests to check in on? Don't let us monopolize all your time."

"Don't be silly, Nadi. Remember what Ammi always

said: family first. Besides, it means a lot that you both came, especially with *everything else* you've got going on." She smiles sweetly at Nadia, who glares at her with narrowed eyes.

"Say, is Shoaib around?" Aman asks.

"He's out back with everyone else. C'mon." Zeba leads them past the living room and into the kitchen. The back of her kaftan billows behind her, forming loose ripples as she walks. As she reaches out to open the back door, Alim rushes into the kitchen wearing nothing but a pair of Spider-Man briefs.

"Mummy!" he shrieks, charging past Nadia and into Zeba's arms.

"Whoa, buddy! Look how big you've gotten!" Aman exclaims as Zeba lifts the boy up. He holds out his hand to offer a high five, but Alim turns away, shyly burying his head into Zeba's neck.

"Alim, I told you to wait!" a harried voice calls from the hallway. It belongs to a college-aged girl with ripped jeans and a cropped sweatshirt, her appearance matching the frenzy in her voice. "I'm so sorry," she apologizes to Zeba. "The boys were horsing around and Alim shat his pants. He ran out before I could get his clothes back on." The girl exhales, blowing the bangs out of her eyes. Her gaze falls upon Nadia and Aman, and she immediately turns a deep shade of pink. "I'm Maggie, by the way," she says, extending her hand.

Nadia shakes it reluctantly, the word *shat* still ringing in her ears.

"Maggie's a former student of Shoaib's. She's helping baby-sit for the night," Zeba explains. She turns and kisses Alim on the forehead. "Are you giving Ms. Maggie a hard time?"

Alim giggles and blows a wet raspberry into her face.

"Here, do you want me to take him?" Maggie offers.

Zeba hands him over and turns to Nadia. "Why don't you guys head outside while I check on the other one. If one is up to no good, it usually means the other is too."

As she and Aman step into the backyard, Nadia is stunned by how lovely and welcoming the outdoor space has been made. The last time she saw it, the small yard was overgrown with weeds and covered in playthings left behind by the boys. But now, there's not an unwanted plant or toy in sight.

Edged along the perimeter of the wooden fence hangs a single string of twinkling lights. At the corner of the yard, the lights continue, spiraling neatly around the trunk of an avocado tree all the way up to the candle lanterns that hang off the branches, casting warm shadows across the freshly cut lawn. There is a long table in the center of the yard, and around it, Zeba's guests cluster together with glasses of cold nimbu sharbat in their hands.

In the corner, she's surprised to spot Sheila conversing with a well-dressed woman in a white open-front abaya and cropped high-waisted pants. "Look who's here," she says to Aman, and points as Sheila gives them a wave.

"I wonder if that's Damien next to her," Nadia continues, examining the dark, handsome man standing beside her friend. Though he is younger than she imagined, she must admit they make a fine-looking couple.

As she glances around the yard, Shoaib sneaks up from behind and grabs Aman by the shoulders.

"Hey, salaams! Long time!" He wraps his arms around him, enclosing him in his large frame. "Salaams, bhabi," he acknowledges Nadia with a wave.

"Looking sharp, man. I almost didn't recognize you," Aman says, stepping back to admire Shoaib's sophisticated ensemble—a dark linen suit jacket with well-fitted jeans and white low-top trainers.

Shoaib adjusts his bow tie. "Just trying to keep up with you." He chuckles, the deep sound of his laugh vibrating in his throat. "What's new with you?"

Aman responds with the same answer he gave Zeba; however, Nadia notices he looks a little less nervous this time. "What have you been up to?" he asks, running his fingers through his hair.

"You know, a little of this, a little of that." Shoaib offers him two cups of sharbat, one of which Aman hands to Nadia. "I was meaning to ask, are you still doing the photography stuff? I've been thinking of getting a DSLR—"

"A what now?" Zeba asks, walking up to rejoin them.

"Jaan," Shoaib says, wrapping his arm playfully around her shoulder. "You know I've been talking about getting a new camera ever since Alim's birthday party. Don't you want me to be a good Instagram husband for you?"

"Oh, you mean for the four photos I post annually?"

"You're the one always saying that we need to take more pictures as a family," Shoaib says as Zeba slips out from under his arm. "Am I right or am I right?"

Aman holds back a laugh as Shoaib turns to him. "But about that camera, I could use some pointers if you have any."

"Aman is more of a film guy, aren't you?" Zeba asks, as if she just took a guess.

"I mean, I have my preferences," Aman says. "But I'd be down to discuss the specs on digitals too if you want."

"I'm curious: Where can you even go to process negatives these days?"

Nadia almost spits out her drink. She's not sure what Zeba is doing but wishes she'd stop.

"I usually do it myself."

"I don't know about all that. I'm looking for something a bit more instant," Shoaib says, pulling out his phone. "Do you know anything about image sensors? These are the types I was looking at." As Aman leans in to look at the screen, Nadia grabs her sister's hand and pulls her away.

"Oh, was that our cue to leave?"

"More like *your* cue to tone it down," Nadia rebukes once they're at a safe distance from the husbands. "I mean, '*Where do you go to process negatives?*' Seriously, Zeba? This isn't an episode of *Veronica Mars.*"

"It was just a question!" Zeba exclaims. "Besides, aren't you trying to figure out who this L person is? I'm just trying to help."

"I appreciate it, but this isn't how we're going to find out." Nadia sighs, kneading out the knots along the base of her neck. All the stress she's been shouldering these past couple of weeks is beginning to manifest in different parts of her body, and her sister's "help" has only seemed to exacerbate it further.

"Fine," Zeba says. She waves to one of the guests, who calls her name from across the yard.

"Go," Nadia suggests. "I'll catch up with you later."

"Come with me. Let me introduce you to everyone." She braids her fingers into Nadia's, and they circle the yard to meet the others. After a quick chat with Sheila and Damien, Zeba introduces Nadia to Alyzeh, the well-dressed woman in white, who Nadia learns is part of Zeba's "mother group." With her is her husband, Wasim, and a young Bengali couple—Rohma and Dev Banerjee, who have recently moved to the neighborhood from Seattle. There's also a handful of people from Shoaib's flag football team and, of course, Ali, his colleague whom they met at Target the week prior.

"Hello," Ali says, brightening when he sees Nadia. "We meet again, this time minus the laundry detergent."

Nadia smiles, her mind once more too distracted to come up with an adequate reply. She notices, however, that his stubble has thickened into the beginnings of a beard, which has been neatly groomed to match the rest of his appearance. Her mom used to say that beards made a man, but since Aman always preferred the clean-shaven look, she never pushed him to grow his out.

"You've outdone yourself, Zeba," Ali remarks, pointing to the elegantly dressed table lined with platters of food. "Hopefully Shoaib gave you a hand in putting this all together."

"He did," Zeba agrees. They spot Shoaib hovering near the appetizers, plucking samosas from the tray onto his plate in between bouts of conversation. "In his own way, of course."

"Of course." Ali laughs.

After a brief chat, they follow the other guests to opposite ends of the table—men on one side and women on the other. Nadia takes a seat next to Sheila, amused by how naturally everyone segregated themselves without even being explicitly instructed.

"Poor Damien," Sheila says, looking wistfully down the table. "He doesn't know anyone here but me." They watch

Damien pace around the table, looking slightly lost. "I hope he'll be able to manage on his own." Just as she's about to jump to his rescue, they see Ali wave him over to the empty chair beside him.

"See?" Nadia says, gently pulling Sheila back into her seat. "It looks like he's managing just fine." She smiles at the relief that washes over Sheila's face. As Sheila converses with a few ladies on the other side of her, Nadia scans the far end of the table for Aman. She spots him next to Shoaib, chair pulled back, neck bent as he types away on his phone. Nadia turns away.

Once everyone is seated, the sound of silverware echoes in the air as platters of food prepared by their gracious host make their circulation. Seated at the center of the table, Nadia catches Zeba orchestrating the pass around, making sure each guest gets a full plate. She finds herself in awe at how seamlessly Zeba is able to pull things like this together. While some of the dishes, like the biryani and garlic naans, are catered from a nearby tandoori restaurant, everything else is homemade and delicious.

Nadia tries a sampling of everything, looking forward to a meal that doesn't involve digesting some type of liquidy sludge. "How are the kids?" she asks Sheila, squeezing fresh lemon over her haleem.

"They're good! Alina is turning thirteen next month. I'm not sure this mama is ready for that just yet."

"I can't believe you're going to have a teenager," Nadia exclaims. "It seems like just yesterday she was a precocious seven-year-old who wrote moody poetry and listened to Lana Del Rey on repeat."

"Oh dear." Sheila clutches her chest. "Who am I kidding? We all know Alina's been a teenager most of her life."

Nadia laughs. She remembers all the birthday parties she and Aman attended for Sheila's kids throughout the years, until they finally stopped when it became too painful being the only childless couple. "How's everything else going?" she asks, changing the subject. "You and Damien seem to be doing well."

"We are." Sheila smiles. "I just never imagined I'd be given a second chance at love."

Nadia squeezes Sheila's hand. She knows these past couple years have not been easy on her since her husband Naveen's death. Aside from the grief, the loneliness created by his absence left Sheila isolated in ways she never imagined. Though Nadia can't fully conceive of the challenges her friend has been up against, she is aware of the stigmas surrounding widowhood as they remained as affixed within their community as did the shame attached to divorce.

"Damien was the first one who met me with compassion when he learned of my situation. I can't tell you how wonderful it feels to be accepted as I am—that too, without pity or judgment. And the clincher is the kids just adore him!"

"I can tell he makes you happy."

"What about you? How are you and Aman?"

"We're good," Nadia says with a pause lengthy enough for Sheila to take notice.

"Do you want to talk about it?"

Nadia shakes her head. "It's nothing," she lies.

"All marriages have their ups and downs. It's perfectly normal to feel a little out of sync now and then."

Though Nadia appreciates Sheila's attempt to reassure, her situation is not so straightforward. She twists the gold band around her ring finger, wishing it were that simple. As the dinner platters empty, she ambles over to the dessert table to find something else to satiate her cravings.

"Have you decided yet?" She turns to see Ali standing behind her. His hand cups his chin and a thoughtful expression covers his face.

"I'm sorry?" she asks.

"Which one you're going to try." He points to the various dessert trays lining the table in front of them. "I'm terrible with so many options. I was hoping you'd have some advice on how to choose."

Nadia hands him a small plate, also taking one for herself. "The secret to choosing is to not. Just try a little of everything."

Ali lifts his forehead, impressed with the bold suggestion. "Isn't that a marvelous secret?" He takes the sharp, serrated knife sitting on the table and cuts himself a generous sliver of coconut cream pie. He pairs it with gulab jamuns, a small piece of baklava, and a few spoonfuls of fresh fruit topped with custard. Nadia waits until he finishes before making her choice. After careful thought, she spoons a small handful of berries onto her plate, minus the custard.

"Was the 'try everything' not meant to be taken literally?" Ali asks, looking embarrassed.

"It was." She laughs, eyeing his selection. "It's just . . ." She hesitates, staring at her own plate of fruit. "It's actually a little embarrassing to admit."

"Oh?"

"I've just gotten so used to sneaking sweets like this in private that it feels almost weird to eat it out in the open."

"You're on a diet?"

"Sort of." Nadia shakes her head. "Well, my husband is. Low-carb. No sugar. I initially joined in for moral support."

"Ah." An understanding washes over Ali's face. "Hence the sneaking in private."

Nadia nods. Behind them, on the patio, laughter erupts from where Zeba has corralled the other guests. In between bites, they watch Shoaib and Zeba stand opposite each other in what appears to be a face-off. Zeba's phone is held to her forehead while Shoaib gestures in front of her as she tries to guess whatever word is displayed on the screen.

"Uh-oh," Nadia says.

"This game they're playing, it definitely looks . . ." Ali cocks his head, searching for the word. "Intense?"

She turns to him with a look that says *you have no idea.* They continue watching as Shoaib grunts loudly, hopping from foot to foot while scratching the top of his head. Zeba shouts words at him while the others rally behind her. Nadia looks around, spotting Aman near the grill, his face buried in his phone.

"Unbelievable," she mutters.

"Hmm?" Ali says.

Nadia turns; she forgot for a second that Ali was there. As she watches him shovel forkfuls of pie into his mouth, the inside of hers fills with saliva. The phantom taste of honeyed coconut teases her taste buds, tempting her with its toasty sweetness. "You know what, fuck it," she says, grabbing the knife and carving a fat slice of pie. Ali watches with amused admiration as she adds it to her plate along with some baklava and two generous helpings of custard. Ignoring his gaze, she uses her spoon to cut into the soft creamy layers of pie and sinks her teeth into each bite. "Oh, this is exactly what I needed," she says, closing her eyes, savoring the flaky goodness. She cleans her plate before tossing it into the trash bin. "I'm gonna catch up with the others before I do something I'll really regret."

"Have fun," Ali replies, biting into a gulab jamun. "I'll be over here in case anyone asks."

Nadia walks over to the patio and sidles up beside Aman just as the timer goes off.

"I said gorilla! That last one better count!" Zeba exclaims as the screen tallies up her answers.

"Do you remember the last time these two went head-to-head?" Aman whispers to her.

"I do. I almost got hit in the face with a chappal." Though her sister's nature is typically calm, there's a competitive side to her that emerges anytime a game is involved—especially one resulting in winners and losers. Even when they were children, Nadia knew better than to be paired up as Zeba's opponent. There was always less risk of injury if she and Zeba played for the same team, a lesson she learned from experience.

Aman's phone vibrates loudly, its distinct buzz separating from the sounds around them.

"I thought you silenced that thing?"

"Hmm? Oh, yeah, I turned it back on in case of an emergency." As he twists his body to peer at the message, Nadia's face turns hot. Even Zeba and Shoaib's playful banter can't drown out the clanging in her chest. She wonders if L's texts constitute an emergency, and if so, what excuse he might use to sneak away this time. To her surprise, though, he closes the screen and returns his attention to the game.

"Everything okay?" Nadia asks, trying to keep her voice steady.

"Yeah." Aman looks at her. "Nothing important." He smiles and slides the phone back into his pocket.

"Okay, okay, you win!" Shoaib calls out, settling the score with Zeba. He throws up his hands, feigning annoyance, but the hint of a smile gives away his amusement.

Zeba grins, twirling the ends of her kaftan as she gracefully performs a curtsy.

"But now," Shoaib says, giving her a gentle kiss on the forehead, "it's time to switch things up." He grabs a guitar standing upright behind him and slings it across his shoulders. "Who's ready for some Antakshari?" he asks, strumming a few chords.

Nadia locks eyes across the patio with Sheila, who immediately perks up—a familiar mischief flashing across her face. She steps forward, wagging a finger at both Nadia and Aman.

No way, Nadia mouths, making it clear that she will not—under any circumstances—give in to whatever crazy thought is crossing her friend's mind.

"Karaoke night, part two?" Sheila says, shimmying her shoulders.

"Absolutely not," Nadia declares, as Sheila attempts to pull her forward. She has no desire to relive any part of that performance. Aman, however, appears mildly intrigued by the invitation. "Tell me you're not considering it?" she says to him with a horrified expression.

"I mean . . ." He shrugs as Nadia stares in disbelief.

"Now it's a party!" Shoaib calls out excitedly. He holds out his fist and bumps it against Aman's.

"I'm not much of a singer, though," Aman admits.

"That's not what I remember," Sheila teases.

"Karaoke is one thing, but I'm awful at Antakshari."

"I doubt that," Zeba says, stepping in. "All you have to do is make things up on the spot. Something tells me you're better at it than you think."

As Zeba goes over the rules, Aman and Sheila arrange themselves beside Shoaib in the center of the patio. "Now, remember," Zeba says, trying to get everyone's attention. "You can sing in whatever language you choose, just make sure whatever sound the singer before you ends with is the same sound you begin your song with. Oh, and no repeated songs."

Aman loosens the tie around his neck and glances at Nadia. She's not sure what to expect but is relieved that his willingness has gotten her off the hook. He whispers his song choice into Shoaib's ear. Though he looks slightly nervous, the moment Shoaib strums the first few chords, his voice comes out clear and strong. *"Pehli nazar mein kaise jaado kar diya."* Nadia's heart skips as she recognizes the song immediately.

When she and Aman first started dating, Atif Aslam's songs would always be playing in Aman's car whenever he would come to pick her up. Though she wasn't familiar with Aslam's music like Aman was, she eventually developed a fondness for it and often teased Aman about using songs like "Pehli Nazar Mein" to try to woo her at the start of their relationship. Hearing the lyrics again after all these years transports her back to that time. Her body sways along with the memories appended to every line.

"Main hoon yahan. Tu hai yahan." Aman grins when he sees her lip-syncing the words. He holds out his arms while singing out the last lines. *"Meri bahon mein aa bhool ja-aa."*

"Wah, wah, wah," Zeba says, clapping along with the others. She looks at Nadia with a surprised expression. "Who knew we were having a full-on concert tonight?"

Aman gives a quick bow as Nadia lets out a small whistle.

"Okay, *JA*. That's what we ended on—" Zeba says, pointing to Sheila, who only has to think for a moment before turning to Shoaib.

"Just follow along, okay?" she tells him. She shuts her eyes and draws in a deep inhale. *"JA-ust a small-town girl,"* she sings.

Shoaib strums the next chord, instantly recognizing the Journey song. Sheila holds out a pretend microphone and leans into the song: *"Livin' in a lonely wooorld."* Damien cups his mouth and lets out an encouraging whoop as Sheila points at him to join her. He grabs her by the waist, and together they sing the next verse leading up to the pre-chorus.

With their audience captivated, Sheila steps forward with her arms outstretched, and it suddenly becomes a group performance. Zeba motions Nadia to join her beside Aman and wraps her arm around her neck as they, along with everyone else, shout-sing the rest of the song. Aman pulls out his cell phone and turns on the flashlight, waving it around like a lighter. By the time they hit the chorus, Nadia is grinning so hard her cheeks feel like they're going to burst. She looks around at everyone's faces and can't remember the last time she had such fun.

When they reach the second refrain, the crescendo builds further. As more cell phones light up around them, Nadia feels a sharp elbow at her side. She notices that Zeba is no longer singing. Instead, she motions to Aman's phone—specifically the screen, which is facing in their direction. They see a row of messages all stacked up, one notification over the other. Aman doesn't seem to notice as Zeba pushes Nadia forward so she can get a closer look at what the messages say. Her stomach immediately drops when she sees they are all from the same sender: L.

Call me when you're free.

What time are you coming over?

Can't wait to see you tonight.

<3 <3 <3

Nadia's breath on the back of Aman's neck causes him to turn around. "Hey." He smiles just as the song nears its dramatic end. But the edges of his mouth immediately drop the moment he sees her face—twisted into equal parts anger and betrayal mixed with a deeply wounded pain.

"Don't stop believin'."

Aman looks down at his phone as L's messages illuminate across the screen.

"Hold on to that feelin'."

"Nadia," Aman whispers. His voice cracks as Zeba steps up, glaring into his eyes. "Nadia," he says again, but before he can get out the rest of the sentence, Nadia backs up, distancing herself from him. As she moves away, Zeba turns to follow, but Aman stops her. "Don't," he says. "Please."

Perhaps it's the desperation in his face or the pleading in his voice, but the protectiveness in Zeba's eyes momentarily abates and she moves aside. As a thundering applause erupts at Sheila's performance, no one else takes notice of what has just happened. Zeba remains quiet, chewing the inside of her lip, watching as Aman crosses the yard to follow Nadia into the house.

12

N adia, please," Aman calls, trailing Nadia into the kitchen. "Talk to me, will you?"

Nadia turns around, her face small, gray with anger. "What do you want me to say?"

"Anything," Aman says, his shoulders slumped forward.

"Who were those messages from?" she asks without pause.

"No one. Just—a friend."

Nadia shakes her head, disappointment crossing her face. After all this, he's still unwilling to tell her the truth.

"Hear me out, Nadia. It's not what you're thinking—"

"I've seen the photos, Aman. The negatives you threw out in your study." Her eyes search his, hoping to receive some acknowledgment or explanation, but there is nothing, only confusion clouding his expression.

"I even found the card on your bookshelf. *Happy anniversary, baby*," she reminds him.

"Nadia," Aman says, reaching for her as he steps forward, but Nadia slips away from his grasp.

"What are you keeping from me?" she whispers, her voice breaking with emotion.

Aman places his thumb and forefinger between the ridges of his brows, her question clearly catching him off guard. "Nothing," he stammers, his thoughts failing to form a coherent sentence. "Nadia, I care about you—"

She looks away, hot tears pushing against her eyes.

"It's . . . it's hard to explain."

"Try. I deserve that much at least."

Aman sighs. "It's complicated." He peers into her eyes, but she looks away. All she wants is to hear him say what she already knows to be true, and as he stares into her face, she almost believes he might. But when he speaks again, it's only more lies. "Nadia, I don't know what you saw. Or think you saw. But those messages . . . they were nothing," he says, pressing down on his words to give them more weight. It pains her that even in this moment, his protection over L exceeds his compassion for her. As she struggles to cope with her overwhelming sadness over that fact, the back door opens and Zeba walks in. Faint sounds of laughter carry into the kitchen briefly before being shut out by the door. Zeba looks from Nadia to Aman, visibly uncomfortable at the solemn expressions on their faces.

"I can leave if you want," she says, focusing mainly on Nadia. "But I just wanted to check in on you."

"Zeba, we need some time to finish our conver—" Aman begins before Nadia cuts him off.

"There isn't anything else to say."

"I think if we just finished talking about this—"

"No," Nadia says. She looks at him, summoning every effort to keep her voice firm. Zeba inches toward her, placing her hand into Nadia's, their elbows touching gently.

"Nadi." Aman lowers his voice, defeat coating his words. "Can we talk about this at home? Just the two of us?" As his eyes plead for her response, Shoaib comes in, struggling to hold a large tray of biryani with both his hands.

"There you are," he says when he sees Zeba. He tilts his body sideways, wrestling with the door as he tries to shut it with the heel of his foot. "Some of the guests are leaving, so I brought this in in case you wanted to pack them a box." He sets the tray down beside the sink and releases a soft whistle. "Who knew carrying a tray of biryani could get you so winded!" he says, suddenly noticing Aman and Nadia. "Hey, you guys are still here!"

"Shoaib," Zeba says, trying to get him to read the mood in the room. However, without any context, Shoaib misses the cues that trouble is brewing.

"I was wondering where you two lovebirds snuck off to!"

Sensing Nadia's discomfort, Zeba releases her sister's hand and motions Shoaib toward the door. "Come help me grab some Styrofoam boxes. I think there's a whole stack in the garage."

"Actually"—Shoaib taps open the cabinet over the stove—"I brought them in earlier. I had a feeling you'd be needing them." He lowers a tower of white boxes. "I also brought in these plastic containers, so you can pack up some of the curries and desserts." He drops the items into a neat pile near the sink, looking pleased with himself. But even the grin on his face can't diffuse the tension lingering in the air.

"So, uh—I think we're going to head out now," Aman replies, his voice shaken. He looks to Nadia, but she stares at her hands, refusing to meet his gaze.

"Already?" Shoaib asks. "You sure you don't want to hang around for another round of Antakshari?"

"*Shoaib*," Zeba cuts in, placing her hand on Shoaib's chest. "It's getting late," she says, stressing her words, hoping he might take the hint.

"I know. I just thought since we haven't seen them in a while—"

"Unfortunately, Aman already has another commitment tonight. Isn't that right?" Nadia says, facing him directly.

Aman's cheeks redden. "We'll definitely have to do this

again," he says with a strained smile, uneasiness written all over his face. "But for now, we should go. Ready?" He glances at Nadia, waiting for her confirmation, but her body reveals her unwillingness to yield.

"I'm staying," she says, her voice staunch.

"Nadi," Aman gently coaxes her. "Let's just go home. We can discuss this some more. Please—" He reaches for her hand, but she instinctively pulls back.

"I'd like to stay here tonight," Nadia repeats, "if that's okay with you guys?" She turns to Zeba and Shoaib, both taken aback by her request.

"Of course you can," Zeba stammers, turning toward Shoaib. "It's fine with us. Right?"

"Uh—yeah—I mean, of course." Shoaib nods, confusion settling between his brows. His eyes shift from Nadia to Aman, unsure of what to make of everything left unsaid.

"Nadi," Aman repeats, but the rigid expression on her face prevents him from asking again. He turns to Zeba and Shoaib, the corners of his mouth weighed down with frustration. "Thank you for the lovely dinner, Zeba," he says. "Everything was delicious. And Shoaib—"

"It was good seeing you, brother," Shoaib replies, placing a palm to his chest.

"Can I pack a box for you to take home?" Zeba asks, reaching for one of the to-go boxes. Despite the anger she feels for her sister, her natural inclination to be a good hostess supersedes.

"Thank you, but that's not necessary." Aman turns back to Nadia, who remains quiet. "I'll, um, I should get going . . ."

"C'mon, I'll walk you out," Shoaib offers, filling in the awkward silence. The moment the front door shuts, Zeba turns to Nadia, her forehead lined with worry.

"Are you okay?"

Nadia shakes her head. "I can't do this anymore, Zeba," she says, dropping her face into her hands.

Zeba wraps her arms across her sister, rubbing small circles into her back. "What did he say about those messages?"

"That it was complicated and not what I was thinking."

"Oh, please," Zeba scoffs. "We saw the heart emojis. And the flirty invitation asking him to come over. He can't be serious, can he?"

Nadia shrugs. "I even told him about the photos and the card I found, but he kept feeding me the same lies. I couldn't listen to it anymore, Zeba. I just—"

"I'm so sorry," Zeba murmurs as Nadia's shoulders heave with pain. There's nothing her sister can say to help, but just having her there to nurse her heartbreak is what she needs more than anything. "So, he didn't tell you who L is?"

"I don't think he's going to," Nadia replies, her voice muffled beneath the tears.

"Then we'll just have to find out on our own," Zeba says. "Aman can deny it all he wants, but he's not the only one involved in whatever is going on. If he won't tell you the truth, we need to find this woman and get it from her."

"But how?"

"I don't know," Zeba admits. "But we'll figure it out."

NADIA KNEADS THE pillows, giving them a few hard squeezes to try to plump them up. She is crouched on the bottom bunk in Noman and Alim's bedroom, her neck curved forward, creating a sliver of space just between the top of her head and the mattress above.

Zeba tried setting her up in the spare bedroom their mom used when her health was failing, but Nadia refused. She couldn't bring herself to enter that room, let alone sleep in the same bed that her mom last slept in. After what just transpired between her and Aman, the thought of immersing herself in a space surrounded by her mom's memory—and the silent judgment that was so characteristically hers—would only compound the shame, embarrassment, and sadness Nadia already feels. But she is careful not to mention any of this to Zeba for fear of provoking an argument. Instead, she stresses that she does not wish to sleep alone, which is not entirely false. If bunking with her nephew will prevent her from further emotional distress, she is willing to sacrifice her comfort for that exchange.

She piles the pillows one on top of the other and plops her head down with a sigh. From under the covers, her phone beeps with low battery. Instead of plugging it in, she slides her hand over the screen and presses the side button to power it off. Aman tried calling her a few times on his drive home, but she ignored the rings, letting them go to voice mail. Now, as she lies in bed, staring at the swirly patterns of the mattress no more than a foot from her face, she wonders if Aman ended up at L's after all.

Not wanting to enter that dark corner of her mind, Nadia wishes she felt as confident about finding L as Zeba does. However, with no leads, she can't see how it's possible when the only information Aman has given are lies. In some ways, his refusal to speak honestly with her feels almost as painful as the truth.

A light knock interrupts her thoughts, and Nadia turns as the bedroom door cracks open. "Just checking on you," Zeba says, poking her head in through the opening. Her thick hair is tied up in a ball-shaped topknot, and her face is scrubbed clean of the winged liner from earlier, swapped instead with clear undereye gel pads. "You have a visitor," she says, pushing open the door. Holding her hand is Noman, who appears ready for bed in a Batman onesie, a stuffed bunny clutched to his chest.

"Hey, buddy," Nadia says, sitting up too quickly and knocking her head on the wooden planks above her. "Ouch," she cries as Noman giggles into the furry top of his stuffed animal. She rubs her scalp with the heel of her hand and laughs too. "Come sit with me," she says, beckoning him with outstretched arms. She clutches him close, sinking her chin into his hair and closing her eyes. He smells of crayons and baby shampoo, and for a moment, all her worries are forgotten as she soaks in the warmth from the small human in her arms.

"Do you need another pillow or blanket or anything?" Zeba asks, leaning against the door.

"I'm okay," Nadia says, squeezing Noman once more before he pulls away. She pinches back the neck of her oversize graphic T-shirt and folds her legs, tucking her feet underneath her. Since she hadn't planned on spending the night, she brought nothing with her except her party clothes and heels. Fortunately, Zeba lent her some sweats and the necessary toiletries to keep her comfortable. "Thank you . . . for everything," Nadia expresses with gratitude.

"Feel free to stay as long as you want." Zeba smiles. "Alim's already fast asleep in our bed, so hopefully Noman won't keep you up too long," she says, watching the boy scramble up the ladder to the top bunk. "Be good, okay?" Zeba reminds him before wishing them both a good night.

As Noman crawls under the covers, Nadia gets out of

bed to tuck him in. Securing the blanket tightly around his body, she places his stuffed bunny on the pillow beside him. "What happened to Bunny's little heart button?" she asks, pointing to the empty space on the stuffed animal's underbelly where loose strands of red thread hang.

"Alim ripped it off," Noman explains, pushing his chin out from under the covers. "I gave him Bunny to play with, and he pulled too hard and broke it."

"I'm sure it was an accident."

"But I told him to be careful!" Noman says. He lifts Bunny from the pillow and hugs him to his chest.

Nadia smiles, combing her fingers through Noman's hair and pushing the stray locks off his forehead. "Sometimes hearts get broken. Even if we don't mean for them to."

"Can we fix it?"

Nadia shrugs. "Maybe." Noman looks up, the browns of his eyes shrinking beneath the heaviness of his eyelids. She leans down to give him a kiss, readjusting the blankets around his chin. "I'll look at it tomorrow and see what I can do."

She walks across the room to shut off the light before crawling into bed herself. It takes her some time to get comfortable on the twin mattress, but once she's settled, her thoughts drift back to Aman—dithering from anger to sadness. She questions and doubts whether he is lying in bed thinking of her too. Squeezing her eyes, she tries to quiet her worries by focusing on the staggered, rapid breaths pushing through her nose. In and out, until the silence is interrupted by the sound of Noman's voice.

"Does it hurt?" he asks, his voice small in the darkness.

"What?" she asks.

"Bunny's broken heart?"

Nadia opens her eyes and blinks. *Does it hurt?* How can she begin to answer that question? She thinks of how it felt to see L's name pop up on Aman's phone. *It hurts like hell*, she wants to say. *A crushing sort of pain that most can't fathom until it's the only thing they can feel.* Clearing her throat, she filters back her words. "It does. Sure," she finally says.

"Like a scrape? Or a cut?"

"Kind of. But on the inside." Nadia props herself up on her elbows, thinking for a moment. From the bunk above, she hears Noman stir in his bed. "Do you remember that one time we went to the park, and you jumped off the monkey bars and hit your head?"

"Mm-hmm," he replies.

Although the incident happened a couple of years ago, Nadia still recalls the fear and panic she felt in that moment—from the sound of the *crack* that echoed in the air when his head touched the cement to the immense guilt she carried for months afterward at not being able to stop it in time. "Do you remember how much you cried the whole drive home because your head kept pounding?"

"It was so loud."

"The pounding?"

"Yeah. Like a thunderstorm inside my head that only I could hear."

Nadia is silent, surprised by the accuracy of that description. "Now instead of your head, imagine that storm is inside your heart."

Noman yawns. "Is that what it feels like?"

Nadia nods. "Yes," she says, her voice just above a whisper. She lies back, all her emotions weighing down on her at once. She turns to her side, the wetness of her pillow feeling cool against her cheek. "That's exactly what a broken heart feels like."

13

Sunday morning, and Nadia finds herself up earlier than usual. She hardly slept—partly because the bottom bunk required her to contort her body in ways she didn't know were possible, but also because she couldn't stop thinking about what took place the night before. She and Aman have quarreled in the past, but never have their fights escalated like this. Between his dishonesty and her refusal to come home, they've taken the worst practices of her father and used them against each other.

After Shoaib heads off to flag football practice, Zeba gets the boys dressed and ready for a read-along organized by the local library. "You sure you don't want to come along?" she asks on their way out. "We can grab brunch after and then swing by your house if you need to pick up a few things."

"I'm going to stay back, if that's okay," Nadia says,

covering a yawn with her hand. Between all the sugar she consumed last night, the lack of sleep, and her unbridled anxiety, her body is one crisis away from falling to bits. She rolls her head forward, using both fists to knead out the knots that have formed at the nape of her neck. A few hours of quiet time might give her a chance to figure out her next steps. As Zeba's car pulls out of the driveway, she pours herself another cup of chai and heads outside.

Perching herself on the front bench, Nadia rests her sore limbs. She typically prepares Aman's breakfast at this time, and for a moment she catches herself wondering if he's eaten. But after what transpired last night, she quickly reminds herself that Aman's diet is the least of her concerns. She can't allow herself to arrive at compassion without receiving some answers first.

She looks up at the sky, squinting from the brightness. The sun is out, yet a still coolness hangs in the air, causing her to shiver beneath her T-shirt. Nadia wraps both hands around the coffee mug, trying to absorb the warmth from the liquid inside. A few feet away, a gentle rustling diverts her attention. From the bushes, a fuzzy-tailed squirrel emerges through the leaves and darts up the front steps, its beady eyes focusing squarely on her.

"Aren't you a funny thing?" Nadia says, staring back. In response, the squirrel alights onto its back legs, twitching its tail rapidly. Nadia monitors its movement as it scampers onto the patio and makes its way directly in front of where she is seated. "I don't have any food for you. See?" Nadia holds out a hand to show it is empty, but she already senses that food is not what it's after.

Nadia sighs and sets down her mug. She slides down, kneeling until she is no less than a foot from its whiskered face. "Can we not do this right now?" she whispers. If this is another one of her mom's attempts to connect, she wants to make it clear that she's not emotionally ready for this interaction—at least not today. But the squirrel remains in position, tail twitching back and forth as if trying to communicate something.

While Nadia attempts to shoo it away, she does not notice that another car has pulled into the driveway and has parked in the empty spot where Zeba's car stood before. Too busy convincing her "mom" that timing is not her strong suit, Nadia remains unaware of her present audience until she looks up and sees Ali staring at her from the steps of the patio.

"Hey," he says, looking just as surprised to see her. "I'm sorry to drop by unexpectedly, but I was looking for . . ." His voice dwindles as his gaze darts between Nadia and the squirrel. "Should I come back?"

"No, no, it's fine," Nadia says, standing up. Self-consciously, she pulls back the neck of her T-shirt against her collarbone. "I was just—" She gestures to the squirrel, who immediately scurries away with the arrival of a third. She rolls her eyes. "I was catching up with an old . . . Never mind." Her cheeks burn as she tries to avert the amused expression on Ali's face. "What did you need?"

"Is Shoaib around? Or Zeba? I was hoping to drop off a few things." He lifts a plastic bag that he carries in his hand.

"Shoaib's at practice, and you just missed Zeba. She took the boys to a reading. I can take that from you if you want."

"Thanks," Ali says, handing her the bag. A quick peek through the handles uncovers a few books and empty Tupperware boxes.

"Are these from last night's leftovers?" Nadia asks, pulling out one of the containers.

"Some of them." Ali laughs, running his fingers through his hair. "There's a chance I might've indulged in some late-night binge eating after I went home," he says with a sheepish smile. "*And* I may have polished off the rest for breakfast this morning."

Nadia tilts her head, feeling less embarrassed about earlier.

"But you should know," he continues, "it's been ages since I've eaten a home-cooked meal, and my momentary lapse of self-control in no way reflects who I am when I'm not around delicious food."

"I woke up this morning still thinking about coconut pie,

so no judgment here," Nadia assures him. "Besides, Zeba's cooking isn't exactly meant to be served with a helping of self-control."

"So, is this a shared family trait? Are all the Abbasi sisters amazing cooks?"

"I wish." Nadia shakes her head. "Zeba inherited her cooking skills from our mom, who is—I mean *was*—a master in the kitchen. Unfortunately, that talent stops with me."

Ali's smile withers. "I'm sorry," he says, his eyes crinkling at the edges.

"I'll be sure to relay your condolences to my husband," Nadia jokes.

"No." Ali pauses. "I meant about your mom."

"Oh. That."

He carefully attempts to read her expression before proceeding. "How long ago did she . . ."

"Last summer," Nadia says, taking a seat on the bench. Ali remains quiet, and she begins to feel sorry for unintentionally bringing it up. "It happened suddenly, even though she was sick for a while." She continues giving a small smile to let him know that it's fine. "I think we're still kind of processing it in a lot of ways."

"Zeba didn't mention this," Ali remarks, his voice soft. "Were you close?"

Nadia thinks for a moment. "It was a complicated relationship."

"Mmm," he says, lips pressed together.

"But I suppose most mother-daughter relationships are a bit complex."

"I think relationships, in general, are complex," Ali says. His tone is comforting and without judgment, putting Nadia at ease.

"The last time I saw her, it was at the hospital right before she passed. She was lying on the bed, and I remember thinking she looked so . . . *small.* But then it hit me that that was because I've only ever seen her as the opposite—strong, stubborn, all-consuming . . ."

Ali listens, his silence making space for her to continue.

"I don't know; it just made me so angry. I feel like her whole life, she had overcome so much; this was just one more thing to surmount . . . all she had to do was push through it."

"Grief is complicated. It forces us to grapple with emotions that don't always make sense."

Nadia nods, drifting back to memories from that final day. She remembers the cadence of her mom's labored breathing, the hollow sounds that rattled from her throat, warning them that even the end would not be easy. She remembers the flurry of nurses who ushered them out of the room, and the fear in Zeba's face when it finally hit her that their mom wasn't going to be coming home this time.

"Did you get a chance to speak to her, at least? That last time?"

Nadia shakes her head. "I tried. There was so much I wanted to say—questions left unanswered; misunderstandings that were never cleared up; all the things I had been carrying around for the past thirty years. But none of that mattered. In the end, she just kept asking for our father." She scoffs and looks away. "Even in her final moments, the only person she longed for was the one who abandoned her. It was like our presence didn't even mean anything."

Ali sits down on the bench beside her. "I'm sorry," he says.

Nadia leans back and sighs. "You know, when she and my father split, I thought it was the worst thing that could ever happen to us. But the worst thing was really watching my mom never get past it." Nadia sucks in a sharp inhale. "I just wish that last memory of her could've been different." Her eyebrows press together as she blinks back her regrets.

This is the first time she's fully articulated these thoughts. She feels exposed, vulnerable, and suddenly embarrassed, yet Ali listens attentively, eyes glistening with sympathy. "I lost touch with my parents years ago," he says. "They also had a complicated marriage, so a lot of the anger and resentment you felt? I understand that."

Nadia is surprised by his openness. "Were your parents separated too?"

"No," Ali says. "But their decision to stay together had nothing to do with love. They remained married for the same reason a lot of people from their generation did: they didn't know there was another option. It was not a happy relationship by any means. For most of my childhood, all they did was fight. And then there were years when I can barely remember them even speaking to one another."

Though her father's absence deprived her and Zeba of the normalcy she craved, it spared them from the type of dysfunction Ali describes. "That must've been hard."

"I think when you grow up in a toxic environment, it's impossible not to carry around some residual baggage. But that load eventually gets lighter, especially when you realize you can't choose your family or the circumstances you're given. You can only try not to repeat the same mistakes."

"Has that worked for you?"

"Not quite," Ali admits. The corners of his eyes taper as he smiles.

Nadia thinks of Aman and of her own failed attempts to not repeat her mom's mistakes. "I guess I thought if I just did everything the opposite of what my mom did, I could guarantee a different outcome. But no one tells you that marriage isn't so straightforward. You can do everything right and still have it fall apart."

"I can't speak from personal experience, but my grandmother used to say: 'Taalee bajaane mein do haath lagte hain.' It takes two hands to clap. The same, I imagine, applies to a marriage."

"Are you not—"

"Married?" Ali shakes his head. "Never have been."

This thought hadn't crossed Nadia's mind. She just assumed . . . well, nothing, really; so she's not sure why his disclosure takes her by such surprise. But then again, everything about their conversation has. Though she's never been one to divulge such personal things to someone she barely knows, she almost finds herself wanting to—drawn to him in a way she can't fully explain. As strange as that should feel, the most surprising thing is *it doesn't*, making their exchange all the stranger.

"My parents' marriage was enough to convince me to avoid it altogether." A hint of regret seems to flicker in his eyes. "Although I did at one point, I don't blame them anymore. I just think when you haven't witnessed enough examples of love, it's hard to try and find it for yourself, let alone trust that you'll be able to share it with someone else."

Ali's eschewal of marriage makes sense, but his reasons for that choice sadden Nadia. "I know it's not my place, but hearing you talk of your parents' marriage . . . maybe you have an awareness that perhaps they lacked? I think that counts for something."

"Maybe," Ali says. "But like you said, marriage is not

straightforward. Regardless of the outcome, it takes courage to take that plunge like you did—courage that not all
of us have."

Nadia's not sure whether her choice to marry was cou-
rageous or foolish, but she appreciates Ali's generosity in
his assessment of her and for his ability to help her feel not
so alone, something she hasn't felt in a while. He sits with
her quietly as she tries to form the proper words to convey
these sentiments. But before she knows it, Zeba's minivan
pulls up beside Ali's car. Missing her chance to express her
gratitude, Nadia gets up feeling disappointed. Together
they walk across the yard to greet Noman and Alim as they
bound up the drive.

"Look!" Alim shouts, handing Nadia a picture of a dino-
saur with crayon scribbles all over it. "I dwawed it myself,"
he declares proudly.

Nadia takes the drawing from Alim and affects close examination. "These colors are incredible!" She holds out her
palm, and Alim jumps up to give her a high five.

"I did one too," Noman says, much less enthused. "But
Alim spilled his grape juice all over it, so I had to throw it out."

"I'm sure yours was equally impressive," Nadia says, giving his hair a quick tousle. As Ali chases the boys around,
Zeba emerges from behind the car, both hands full. Struggling to locate the keys in her pockets, she breaks into a
smile as Ali runs up to unburden her.

"Thanks," she says, handing him her bags. "I might've gotten a little carried away on the Instacart while the boys were at the reading, but since it's my turn to get groceries this week, I figured I'd just do a quick pick-up on the way home."

"Not a worry," Ali says, following Zeba up the walkway.

"I didn't know you were coming over."

"I just stopped by to drop off a few books for Shoaib and your Tupperware."

"Finished with them already?"

Ali turns and looks at Nadia with a smile. "I was told this was a no-judgment zone."

"Not judging at all," Zeba insists as they walk up the patio. She sees the boxes he brought sitting near the bench and calls Noman over. "Grab Mummy those boxes and bring them inside," she tells him. "Let me refill them, so you have something for tonight."

"Oh, that's not necessary—" Ali begins, but Zeba is already leading them into the kitchen. Nadia steers both boys inside before shutting the front door. As they push past her and into their bedroom, she rejoins the adults.

"This will only take a minute," Zeba says, opening the fridge and sticking her head in. Her voice is muffled under the hum of the ice maker as she goes through the list. "There's a tray of biryani and tandoori chicken . . ." She pulls out all the leftovers and sets them on the counter.

"You know what, I'm just going to pack up a little of every-thing."

"Really, don't go to the trouble—"

"What trouble?" Zeba scrunches her face. "Now, let's see. I think Shoaib left some extra containers around here someplace." She opens the top cabinets searching for what she needs.

"Let's not pretend you were ever going to win that argu-ment," Nadia teases Ali. "As Zeba's sister, here's some ad-vice: always accept any and all food that comes your way."

"I guess there are worse battles to lose."

"Far worse." Nadia laughs. From the corner of her eye, she notices a flash of new messages on her phone, which is charging at the table. She walks over to find exactly what she suspected: messages from Aman.

When are you coming home?

Can we please talk?

Nadia, I'm sorry.

It's different to be receiving messages from Aman rather than sending them. But as gratifying as the reversal feels, unless Aman is willing to lay out the truth in all its ugli-ness, Nadia's not interested in perfunctory lies and empty excuses. It will require more than a simple apology to remedy their situation.

"Everything okay?" Zeba asks, noticing the expression on her sister's face.

"Yeah. Fine," Nadia responds. Leaving the messages on read, she sets the phone down and turns back to the others. "Don't forget to pack the dessert."

"Maybe a few slices of coconut pie?" Ali suggests.

"As long as you save some for me too."

14

"Your one o'clock is here, Dr. Abbasi."

Nadia is so focused on updating patient files that Julie's interruption startles her. "Okay, send them in," she says, typing the final entry before minimizing the page. Two days have passed since the events at Zeba's party unfolded, and as grateful as she is to have a place to stay, sleeping on a twin-size bed has been more of an adjustment than she signed up for. While she waits, she uses the pads of her fingers to knead out the sore muscles in the soft part of her lower back. She groans as an older woman with bright red semi-rimless glasses, matching nails, and a nose piercing walks through the door.

"Bad time? 'Cuz I can mosey on back if you'd like," the woman says as Nadia spins around in her chair.

"No, not at all. Come on in." She takes the new-patient folder that Julie hands her before shutting the door. "Mrs.

Paula *Guarionex*?" she sounds out the name scrawled on the paperwork. "My apologies if I mispronounced that."

"No apologies needed," the woman says, taking a seat on the green cushioned exam chair. She speaks with a slight Southern drawl, her voice steeped in the sweetness of a carbonated drink. "A last name like Guarionex is destined to be butchered, and believe you me, I've heard it butchered far worse than that."

"Perhaps we stick to just first names then?"

"That I can do, Dr. Nay-dee-ah," Paula says, slowly yet incorrectly, enunciating the name embroidered on Nadia's lab coat.

"So, Paula," Nadia says, not bothering to correct her. "It says you're here for an eye exam today?" She flips through the pages of the file as Paula tells her about her eye history and the reason for her visit. She also informs Nadia that she has just moved to the area from Atlanta and was referred by a neighbor in her building who also happens to be a patient.

"You're a li'l younger than my previous optometrist, Dr. Ricci, who checked my eyes for *twenty-seven* years. Prolly longer than you've been alive!"

Nadia smiles. Though she is often mistaken as younger, she enjoys the satisfaction that comes from revealing her true age. She likes seeing the surprise in people's faces, and as expected, the reaction she gets this time doesn't disappoint.

"Heavens to Betsy!" Paula exclaims when Nadia tells her that she has, in fact, been alive longer than she might think.

"I will gladly accept your initial guess as a compliment, however," Nadia says. They continue chatting as Paula bombards her with a stream of questions, most related to her vision. Nadia does her best to answer each one while at the same time hovering a lighted magnifying device over each eye, checking her retinas, corneas, and the membranes covering the whites of her eyes. After careful examination, she lets Paula know that she can rest assured that both eyes look quite healthy for someone of *her age*, to which Paula emphatically cries out, "Hallelujah!"

Once the refraction test is completed, Paula sits quietly, for the first time since entering, while Nadia fills out the remaining information on her paperwork. She taps her fingernails on the brass buckle of her handbag as she awaits a prescription for her new eyeglasses. The silence is short-lived, however, as a framed photo sitting beside Nadia's computer catches her attention. "Oh, that's the handsome fellow from my yoga class!" she says, pointing at the image of Nadia and Aman standing in front of the Blue Mosque from their trip to Istanbul several years ago.

"Hmm?" Nadia says, tearing along the perforated line and handing her the prescription.

"In the photograph," Paula says, still pointing at Aman.

"He attends my weekly *vin-yah-suh* class over at Purple Clover Studio."

"Aman?" Nadia shakes her head. "That's my husband. He doesn't do yoga."

"Oh, he does yoga just fine. I seen him and alls them young'uns contortin' and twistin' like it's gravy. Let me tell you, this old lady just done her best to keep up."

Nadia furrows her brows. "You must be mistaken, Paula. My husband's not much of a . . . contortionist. Perhaps you're thinking of someone else?"

"I'm terrible at names, honey, but I never forget a face. That's him, all right." Paula slides off the exam chair, her tortoiseshell heels making a clacking sound as they hit the floor. "You tell him I'll see him at the next class," she says, stuffing her prescription into the front flap of her handbag. She follows Nadia to the front waiting area so Julie can take down information for her next appointment. Nadia steps back, racking her mind over Paula's comment. Why would Aman sign up for a weekly yoga class? But more importantly, why had he not mentioned it to her? Is there more to what he's hiding?

15

About twenty minutes north of Cedar Heights, heading toward downtown, sits Purple Clover Studio. The building, with its Spanish tiled roof and large mirrored windows, looks identical to the other stores attached to the shopping megacomplex right off the freeway. A faded GRAND OPENING banner hangs above the Whole Foods anchored at the corner while multicolored balloons wave from the entrances of the specialty stationery store, the gourmet boba place, the nail salon, and the yoga studio. Although the parking lot is filled with cars, there are no people walking around. In fact, the whole mall appears to be empty, giving Nadia a sense of uneasiness the moment she pulls in.

AFTER PAULA LEFT, Nadia went back to updating patient files, pushing the yoga comment out of her mind. It was clearly a mistake. Paula's need for new eyeglasses was the only explanation. There was no other way to make sense of that conversation. But it was the certainty with which she identified Aman that was hard to shake. Once the final report was completed, Nadia opened a new tab and searched for *Purple Clover Yoga*. Though nothing initially jumped out, when she pinned its location on a map, she discovered it was less than a mile from the hospital where Aman worked.

Was it possible that Aman discovered the studio over a lunch break?

Sure.

Would it be easy to swing by for a class once or twice a week after his shift ended?

She supposed.

But that doesn't change how out of character attending a yoga class would be for him. Despite his recent health kick, Aman's medical background has always made him wary of Ayurvedic practices—a skepticism she's heard him express on countless occasions whenever friends of theirs would bring up self- and spiritual-development techniques. The very thought of Aman *voluntarily* signing up for a class centering around contorted posing while reciting affirmations and platitudes seemed . . . *odd*. But not any odder, she realized, than the other things he had been keeping from her . . .

As soon as the last patient left for the day, Nadia tasked Julie with locking up the office so she could give Purple Clover Studio a call from the privacy of her car.

Initially, her rationale was simply to get more details on their weekly vinyasa class. Making note of the days and times, she figured, would be a good place to start, even if only to file away with the other "finds." But when her call was answered by a breathy-voiced woman named Lena wishing her a "bright and balanced day," Nadia choked on her words and hastily ended the call.

Lena? Lena with an L? Could it be possible?

"Is Aman having an affair with a woman named Lena who works at a yoga studio?" Nadia's reflection stared back at her from the phone screen as she spoke the words aloud. Could this be why he never mentioned the class to her? Could this explain all the late nights at the "hospital"? And his whereabouts on his last day off from work? The missing clues she had desperately been searching for suddenly fell together. Though a part of her had hoped it wasn't so, hearing Lena's voice eviscerated those hopes, taking her suspicions—which until then were still hazy and uncertain—and shaping them into something tangible and real. Without another thought, she started the car, and twenty minutes later was parked in front of Purple Clover Studio with the engine off, but her heart racing.

TAKING A FEW breaths, she tries to think out a logical plan of action. These past few weeks, her waking hours have been haunted by thoughts of this anonymous person—a person

she's convinced herself is the cause for Aman's changed behavior. Now the only thing between her and the answers
to the questions she's been grappling with is less than a
hundred yards of parking lot. All she must do is walk into
the studio, ask for Lena, and the mystery will be solved.
But the thought of *seeing* Lena; of attaching a real person
to that breathy voice—the texter of the messages that fill
Aman's phone; the sender of those flirty emojis—fills her
with a terror great enough to eclipse even the confusion
that consumes her and the confirmation she seeks.

"Get it together, Nadia," she tells herself. "This is what
you've been waiting for. The missing link that will explain
everything." Even so, she can't bring herself to get out of
the car. Grasping the weight of the moment, she stays put
as she rallies the courage needed to go in. Though it takes
a while, her heart eventually slows and she steps out of the
car. At the entrance, her reflection in the mirrored windows reminds her that she is far from yoga ready in her lace
blouse and ivory pleated skirt, but she marches forward
nonetheless. It's too late to turn back.

Pushing the doors open, she's welcomed inside by the
sweet, earthy scent of sandalwood. Nadia looks around, her
gaze drawn to colorful mandalas painted on white walls
and the natural daylight pouring through the rectangular
skylights that panel the surface of the high ceiling. To the
left of the entrance, a selection of leggings, sports bras, and

cropped sweatshirts hang from carefully curated racks beside clear glass shelves that display an array of water bottles, yoga mats, and towels—all overpriced and branded with the Purple Clover logo. A handful of attractive young men and women sporting fitted tanks and ponytails browse this section, a thin layer of sweat coating their perfectly hairless, toned bodies.

On the other side, she notices a bold hand-woven rug under a large wooden slab table decorated with dozens of white porcelain hand sculptures, their lifeless fingers all angled upward as if summoning a higher power. Crystals and amulets of all shapes and sizes nestle in the palms of these sculptures—each more brilliant than the next. Nadia restrains the temptation to touch the translucent gems, admiring instead how they gleam beneath the slatted sunlight.

"Can I help you?" a tall, good-looking man behind the counter asks.

Nadia turns, blushing at the upper chest on full display through his netted T-shirt.

"Is this your first time visiting Purple Clover Studio?"

"Yes," Nadia says, feeling self-conscious. She leans forward to grab one of the folded schedules stacked on the counter. "I just wanted to take a quick peek at the list of classes."

"Of course! We have all sorts of options depending on

your level of experience. If you want something a bit more conventional, we have a weekly hatha class that's quite popular. There's also an intentional flow class that gets you familiar with the fundamentals of yoga sequences so you can experience the sensations of asanas—"

Nadia nods as he speaks, hoping to give off the impression that she understands. "I'm just going to look over this on my own." She smiles, trying not to be rude but wanting to stay focused on her initial plan to find Lena.

"Take all the time you need!" He leans down to grab a rolled-up towel from a shelf beneath the counter. "I've got a six o'clock class now," he says, wrapping the towel around his neck, "but Lena will be out shortly to cover the desk if you have any questions."

"Oh," Nadia says, her stomach plunging at the sound of *Lena*'s name. Nadia's throat dries as if she just swallowed a shot of sawdust. "Great," she whispers, watching him walk toward the studios before clearing her throat and trying again. "Thank you—"

"Rick," he says, turning and pointing to the name tag hanging from the lanyard around his neck. He grins; the white of his teeth matches the brightness of the walls behind him. "See you around!"

As he turns the corner, Nadia withdraws from the counter, frantically searching for someplace less conspicuous to await Lena's arrival. Overcome with a sudden rush of panic, she bumps into a rack of brightly colored yoga shorts. "Oof!" she cries, catching it right before it topples over. Beside her, a young woman browsing the next rack eyes her with annoyance. "Sorry," Nadia mutters, hiding her embarrassment behind the class schedule still clutched in her hand.

Nadia's clumsiness causes her to second-guess whether she's truly ready to face Lena. This, after all, could be Aman's mistress: the woman he has been sneaking around with behind her back; the one he's willing to risk his marriage for. What can Nadia possibly say to her? What words could she even utter that might adequately convey the hurt, anger, and confusion she feels? Whatever she was hoping to accomplish by confronting her suddenly seems juvenile. Embarrassed, she turns to leave just as one of the studio doors opens and a herd of sweaty, red-faced, half-naked people exit into the front lobby. The previous quiet of the space now fills with voices—one, in particular, standing out from the rest.

"Make sure to drop your towels off in the bins to your right!" Nadia turns in its direction and is immediately transfixed. The light in the room brightens as a slender, sun-kissed gazelle moves gracefully toward the front counter, her honey-blond hair pulled back into a high, voluminous ponytail, with a tie-dyed tank dress wrapped tightly around her waifish frame. It is like she is lit from within, and for a moment, Nadia's breath catches in her throat.

"See you ladies next week!" Lena waves to a group of older women leaving the building. She leans effortlessly against the counter, her back perfectly flat, and chats with the other students from the class. As the sound of her laughter carries through the space, Nadia looks away, feeling a sharp pain in her chest. She never imagined the sender of Aman's texts to be so attractive. Even without any makeup on, Lena is stunning, her skin smooth and luminous with a youthful glow.

But it's more than her looks. What bothers Nadia most is how different Lena seems from her—almost the exact opposite. If Nadia is pensive and reserved, requiring time to open up and, even then, doing so with caution, Lena appears friendly and free-spirited, unmarked by the trials of life. If Nadia is insecure, Lena radiates confidence from every pore of her body. Even her laugh is open and unassuming, almost fearless in a way that Nadia's feelings of inadequacy would never allow.

"Do you mind?"

Nadia turns around, her thoughts interrupted by one of the sweaty, half-naked patrons from the five o'clock class.

"Do you mind if I just—" the woman repeats as she reaches out to grab a sports bra hanging from the display in front of Nadia. "I just need one of the yellow extra-*extra*-smalls."

"Of course," Nadia murmurs, stepping aside. But as she

backs up to make room for the woman, her purse knocks into the glass shelves on her other side, and an entire section of aluminum water bottles spill onto the floor like a row of dominoes. Panicked, Nadia bends down to grab the fallen merchandise and bumps directly into Ms. Extra-Extra Small.

"Excuse me!" the woman cries, rubbing her rear.

"Sorry!" Nadia says, her skin prickling from all the eyes in the front lobby staring at her. Even the students at the counter peer curiously in her direction, distracted by the commotion. Struggling, Nadia stumbles back with an armful of bottles, apologizing once more to Ms. Extra-Extra Small and anyone else she passes. But as she pulls away from the racks, she turns around to find herself face-to-face with Lena.

"Are you okay?" Lena asks, her grayish-blue eyes wide with concern. Nadia nods, immediately forgetting her words. Up close, Lena's beauty is even more disarming. Thick, perfectly shaped brows frame her expressive eyes, and tiny freckles sprinkle the bridge of her small, upturned nose. She reaches out, gently touching Nadia's shoulder. "I hope you didn't hurt yourself—"

"I'm fine," Nadia says, jerking her shoulder so abruptly that it takes Lena by surprise. "Really, I'm fine. Thank you," Nadia stammers. Unsure, she holds out her arms, awkwardly waiting as Lena takes the bottles one by one and places them onto the counter. "I'm sorry," she says when she is relieved of the final one. Her hands now free, she tucks a loose curl behind her ears, feeling the heat rise to her cheeks. "I'll get out of here," she says, backing up. "Have a good evening. Sorry again for . . . I'm sorry," she repeats before exiting the building.

A rush of warm air slaps her face the moment she steps outside. Nadia exhales. The late-day sun hovers over the horizon, casting its golden rays across the parking lot. Now that she has seen Lena, she isn't sure whether she feels better or worse. Any plans to remain inconspicuous went completely awry, her humiliating stumble drawing more attention to herself than intended. But worst of all is that she ended up apologizing to the woman having an affair with her husband. Of all the things she should've said to Lena, *I'm sorry* was the least appropriate. "Stupid, Nadia. So stupid," she whispers to herself.

When she reaches the car, she checks her phone to find new messages from Aman.

Coming home early tonight. Can we talk?

She presses against the headrest and sighs. She can't avoid Aman forever, but her encounter with Lena height-ens her insecurities as she is confronted with the reality of what she's up against: Lena is the new object of Aman's affection—a position she no longer occupies. With so much at stake, she stares at the messages glowing on the screen. Unsure of how to accept this truth, she leaves her phone abandoned on the seat and pulls out of the parking lot.

16

Across the kitchen table, Zeba sits, head cradled in her hands. "I can't believe it. An instructor at a yoga studio?" She looks at Nadia, face weary with disbelief. "I can't believe Aman would do this."

Nadia swallows, but her mouth is too dry to even respond. After dinner, Shoaib took charge of the boys' bedtime routine so she and Zeba could talk without distractions. But after recapping the events of her visit, Nadia feels panicked as her regrets about the situation fester. She never should've gone to Purple Clover in the first place. Now that she knows who the mystery woman is that Aman's been texting, she wishes she didn't.

"You said you spoke with her?" Zeba asks.

"Sort of . . ." Nadia shrugs. "Words were exchanged, if that's what you mean."

Zeba leans forward, her long arms draping over her

knees. A tiny crease forms between her brows as she carefully weighs her next question. "So . . . what is she like? Is she what you expected?"

Nadia hesitates, swallowing the description of Lena that immediately comes to mind. She's not sure *what* she expected. She wishes she could say with confidence that Lena is not a threat. That she is nothing more than a dim-witted floozy whom Aman will likely dump out with next week's trash. But those are not statements she can make. Now that she's seen Lena in the flesh, she understands why Aman would be drawn to someone like her—her poise and unreservedness, her undeniable allure. But admitting that to Zeba means she'd have to admit it to herself. The shame of that is too much to bear.

"You don't have to answer that if you don't want to," Zeba says, noticing her sister's discomfort. "I'm sorry—"

"No, I just . . ." Nadia's voice trails off. "I don't know. I guess if you're curious, you could stop by the studio and see for yourself?"

Zeba presses her lips together, considering Nadia's suggestion. "I've got a better idea," she says, getting up. Nadia waits as Zeba leaves the kitchen. A few minutes later, she returns with a laptop and renewed vigor in her eyes.

"Purple Clover Studio, you said?" Zeba confirms, typing it into the search bar along with Lena's name. As she presses "enter," the two of them lean in—Nadia more anxious than curious. She worries how another glimpse of Lena might affect her self-esteem but can tell by Zeba's expression that she's fully committed to the investigation. To their surprise, however, the search garners few results. Besides a brief instructor bio on the yoga studio website and a defunct Pinterest page, nothing else for Lena shows up. Not even a social media account, which Nadia finds shocking.

"What now?" she says, turning to Zeba, who is clearly frustrated.

"How is that possible?" Zeba says, trying another spelling. "What kind of twentysomething has no online presence?"

Nadia shrugs. Though it strikes her as odd too, it also adds another layer of intrigue.

After a few more tries, Zeba shuts the laptop with a sigh. "I guess we can make another trip to Purple Clover."

"*We?*" Nadia shakes her head. "There's no way I'm going back there. Not after the total ass I made of myself today."

"Aren't you the slightest bit curious to know more about this woman? Besides the fact that she works at a yoga studio?"

"I can't," Nadia says.

"You're not serious, Nadi? If this is who Aman is cheating on you with, you at least owe it to yourself to dig a little deeper."

"What for?"

Zeba scrunches her face, bewildered by Nadia's resistance. "To gain some insight into who she is? To find out what she's like? And what it is about her that would cause Aman to risk his *ten-year marriage with you.*" She gesticulates emphatically to emphasize each point. "We both know you're going to get zilch from Aman. If you want answers, you're going to have to go to the source."

"Who says I want more answers? What if I've already gotten what I want?"

"Please," Zeba scoffs at Nadia's argument. "You don't believe that. Otherwise, you never would've gone there in the first place."

Nadia is quiet. Even if her sister is right, what good will come of more answers? That brief yet humiliating encounter with Lena has already proven to be more than she was ready for. What she knows is this: Lena is gorgeous. She's young. She's vivacious. And whatever hold she has on Aman is no longer a mystery. Beyond that, what else is there to know?

"At least just come and point her out to me," Zeba continues. "No pressure; I promise. You can even let me do all the talking."

"I know you're trying to help—" Nadia begins, unsure

how to explain how painful the situation is to process. "I'm just not there yet."

"I get it. I do," Zeba says, leaning forward. "But this is *you and Aman* we're talking about. All I'm asking is that you think about it. Okay?"

Nadia looks away. "Okay," she concedes, relieved that thinking is all she has agreed to.

17

---

his is crazy," Nadia whispers into Zeba's ear. It's Thursday evening, and they are back at Purple Clover Studio. After taking a few days to get past the humiliation of that first visit, Nadia realized her sister was right. This is her and Aman. If there's even the slightest chance of saving her marriage, she first needs to find out where things went wrong. And to do that, she'll need more answers.

With the boys off at their karate class, Nadia agreed to meet up with her sister after work. Her plan was to wait in the car while Zeba went in and took a quick peek. But her sister insisted that she come inside so the two of them could collectively get a better sense of Lena. The moment they walk in, and Nadia sees the front counter, she immediately has second thoughts. "I don't think I can do this," she says, inching toward the exit.

"You *can*," Zeba says, firmly pulling her by the arm.

"You're already inside. All you have to do is stay by my side; you don't even have to say anything."

"I don't know, Zeba." Nadia bites the inside of her lip; the taste of old pennies fills her mouth. "How do we know if she's even working today?" Although she kept the class schedule from her last visit, it notably left out the names of the instructors teaching each class. "We probably should've called first . . ." She looks around the front lobby, which is empty save for a few people browsing the racks.

"Let's find out," Zeba says, marching up to the counter.

"Hi, can I help you ladies?" the woman behind the desk asks. She has dark wavy hair and olive-colored skin with that same dewy smoothness as Lena's. *Is being a bombshell a baseline requirement for every employee at this establishment?* Nadia wonders, her insecurities resurfacing.

As Zeba proceeds to feign interest in the turquoise ornament strung around the woman's neck, Nadia stands distanced, one foot crossed over the other, a list of worries scrolling through her mind like a digital marquee sign. What if Lena comes out and recognizes her from last time? Even worse, what if Aman walks in for his yoga class and sees the two of them? What explanation could she give to him about why they're there?

"I think we should *go*," she whispers through clenched teeth as the woman turns away to grab a fresh stack of schedules. Zeba shushes her with narrowed eyes, reminding her that she's in charge.

"So, these are all the classes we offer." The woman hands them each a folded pamphlet before placing the rest on the counter. "There's also flyers here for our upcoming wellness retreat and the special promo we're offering for our partner yoga workshop at the end of the month."

"Partner yoga?" Zeba exclaims. She turns to Nadia with an arched brow. "That sounds fun," she says, taking one of each flyer.

"Let me know if you have any questions!" The woman smiles, her teeth straight and perfect.

"Well, actually, I do have another question," she hears Zeba say. Nadia feels sick. Her stomach is so warped into knots that she can barely stand upright. "Is Lena teaching today?" Nadia's heart pounds against her ears in anticipation of what follows.

"Oh, hey!"

Not catching the woman's response, Nadia turns to see Rick, the attractive young man who greeted her the last time she was here.

"Are you back to try the intentional flow class?"

Nadia's face burns. The fact that he remembers her proves there's no way Lena won't, and all she wants to do is bolt through the front doors.

"They were asking if Lena was teaching today," the woman tells Rick as he walks around the counter and reaches underneath to grab a rolled-up towel.

"Why don't you check the class log?" he says, clicking open a digital spreadsheet on the monitor. As the three of them, including Zeba, huddle around the screen, Nadia holds her breath, watching the woman scroll through the document past the vertical segments of each column. "There she is," Rick points out, as Nadia feels the oxygen slow to her brain.

"It looks like her last class ended at five today."

Zeba's mouth wilts with disappointment. "I see," she replies, glancing at her watch. It's barely half past five. They missed Lena by a mere twenty-eight minutes.

"Excuse me," Nadia says, backing away from the counter. Her legs feel wobbly as she pushes through the doors. Behind her, she can hear her sister finishing up the conversation with Rick and the woman.

"Is there anything else I can look up for you?"

"Did you need more information on that flow class?"

"No, no, that won't be necessary. Thank you for the help," Zeba replies, rushing to follow Nadia, who is stooped outside, palms pressed into her knees as she tries to catch her breath. She fills her chest with deep lungfuls of air until she feels the blood rushing back.

"Are you okay?" Zeba asks, placing a hand on her shoulder.

"I told you we should've called first," Nadia says, standing up. Though she's managed to avoid another encounter with Lena, she feels foolish for not having a better plan in place.

"It was worth a try," Zeba says, flipping through the flyers she's collected.

Nadia walks toward the parking lot. Considering the amount of anxiety this visit has cost her, she is angry at the time and mental energy that's been wasted. "I knew this was a bad idea, Zeba. We shouldn't have come."

"Nadi, look—"

"I mean, even on the off chance that she had been working, what were you going to say? It's not like we can tell her *why* we came, not without offering some context first."

"Nadi, look at this—" Zeba's voice tangles in her throat as she hastens to catch up.

"*She* probably has no idea that she's in a relationship with a married man. Why would she?"

"Nadi, look—"

"And even if she did, what difference would it make? Clearly she's not broken up about it based on the frequency of their texts."

"Nadia, STOP!" Zeba reaches out and pulls Nadia by the elbow, forcing her to halt. "Will you listen to me for a second?" The two of them face each other, chests rising with frustration. Zeba holds up one of the flyers. "Can you *look* at this?"

Nadia snatches the flyer away. "What is it?" she says, her voice sharp. "What do you want me to look at?"

"*This*," Zeba says, lifting Nadia's hand. She points to the writing on the flyer.

Three-day wellness retreat . . . Foothills of the Santa Monica Mountains . . . Guided meditation . . . Daily hikes and yoga classes . . . Plant-based meals.

"It looks like a wellness retreat," Nadia says, scanning the words on the page. "So what?"

"*Look* at the list of instructors," Zeba says, pointing to the bottom.

Shaman Osiri, Quinn Perry, Eldrick Walkner, Lena Dewan . . . Lena Dewan.

Nadia turns to her sister.

"Nadi, this is your chance," Zeba tells her, her mouth wide with excitement. "Three whole days. In the mountains. You can find out everything you need to know about this woman—"

"Have you lost your mind?" Nadia exclaims, the sick feeling in her stomach returning. "I'm not signing up for this." She hands Zeba the flyer, but her sister pushes it back.

"Think about it, Nadi. She has no idea who you are, which gives *you* the advantage of catching her with her guard down."

"What are you suggesting I do? Tackle her in the middle

of the mountains and tell her to stay the hell away from my husband?"

"Actually, I'm suggesting you do something better than that," Zeba replies. Her eyes twinkle in a way that Nadia hasn't seen before. "*Befriend* her. Get her to trust you enough to confide in you about her personal life and who she's dating."

"And then what?"

Zeba hesitates, her lips breaking into a small smile. "Then you convince *her* to leave *him*."

Nadia is shell-shocked. *She* convince Lena to leave Aman? How would that even work? "I think you're forgetting the third person in this relationship. *Aman*. Even without Lena, how can I get past all the lies? And how do I know what happened with Lena won't happen again?"

"Look, I understand that you and Aman have a lot to work through. But at the end of the day, you still want to save your marriage, right?"

Nadia nods. She does want to save her marriage, hurt as she is. She loves Aman. And while that alone is reason enough, for Nadia it goes even deeper than that. There's a need to prove herself. To prove that her marriage isn't doomed like her mom's. To prove that Aman won't abandon her like their father did. To prove that she's worthy of being loved by him, even if her mom didn't believe that she was . . .

"Trust me, Nadi, it'll be a lot easier to work on your marriage once you remove the biggest obstacle standing in the way."

Nadia considers her sister's plan. "This is crazy." She shakes her head.

"Maybe," Zeba agrees. "But how else would we do things? We're Abbasis, remember?"

18

Nadia sits in the car processing everything that's just happened. After their failed attempt to confront Lena, Zeba left to pick up the boys from karate. Although Nadia agreed to meet back at Zeba's for dinner, she decides to make a quick stop on the way.

As she drives past the sign for Cedar Heights, it hits her that it's been almost a week since she's been home. She and Aman have barely spoken to each other since the night of Zeba's dawat. Though she's far from ready to slip back into her old life—especially after seeing Lena—pulling into the driveway triggers in her a longing for the ease of what once was. She misses the life they built together, a life that up until now seemed stable enough to withstand any trials thrown its way. She pushes those feelings aside and reminds herself: *Everything is different now.*

It's a relief to find Aman's car absent from the garage;

however, she has no way of knowing when he'll be home. Though she doesn't plan to stay long, she hopes to have enough time to grab some extra clothes and necessities and leave before he has a chance to know she was there.

She walks through the garage door and into the kitchen. She can't help but notice how everything looks the same yet feels different. It's more than just extra dishes piled in the sink, or bread crumbs scattered in front of the toaster oven. The hum of the refrigerator sounds louder, more pronounced. The marble on the counters shines a bit less; the stainless steel appliances appear duller. It's an overall disquiet that makes her feel as if she's snooping around in someone else's house. How quickly the strange settles into the familiar, she thinks.

On her way to the bedroom, she flips on the light switch near the stairwell and pauses as it flickers a moment before fully illuminating. For months she's been telling Aman to replace the lightbulb, but his excuse was always that he was too busy. She stares at it a moment before continuing up the stairs.

From the top shelf of her closet she grabs a small duffel bag and begins packing it with undergarments, work clothes, and anything else she thinks she might need. She tries to stay focused, but her mind keeps drifting to Zeba's suggestion of attending Lena's retreat. The idea of manipulating a friendship with Lena just to break her and Aman up seems so . . . circuitous? But what are her other options? The fact is, she does need answers. What pushed Aman toward Lena to begin with? What is the nature of their relationship, and what does that mean for her and for them? How easy it would be if she could get these answers directly from Aman. If he'd be willing to share with her honestly and openly, allowing them to clear the air and move forward. But Nadia knows better than to hold on to that hope.

She is immersed in these thoughts when Aman's car pulls into the garage. Nadia does not hear him walk through the front door. Nor does she notice the weight of his footsteps on his way upstairs. It is not until he is standing right behind her at the entry of their closet that she finally notices his presence.

"Hi," Aman says, dropping his briefcase against the armoire. His face looks tired, and the edges of his mouth are turned downward. "I didn't realize you were coming by. I would've come home sooner."

Nadia zips the duffel bag and stands up, facing him. "I just stopped by to pick up a few things." She can feel herself softening at the sight of him. His typically pristine appearance is no longer intact, and she fights back the urge to reach out and fix the sagging collar of his untucked shirt. Now is not the time to get distracted, she reminds herself. Not when the future of their relationship still hangs in the balance.

"How have you been?" he asks, peering into her eyes. The sound of his voice is so gentle, so tender that it almost brings her to tears.

"We don't have to do that."

"I miss you, Nadi," Aman says, his shoulders dropping with a sigh.

Hearing those words causes Nadia's chest to ache. She misses him too. His skin; his smell; his touch. But none of that negates the betrayal she feels. She cannot allow Aman to pull her back in unless he is willing to give her the answers she needs. Abandoning the duffel bag on the closet floor, she perches herself on the edge of their bed, her mind flashing back to the countless nights spent staring at the vacant space on his pillow, waiting for him to return. "I'm willing to listen. But only if you're ready to tell me— everything."

Aman walks over and takes a seat beside her. "I don't know where to begin," he starts. Nadia waits, giving him a chance to collect his thoughts. She watches quietly as he stares at his hands, twisting the wedding band on his left ring finger as he tries to find the words. "I just—" He pauses before starting again. "It's been a while since I've been happy. I mean, I've been trying—*we've* been trying," he corrects himself as he struggles to look at her. "But it's been hard."

Nadia is quiet, unsure how to respond.

"Are you happy, Nadi? Be honest," he asks, his eyes searching her face as if trying to read her thoughts through her expression.

She reflects on what he's asking, refusing to avert her gaze. *Am I happy?* She swallows, parsing each word to figure out the answer. *Happy?* The more she thinks about it, the more obscure the word becomes. What does it mean to be happy? "I want us to be together," she eventually says.

"That's not what I'm asking."

"What do you want me to say?" How can she boil down their entire marriage to this one single question? Ten years they've spent together. It's not so simple, she wants to tell him. There have been enough highs and lows over the years that it'd be impossible to analyze them all in that moment. But living apart hasn't been easy either. If this past week has shown her anything, it's that she's willing to do whatever it takes to get back to where they once were—before doubt and uncertainty made themselves a permanent fixture in their marriage.

Aman leans forward, dropping his head into his hands. Everything about his body language points to his discomfort. "I'm just wondering, Nadi . . ." He rubs his face as loose strands of hair fall over his forehead. ". . . if this is the life you had imagined for us?"

Nadia blinks, feeling hot tears press against the bottoms of her lids. Their struggles to start a family have not been a secret; they've been the primary focal point of their marriage for years. Even so, it's frustrating to rehash them now. "Of course this isn't the life I imagined for us. But we tried everything we could, and I thought we both agreed after that last round of IVF that it was time to move on—"

"I'm sorry." Aman shakes his head. "I wasn't trying to make this about that."

"I know this isn't how we planned it, but—" Nadia takes a deep breath. "I've told you before, if you want to try again, we can talk about it—"

"No." Aman rubs his eyes with the tips of his fingers. "That's not what this is about."

"Then what is it, Aman? What else are we talking about?"

"What if it's not *just* about starting a family? What if there's more to it than that?"

"Like what?" Nadia says, her voice thick with emotion. When he doesn't immediately respond, her insecurities take over. "Just say it, Aman. What am I missing? Is that why you've been lying to me? Why instead of coming to me, you've decided to go somewhere else to find it?"

Aman looks up, stunned by the accusations.

"Did you honestly think I wouldn't find out? All the phone calls, the text messages, the late nights, the excuses . . ." Her face twists with pain reliving it all. "Just because I haven't said anything doesn't mean I don't know what's going on right in front of me."

"It isn't what you think, Nadi—"

"Stop, Aman." She holds up her hand, letting him know that she's done listening to any more untruths. "It's exactly what I think, so just stop. I know you've been seeing someone. I know you've been—" She can't bring herself to end that sentence.

Aman stands up, running his fingers through his hair. He walks over to the window and grips the sill. "You're right," he says, pressing his forehead against the glass. "I have been seeing someone." His admission is unexpected; his words knock all the air from the room. Nadia's breath lurches in her throat as she tries to grasp whether she heard him correctly. "But it's not just some steamy affair like you're thinking, Nadia." He turns to her, his voice heavy with remorse. "I'm trying to explain to you *why* I haven't been happy."

"*Happy?*" Nadia scoffs, her entire body rejecting the word. "You've just admitted you've been cheating on me, and I'm supposed to sit here and listen to why things have been hard *for you*?"

"Nadia, listen to me—"

"I'm done listening, Aman." Nadia stands up and grabs the duffel bag from the closet. "If you were unhappy, you should've told me. We could've worked on it. *Fixed* it. It's not something you bring up after you've already moved on with someone else."

"I never wanted this to happen, Nadia," Aman says, following her down the stairs. "I can't tell you how much this has been weighing on me. I'm just ready for us to be honest with each other."

"Don't you dare talk to me about honesty," she sneers, her speech slurred with anger. "I'm not the one who's been hiding a secret relationship from you." She pushes past him and storms out the kitchen and into the garage, leaving him trailing behind. Fumbling with her keys, she struggles to get her car door opened fast enough.

"Nadia, can you just slow down—" Aman rushes out the door and places his hands on the roof of her car, his face wounded and twisted in a way she no longer recognizes. "Please don't leave like this. Can you come back inside?"

"What else is left to talk about, Aman?" Her chest aches with such an intense pain that it feels like it might shatter. Climbing into the car, she ignores Aman's pleas as she backs out of the driveway. Her heart caught in her throat, she makes the drive back to Zeba's house in total silence. When she arrives, everything she has been holding back finally releases, breaking her in its aftermath. Hunched over with forehead to the steering wheel, Nadia cries, a deep, heaving cry as her body attempts to expel the hurt inside her. Despite all the clues she'd been piecing together, nothing could have prepared her for what it would feel like to hear Aman say those words.

AFTER DINNER, AS Zeba gets the boys ready for bed, Nadia finds herself drawn to the spare bedroom at the end of the hallway, the very room she's been avoiding all week. She turns the doorknob, and a familiar smell urges her forward. It's the same smell that fills the inside of a suitcase housing old saris: the sulfurous scent of sweat and musk that clings to the stiff fabrics. Nadia sits down on the bed. She lifts the pillow, burying her nose in the quilted case. For a moment, she is reminded of coconut. And curry leaves. And the stale aroma of dried jasmine petals crushed inside an old book. They're the smells of her mom.

The last time she was in this room, she and Aman had just begun fertility treatments. She shared details about the clinic they had visited and the optimism shown by their latest consultant. Her mom listened quietly as she massaged amla oil into the shafts of her sister's hair as Zeba sat in front of the mirrored dresser.

Nadia had always been transparent with her mom and Zeba about her struggles to conceive. They knew all about the multiple miscarriages and the grief following each loss; the inability of the doctors to pinpoint anything "medically wrong." During these conversations, it always bothered Nadia how little her mom contributed. She understood that in their culture, certain things were not openly talked about. She understood the discomfort and awkwardness surrounding these topics and the inconvenience it brought on those of an older generation to express compassion outwardly for such matters. Even so, she couldn't help but interpret her mom's silence as a personal affront, as if Nadia's infertility was simply one more disappointment to add to the list of others. If her mom were still alive, she imagines how that disappointment would be further compounded by a failing marriage. At least she can keep that loss to herself for now.

Nadia walks over to the dresser and opens the top drawer. Inside she pulls out her mom's fine-tooth comb and the glass bottle of amla oil she knew would still be there. She unscrews the aluminum cap, smelling the thick greenish liquid that fills the bottom half. Unclasping the claw-shaped clip that holds her hair up, Nadia releases her curls, letting them hang loosely over her shoulders. She uses one end of the comb to part her hair evenly down the middle. Tipping the bottle, she carefully pours oil into the cup of her palm and dips her fingers into the syrupy liquid, allowing the coolness to coat her fingertips. Back and forth, she massages the oil into her scalp until it saturates the top of each strand. She closes her eyes, imagining her mom's fingers rubbing vigorously, her brittle fingernails raking through her hair.

"Here, let me do that."

Zeba stands at the doorway, her mouth lifted in a small smile. Nadia waits as Zeba slides a stool in front of the dresser and then sits down. In the mirror, she sees her sister take her place behind her.

"Remember how much we hated the smell of this when we were kids?" Zeba asks as she generously pours the oil into her hand.

"More than the smell, I hated everyone asking, 'Why does your hair look so greasy?' It always took like three washes to get it all out."

"I bet those girls who made our lives hell are probably wishing they had these thick, luscious locks now, huh?" Zeba says, running her fingers through Nadia's curls. She leans Nadia's head back and gently combs out small sections of her hair, making sure the oil spreads all the way from root to end.

"Do you do this for the boys?" Nadia asks, closing her eyes. She can feel her sister plaiting her hair in the same way their mom used to.

"I wish," Zeba says. "I can never get them to sit still long enough." She pulls a rubber band from her wrist with her teeth and wraps it around the end of Nadia's braid. "There," she says, looking at her sister's reflection in the mirror. "That looks about right."

"Ammi would definitely approve." Nadia smiles, returning the oil and comb to the top drawer. She joins Zeba on the bed, resting her shoulders against the metal headboard.

"You were extra quiet at dinner tonight," Zeba says, rolling onto her stomach. "You're not still upset at me for making you go back to the studio, are you?"

Nadia shakes her head. "After you left, I stopped by the house to pick up a few things and Aman was there."

Zeba looks surprised. "How did that go? Did you tell him about Lena?"

"No. But he finally admitted that he's been seeing someone."

Her sister props herself up on her elbows. Aside from the subtle rise and fall of her chest, she is quiet as she tries to process this information. "Did he say anything else?"

"Only that he hasn't been happy for some time."

"*Happy?* What does that mean?"

Nadia shrugs.

"So, what are you feeling now that he's finally confessed?"

"I can't pretend like I didn't already know, but . . . it still hurts to hear it confirmed, you know?"

Zeba nods. She reaches out and takes Nadia's hand.

"I don't even know where we're supposed to go from here. I mean, what do I do now?" she asks, eyes pleading for answers.

"Have you given any more thought to that retreat?" Zeba asks after thinking for a moment.

"I don't think I can." Nadia leans back, her fingers squeezing the bridge of her nose. "I just hate that I ended up here. In the same place as her." She looks around the room and sighs. "I tried so hard to avoid this outcome, but here I am. Literally."

"You're not in the same place as her," Zeba reassures her. "Your circumstances are different. The choices available to you are different."

But Nadia doesn't see it the same way. "I just don't want to waste my time pining over someone who has already found happiness elsewhere."

"But how do you know that what Aman has with Lena is what he wants? Isn't it worth your time to at least find out before you give up?"

Nadia doesn't say anything.

"So, you're just going to let this irrational fear of ending up like Ammi prevent you from even trying?"

"It's not irrational—"

"When are you going to let it go, Nadi?" Zeba sighs. "So, she loved our father. You can't fault her for that. Not when she sacrificed everything to come here on the promise that he would take care of her—of *all* of us. You act like she should have known that he already had a life here with someone else."

"I'm not faulting her for his mistakes, Zeba. I just . . . wish she didn't hold on for as long as she did. All the lies and the pretending, her refusing to move on once she already knew he had. I know it couldn't have been easy for her, but her choices made it harder for us too."

"You're right. It wasn't easy. For any of us." Zeba pauses. "But I think you forget sometimes that she was nineteen when she married him. She was just *a kid.* Did she have it all figured out? No. But who does when you're faced with things that you never planned for?"

Nadia is quiet. It never occurred to her that their mom's struggles to deal with their father's infidelity could be attributed to youth. When she married and moved to America, she was barely entering adulthood. She had no family. No friends. And the only person she knew and trusted ended up abandoning her—alone with two kids.

"Hers was a story of unrequited love. A story that could only end in sadness. Unfortunately, it just took her her whole life to figure that out." Zeba sits up and looks earnestly into her sister's face. "But your and Aman's story is different. Your story began with love—and sure, it might seem like that love has gotten muddled somewhere along the way, but that's no reason you shouldn't at least try to set it back on course."

"But what if I try only to realize that it's not me, Zeba?" Nadia says softly. "You didn't see what I'm up against."

"All I know is no other woman can erase the years you and Aman already share. When it comes down to it, Nadia, there's no competition. And it might serve Lena well to be reminded of that."

THAT NIGHT, WHILE she lies awake listening to the snores of the small human above her, Nadia thinks of her mom. She desperately longs for one of her signs: the wail of a stray cat or the tap of some night creature at the windowsill. She even watches the goldfish in the small bowl atop the boys' dresser for some movement or signal that might indicate her mom's presence, but nothing. Of all the unexpected visits her mom has paid her this past year, this is the first time Nadia wouldn't mind being caught off guard. But the later it gets, the clearer it becomes that her mom won't be coming. This time, unsurprisingly, she's on her own.

19

On her desk sits the flyer from the yoga studio advertising the weekend retreat. Nadia lifts the folded leaflet, flipping it in her hand, her last conversation with Aman still on her mind. As difficult as it was to hear him confess to cheating on her, their conversation also resurfaced other issues she had been deliberately ignoring. It's not just Aman who feels unhappy. She too has been discontent for some time now, but rather than confront it, she hoped it would somehow resolve on its own. Seeing where that unhappiness has now led them, however, she recognizes how misguided she was in that mindset.

"Dr. Abbasi?" Julie says, poking her head into Nadia's office. "I'm going to take my lunch now."

"Okay," Nadia replies, barely glancing at her.

"I'm thinking of checking out that ramen place around the corner. Want me to bring you back something?"

"No, thanks," Nadia says, expecting Julie to shut the door. But she continues to linger for a few extra moments.

"Dr. Abbasi? Are you okay?"

Nadia looks up, the bottoms of her eyes sunken in darkness. "I'm fine," she says, trying to make her voice as convincing as possible. The brokenness of her smile, however, gives her away.

"You don't look fine. In fact, it looks like you haven't slept in days." Julie walks over and crouches beside Nadia's chair. "Is it because you saw Ms. Papazian's bunions sticking out from the opening of her Birkenstocks yesterday?" She shudders. "I'm surprised I haven't had nightmares myself."

Nadia laughs despite herself.

"Are you sure you don't want me to bring you back anything? It wouldn't be any trouble."

"I already packed a lunch," Nadia explains, pulling out a Tupperware full of steamed quinoa and vegetables from her bag. Although staying at Zeba's means no more green smoothies, seeing Lena in the flesh has triggered a renewed motivation to get back on a healthier diet.

"*This* is what you're eating?" Julie picks up the container, examining it from the outside. "No wonder you look miserable. C'mon, let's go get some real food," she says, gently pulling Nadia out of her chair. "I refuse to take no for an answer."

Nadia relents, eventually standing up. But before she turns to leave, she carefully tucks the flyer beneath the keyboard. "What should I do with this?" she asks, lifting the Tupperware.

Julie uses her foot to expose the trash bin beside Nadia's desk. "What you probably should've done in the first place."

THE WALK TO the ramen place is short, but there is already a sizable crowd lined up when they arrive. Glimpsing the glass-fronted exterior, they see every table in the small, box-shaped restaurant occupied. Fortunately, the turnover rate is quick, allowing Nadia and Julie to nab two stools near the entrance. As they wait for their orders, Nadia confesses to Julie that her previously posed question about cheating was not so hypothetical. When Julie admits that she assumed so all along, Nadia proceeds to fill her in on the recent discovery of Lena Dewan—the equivalent of Julie's Snapchat adversary, Alyssa James.

"I don't know, Dr. Abbasi, I think I'm with your sister on this one," Julie says as the food arrives. With one hand, she pulls back her chopsticks, expertly wrapping the thin noodles around the tips before placing them in her mouth. "Signing up for that retreat sounds like the obvious answer. I mean, unless your husband knows about your encounter with Lena."

"I didn't mention it to him. And since he's never divulged her name to me, he has no reason to suspect that I even know who she is."

"That means you'll have an entire weekend to find out anything you want about this woman without her or anyone else knowing who you are. The setup couldn't be more perfect."

Nadia swirls a white porcelain spoon through her vegan ramen, pushing aside blocks of crispy tofu from the center of the bowl. The sweet tanginess of the miso-roasted vegetables makes her stomach growl, but her waning appetite prevents her from diving in like she normally would. Instead, she dips her spoon gingerly, touching the side of the bowl before bringing it to her mouth.

"Just think about all the information you could uncover. Like what if you find out their relationship isn't even that serious?"

"What do you mean?"

"Maybe they're just friends with benefits."

Nadia cringes.

"Like fuck buddies."

"I know what that means," Nadia says, her insides churning. Just imagining Aman in bed with Lena forces the mushroom broth to rise in the back of her throat. She knows that Julie is trying to spin this as a positive, but she's not sure what is worse: the idea of Aman and Lena having formed some deeper emotional connection, or the two of them just casually boning. "I'm not convinced how finding out more about *their* relationship will help *me*."

"You said yourself your marriage hasn't been happy in a while. This might give you a glimpse into why." Julie sets her spoon down and looks at Nadia. "You know, after that whole Alyssa James sitch, I discovered that one of the main reasons my ex cheated on me was because he felt emotionally disconnected. Even though we were still having sex, we had stopped talking about things, and while it doesn't excuse the cheating—in fact, all cheaters can go choke on an egg roll, for all I care—it is something I've tried to be more conscious of in the relationships I've had since. Especially with Trevor. We talk about *everything*. I don't want us to ever get to a point where we can't share how we're feeling with each other, since I already know where that leads— and I'm not about to go down that rabbit hole again."

Nadia reflects on how she and Aman have also emotionally disengaged over the past few months. To make matters worse, their physical connection has been on a steady decline ever since their last IVF cycle failed. She can't remember the last time they shared that kind of intimacy, and while she expected those issues to eventually resolve, the toll they've already taken on their relationship is clear.

After lunch, Nadia returns to her office and shuts the door. From under the keyboard, she unfolds the flyer. At the very bottom there's an email address listed for the event organizer. She clicks open a new message box and types a short email requesting a link to the registration form before she can think herself out of it. Biting her bottom lip, she hits "send," collapsing into the chair. A three-day retreat in the middle of the mountains with her husband's mistress. What could possibly go wrong?

20

The route east of Yerba Buena Road is narrow, bending and curving at every turn. Zeba shuts off the radio and tightens both hands around the steering wheel. She straightens her back along the edge of the seat cushion, the extra height providing added visibility.

"You want me to drive?" Nadia asks. She notices a sign for a scenic overlook ahead and points it out. "We can pull over there and trade if you want."

"No more stops," Zeba replies, her gaze cemented ahead. "We're almost there."

They've spent the past two hours driving along the Pacific coastline, soaking in views of morning waves slicing through the ocean. Aside from the influx of traffic near Malibu, the drive has been relatively peaceful, almost pleasant, despite the giant knot that's taken up residence in the pit of Nadia's stomach. For most of the journey, Zeba has been providing reassurance: explaining to Nadia why this retreat will be good for her, how something positive will likely emerge from this weekend away. But looking now at the changing terrain of rocky ledges and densely populated trees, Nadia questions her decision to come. Apart from the fact that she's never camped before, the idea of being stuck in the wilderness with Lena is starting to sink in.

She checks her phone to see if Aman has responded to her earlier text.

Going out of town. Will talk when I get back.

Since their last conversation, Aman has besieged Nadia with messages begging to meet again. He claims there is more he needs to tell her, but she's been far too distraught to take him up on the offer. After hearing his admission, she's not sure she needs him to expound any further. He's already made his unhappiness clear; what she can't understand is how to fix it. That will require candor and honesty on both their parts. Though, if she trusted Aman to be capable of either, she wouldn't be driving to this retreat in the first place . . .

Surprisingly, there's been no response from Aman. Not even to inquire about where she's going or when she'll return. She wonders if his nonreply might indicate that he's given up on her . . . and, in turn, them.

The road climbs higher. "How many bars do you have?" she asks Zeba. Keeping her eyes fastened ahead, Zeba feels her way around the center console and hands over her phone. "Perfect," Nadia says, glancing at the screen. "There's literally zero reception out here."

"You say that like it's a bad thing," Zeba remarks.

"What if I need to contact you over the next few days? What if there's some sort of emergency? Am I just supposed to be stranded out here like it's the early nineties?"

"Maybe disconnecting is what you need, have you thought about that?" Zeba asks, looking at her. "It might help you focus better on what you're here to figure out."

Nadia leans back into her headrest. Her situation would be a lot less complicated if she didn't still love Aman. As hurt as she is by his actions, she can't bring herself to *hate* him. In fact, if given a choice, she would still choose to be with him rather than without. Yet she also recognizes that she and Aman cannot continue down the path they are on. If they both remain as unhappy as they have been, a divorce might be inevitable even sans the added barrier of Lena Dewan.

So much is contingent on this weekend, Nadia thinks. Not only must she uncover the nature of Lena and Aman's relationship, but she must also find a way to break whatever hold Lena has over him. She just wishes she felt as confident as Zeba that she's the person to do this. Despite the mounting pressure, Nadia remains hopeful. If all goes to plan, she and Aman will be reminded of why their marriage is worth fighting for. Regardless of how attractive or free-spirited Lena might be, Nadia and Aman are meant to be together—in this life and the next, just as they promised each other at their nikkah ten years ago. These are the thoughts running through her mind as Zeba pulls up to a makeshift parking lot.

About a hundred yards away, they see a circular dwelling atop a wooden platform in the middle of a raised clearing. "This is it," Zeba says, shutting off the engine. In the rearview mirror, they glimpse a handful of people standing near the dwelling, bags of luggage dropped at their feet like misshapen boulders. Of the faces she can make out, Nadia recognizes only Rick, the man she met both times at the studio.

"Shit," she mutters, disappointed her presence won't be as covert as she had hoped. "That's the guy who helped us look up Lena's schedule." She points to Rick, who stands with arms crossed, peering across the vista at the surrounding mountains. "He'll remember me for sure."

"It'll be fine. Don't worry," Zeba reassures her. "Most of these people are patrons of the studio anyway, so one more familiar face is nothing out of the ordinary."

Nadia bites her lip. She glances at the others, their craned necks stretching toward phone screens juxtaposed against the natural setting. "I thought this would be a larger group. Do you think more attendees will come?"

"Maybe," Zeba says, climbing out of the car. "Let's unload your things."

"Wait." Nadia hesitates as the opened door beeps in the background. "I'm not ready yet; can we wait here for a few more minutes?"

"Nadia, I didn't drive all this way for you to change your mind now."

Nadia sighs, pushing aside the apprehension she feels. One by one, she takes the bags Zeba hands her as she empties out the trunk.

"Are you sure you packed everything?" Zeba asks, wrapping the straps of Nadia's duffel around the handle of her suitcase, making it easier to pull both. "Because I won't see you again until Sunday, when I come back to pick you up."

"I should be okay," Nadia replies. Along with the registration code, the retreat coordinator emailed her a packing list, which she followed very precisely. Besides the necessities—fitness clothes, hiking shoes, toiletries, sunblock—she packed all the optional items as well, just in case. She didn't want to take any chances. As they see Rick and the others make their way inside the dwelling, Nadia looks on anxiously.

"It's going to be fine," Zeba says, noticing the trepidation on her sister's face. "*Andheri.*"

Nadia nods.

"Come here." Zeba holds out her arms as Nadia leans in to give her a hug. "Remember: no one knows why you're here besides me. Take this opportunity to make of it what you want."

Nadia squeezes her eyes closed and rests her chin against Zeba's shoulder. The scent of jasmine from her sister's hijab fills her nose. It's only laundry detergent, but she feels homesick already.

"You got this, okay?" Zeba places both hands on Nadia's shoulders and pushes her back, looking directly into her face. "*Okay?*"

Nadia nods again. She swoops her hair to one side and slings her backpack over her shoulder, carrying it by a single strap. "I guess that's everything."

"Keep me posted," Zeba says as she shuts the trunk and gets back into the car. "I want all the details—in real time."

"With this reception? I can't make any promises. But I'll try my best." She grabs the handle of her suitcase and steps back as her sister's minivan reverses into the road. With a small wave, she continues to wait, watching until the green of Zeba's car is swallowed up by the wilderness surrounding it.

21

The bright, expansive interior of the dwelling belies its modest exterior. Wooden rafters extend from the center skylight across a dome-shaped ceiling. Everything is touched with a golden hue, lit by warm rays pouring in through the windows that surround the curved structure. While the temperature outside rises, Nadia is surprised at how cool and comfortable it is inside.

The decor is simple, yet luxurious in its minimalism. A long wooden table acts as the centerpiece of the dining area, while oversize sofas facing a vintage freestanding fireplace complete the cozy living space. Leafy palms brighten the indoors with green and pliant foliage, and freshly picked wildflowers adorn the surfaces, infusing the air with a sweet, citrusy aroma.

Nadia drops her bags against a lattice-covered wall and spots an empty seat on a couch. Though she hasn't caught sight of Lena yet, she tallies about seven other guests—in addition to herself. She had hoped for a larger group to better blend into the background and observe Lena unnoticed. The intimacy of the gathering, however, is something she'll have to factor into her plans. Feeling uneasy, she takes a seat.

"First time?" a heavily tanned woman sitting beside her asks. The name tag on her T-shirt reads PATRICIA, and she wears knee-length bike shorts over what appears to be a one-piece bathing suit, judging from the bright blue straps peeking over her shoulder blades. "I can always pick out the virgins."

Nadia looks down at her high-waisted culottes and floral-printed blouse and realizes how unready she is for the weekend—in both emotion and apparel.

"This is my fourth time attending," Patricia announces as curved lines wrap around the edges of her mouth. The expression on her face is smug, like she's about to flash Nadia a frequent-flyer card reserved for retreat-goers.

"Wow, that's . . . *something*," Nadia says with a tight-lipped smile. Though the woman seems friendly enough, Nadia is not in the right headspace to maintain small talk. As she considers the politest way to disengage from the conversation, Lena enters the dwelling through the fiberglass doors. Her honey-blond hair is down this time, flowing loosely to her midback in long, natural waves. Nadia's throat clams up as she watches Lena walk over to Rick and two other women clustered around the dining table, the four of them in matching green T-shirts.

"Hopefully you brought more comfortable shoes with you," the woman beside her remarks, pointing to Nadia's lace-up espadrilles with a quiet but obvious judgment.

"Huh? Er, yes, I have everything," Nadia responds, surprised that the conversation between them hasn't ended yet. Behind her, Lena laughs, her voice blooming like sunflowers on a warm summer afternoon. Nadia shrinks into the cushions. Atop one of the end tables sits a Buddha statue: eyes closed with both hands clasped in its lap. She reaches out to touch it, admiring its bronzed visage.

"Don't forget to fill out a tag," the woman says, pointing to a handful of blank name tags scattered across the coffee table. Nadia grabs a marker and neatly writes her name across one. As she peels off the backing and affixes it to the front of her blouse, Lena and the other green-shirted instructors make their way to the center of the living space. They arrange themselves in a straight line, preparing to address the attendees.

"Hello!" one of them calls out. Her bright red hair is swept into a side braid, and she holds up an arm, patiently waiting for the room to quiet. "Welcome to the Ashram, a weekend wellness retreat designed to rejuvenate your body, mind, and soul. My name is Quinn Perry, and I am your retreat leader." Quinn looks around, placing both hands on her chest and smiling warmly. "This lovely dwelling that we're currently seated in is called 'the hive.'" She gestures around drawing attention to the space. "This is where we will congregate as a group, morning and evening, for meals and reflections."

Nadia swallows. She had no idea there would be so much together time. Her uneasiness intensifies.

"I thought we could begin with a quick icebreaker. Why don't we go around the couches and have everyone introduce themselves—tell us your name, where you're from, and how you practice self-care. Who would like to start?"

The woman beside Nadia shoots up a hand. "I'll go," she offers, repositioning her body to face outward. "My name is Patricia," she says, stretching its pronunciation into four syllables. "And this is my fourth time attending."

Nadia resists the urge to roll her eyes.

"For those who don't know me, I'm from Ventura County. Recently, I joined a Booze and Brews group in Ojai as self-care, and I enjoy making homemade wine."

As Patricia describes at length the challenges of her new hobby, Nadia racks her brain for something interesting to share about herself. Her preoccupation with Aman these past few weeks hasn't left much time for self-care—though it was never something she was big on regardless. Failing to come up with a single example, Nadia is anxious; her stomach churns at the thought of her turn.

Fortunately, after Patricia, the older gentleman seated on the couch across from her speaks out. "My name is Gary, and this here is my partner—"

"Also Gary!" his partner interjects with a grin. "You can call us the two Garys."

"Gary 2.0."

"I'm the upgraded version!"

While the others seem amused by the twosome, Nadia is more struck by how alike Gary and Gary look. If having the same name isn't odd enough, they also share the same cropped haircut and affinity for tie-dye, based on their matching sweatsuits.

"We're from Seattle—"

"Home of the Seahawks!"

"We *loooove* bingeing crime and murder documentaries."

"We're partial to cults too—"

"But only from an outside perspective . . . we don't actually belong to a cult, although I could see this guy joining one accidentally!" He points to Gary beside him.

"Who doesn't like making new friends?" Gary admits.

Nadia's fascination peaks as the Garys continue, their sentences bouncing from one to the other, seamlessly interwoven.

"We're also big on farm-to-table cooking—"

"It's all about local sourcing."

"And environmental sustainability. But enough about us. Don't let us talk your ears off!"

"Although we gladly would!"

And Nadia would gladly listen if it meant avoiding a turn. Next to introduce herself is Iris, a twentysomething influencer sporting space buns and fringed leggings. Dressed more fittingly for Coachella than a wellness retreat, Iris describes herself as a health and lifestyle consultant whose entire brand is rooted in self-care.

"If anyone is interested in trying out a new product"— she reaches into her waist bag and pulls out a fistful of cellophane-wrapped lollipops—"hashtag: not an ad, but a friend and I just launched Suckers, a stress-relief lollipop. Our handle is @suckerpop. Give us a follow, so you can like/comment your thoughts. I even have a code I can share for twenty percent off your first order."

"What's the relaxing agent?" one of the Garys asks, inspecting the lollipop Iris hands him.

"Essential oils mixed in with a little extra *zhuzh*."

"I didn't know essential oils were safe to consume . . ."

"I could see this pairing well with a glass of wine," Patricia says, taking a lollipop.

"We're still waiting for clearance from the state health department," Iris explains, "but the oils are all-natural—"

"Maybe we should get that clearance before distributing

these to the masses?" Quinn quickly collects all the Suckers and passes them back to Iris. "Shall we move on to our next guest. Brandon?" she says, reading off his name tag.

"Hi everyone," Brandon says. He is young with long, lanky limbs that look like they belong on someone twice his height. His expression is pensive as he looks around the couch. When his eyes meet Nadia's, he presses his palms together and bows. "Namaste."

Nadia looks behind her, uncomfortable when she realizes the special acknowledgment is for her.

"I'm somewhat of a nomad. Traveling and yoga are how I practice self-care. Last year, I spent the summer in South Asia, where I was able to combine my love for both." He turns back to Nadia. "*Tumhaara desh bahut khubasoorat hai*," he says in slow, stilted Hindi.

Nadia's face reddens. She has no idea what he is saying and is nonplussed by his assumption that she does.

Next is Steph, a divorced mom from Orange County, and her preteen daughter, Stacey. "We're here for our annual wellness weekend," Steph explains. "Since the divorce, we've been focusing more on our mental health and equipping ourselves with positive coping mechanisms." She takes Stacey by the hand. "Isn't that right, sweetie?"

Stacey nods, her upper lip curling to reveal her two-toned braces.

"Our goal this weekend is to neutralize any negative chi

and recalibrate our natural cycles of energy." She takes a deep breath and releases it through her mouth.

Nadia takes her own breath as she anticipates what's next.

"We have one more introduction left." Quinn shifts the focus to Nadia's corner of the couch.

Nadia blinks, her heart racing. "Um, hi. I'm Nadia," she says, clearing her throat. "This is my first time attending a wellness *anything*." From her periphery, she sees Patricia break into a pitying smile. "I can't say I practice much self-care . . . unless you count sneak-eating junk food and crying in my car." She expects a laugh, but the room is quiet. Swallowing hard, she looks at her lap, feeling the heat rise to her face.

"That sounds like top-notch self-care to me," one of the Garys says, breaking the silence.

"*You do you*, honey," the other Gary agrees.

Nadia smiles, relieved to move on.

"Our final guest unfortunately had to cancel at the last minute, which means it's going to be a smaller group than normal," Quinn explains. "Now that we've gotten to know each other, however, let's meet the instructors who will guide us through this weekend. This team beside me"—she points to the other green shirts—"is here to work with you, to help purge your minds of worldly distractions and balance your physical and spiritual selves. Together, our goal is to create a transformative experience that you'll be able to carry with you long after you've returned to your everyday lives."

Distracted by the sugary, measured tone of Quinn's voice, Nadia diverts her attention; her eyes drift toward Lena, who stands to Quinn's right, her hands clasped delicately in front of her body as she gently sways to an imaginary breeze. A small smile spreads across Lena's lips as she listens to Quinn, nodding along to her every word. As Nadia watches her, she is wholly transfixed by this woman who up until a week ago was no more than a shadowy figure concocted in her mind. In the time she's spent thinking of her since, she almost feels as if she knows her despite their never having had a real conversation.

"This retreat is meant to help you reconnect with yourself," Quinn continues as she passes out a detailed printout of every class, activity, and meal, planned down to the hour, "not just to balance your exterior, but to help you create a new awareness and relationship with yourself and the metaphysical world. We want our guests to leave this weekend feeling rejuvenated and empowered—confidently equipped with the strength to conquer any mountain." Quinn pushes her fist into the air, her crystal bracelets sliding down her freckled wrist as everyone except Nadia lets out an inspired *whoop*.

Martha, one of the other instructors, follows with the rules and regulations as Nadia stares at the schedule. It's starting to feel a bit overwhelming. She bites her lip, staggered at how easily the other guests are eating up this hokeyness. As Martha discusses the benefits of a "nutrient-dense" diet, Lena comes around with a tray of foamy green liquid. Taking one of the cups, Nadia reluctantly slings back a shot of wheatgrass and ginger, wincing at the foul, bitter taste it leaves in her mouth. She questions how she's going to survive the weekend with her sanity—and appetite—in check.

After a review of the meal plans, Quinn describes the lodging accommodations, urging the guests to double up with someone they wouldn't mind rooming with. With the same panic befalling twelve-year-olds pairing off for their first dance, Nadia glances around, immediately eliminating the two Garys and the mother-daughter duo, both of whom will obviously room together. With four out of the running, she turns her attention to Iris, who is busy snapping selfies at the other end of the couch. Before she can make her move, however, Brandon corners her.

"India is such a beautiful country," he gushes. "There's so much I miss—the people, the sights, the *smells*."

Nadia winces. Though her connection to India is sparse, limited to a handful of stories passed down from her mom, she doesn't remember anything noteworthy mentioned about the smells.

"You're Indian, right?"

Indian American, she wants to clarify, but she doubts that technicality will sway Brandon's already-formed perception of her.

"I guessed it." He smiles, pleased with himself for connecting his own self-constructed dots. "After two months on the subcontinent, I feel a connection with other Indians in a way that's inexplicable." He rubs his chin meditatively. "I'd love to swap stories sometime about your experiences growing up there."

Nadia presses her lips together wondering if she should let him know that she was born and bred in LA. "I should get back to finalizing my room situation . . ."

"Do you need someone to room with? Because I could—"

"No," she stops him. "Thanks, but I'm almost set." She glances at Iris, who is recording a video for her followers. "Check with Iris, though?"

"Sure thing. *Shukriya*."

Nadia waits until Brandon walks away before turning to the only option left. "Patricia is a lovely name," she says, angling her body toward her.

"Patri*c*ia," the woman says, flashing coffee-stained teeth at her. "With a soft *C*."

"Nice to meet you, Pa-tree-*see-ah*." Nadia widens her mouth to get that soft *C* sound. She pauses for a moment, mustering the courage to pop the question. "I was wondering if you'd be interested in rooming together?"

"Sorry, newbie." Patricia shakes her head.

"Nadia," she corrects her, but her amendment goes unheard.

"I already requested a private room for the weekend. That's one of the advantages of booking in advance. Once you've attended as many times as I have, you pick up on a few things."

Private room? Nadia doesn't recall seeing any type of room option when she filled out her reservation. She might've been the last to sign up, but even so, there must be something available. "Will you excuse me?" she says, getting up. If there's even the slightest chance of her surviving this weekend, she must get her hands on one of those private rooms. She walks over to Quinn, who is answering some questions for Steph and Stacey. As Nadia waits her turn, she can't help but overhear bits of their conversation.

"We'd really like a room that is east-facing," Steph explains. "It's important for us to feel the energy of the sunrise when we meditate at the *sattvic* hour. Those sunrise sessions have done wonders in helping balance our moods, right, honey?"

Stacey nods.

"Mmm. Understood," Quinn says. "I know how crucial that natural alignment can be. Let me see what we can arrange."

"Just a quick question," Nadia cuts in when Quinn motions for Martha across the room. "I was wondering if I could request a private room. I'm not really accustomed to rooming with people I don't know, and—"

"I'm sorry, all the private rooms have already been booked. We only have shared rooms available. Were you not able to find someone to pair up with?"

Nadia lowers her voice just in case Brandon might overhear. "I think all the guests have already found roommates . . ."

"Oh, that's right, we have one less guest this time."

"Which is why if there's some way to accommodate my request for a private room—"

"Don't worry." Deep lines furrow across Quinn's forehead. "We will get this taken care of." She turns to Martha, who has just walked over with a clipboard in one hand and a basket of room keys in the other. "Martha, it seems a guest of ours has found herself without a sleeping assignment. Can you help place her?"

"Of course," Martha answers, scrolling through her list to scan for empty beds.

As Quinn returns to her conversation with Steph, Nadia hopes another push might help seal the deal. "You know, Martha, I'd be willing to pay extra for a private room if—"

"The rooms can't be bought for additional payment. They're assigned on a first-come-first-served basis."

"I understand," Nadia says, her face hot.

"But if we shuffle a few people around, it looks like we might be able to create a double occupancy." Martha points to a blank slot on the guest list. "Yes. We can arrange a second bed to be placed in yurt eight with one of our instructors—" She raises her head, looking straight past Nadia. "Lena, can you come join us?"

"Oh, for fuck's sake," Nadia mutters. "Can I look at that list to see if there's another open bed somewhere?" Martha pulls back. Nadia tries again, her voice dripping with desperation. "Is there someone else I can swap rooms with? Or perhaps there's a hotel nearby . . ." The words spill from her mouth, her agitated state preventing her from noticing that Martha is paying her no mind. As Lena approaches them, Martha extends her arm, pulling her into the conversation.

"Lena, would you mind sharing a room with one of our guests here, *Ms.* . . ." Martha waits for Nadia to fill in the blank.

"Nadia," she manages to croak.

"Nice to meet you," Lena says with a broad smile. "Sure, I don't mind sharing."

Nadia recoils at the irony of that statement.

"Have we met before?" Lena tilts her face.

"Er, no? Maybe? I don't know." Nadia's voice catches in her throat. Taking the map and room key Martha hands her, she prattles a quick "Thank you" and rushes outside before Lena can make the connection. Of all the people she could've been roomed with, of course it had to be her.

Struggling to control the emotions coursing through her, she pulls out her cell phone and walks toward the parking lot. Two bars of service. She presses Zeba's name and impatiently counts the rings, praying for a voice of reason to intercept from the other side.

22

———————

Are you crazy?!" Nadia exclaims. The spotty reception forces her to boost the volume all the way up against her ear. "You told me to befriend her, but I can't possibly *share a room with her*!"

"Why not?" her sister's crackled voice responds. "Can't you see that it's the perfect setup?"

"For what? *Murder?* Because that's exactly where this is headed!"

"She's the reason you signed up for this weekend."

"*She's* the woman fucking *my husband*."

Zeba sighs loudly.

"Look, I tried. I can't do it."

"What do you mean you tried? It's been less than an hour since I dropped you off!"

"You have to come back, Zeba. I can't stay here."

Zeba pulls over into the shoulder, startled by the alarm in Nadia's voice. With the engine still running, she attempts once more to reason with her. "Before we do anything rash, will you at least hear me out?" she asks, struggling to keep her tone level. "Most of the weekend will be occupied by activities, right?"

Nadia emits a deep-bellied groan.

"And since Lena is teaching many of those activities, how often will she even be in the room?"

Nadia squats down, resting her elbows on her knees. Her mom used to say that the best way to "cool" a temper was, if standing, to sit down. And if still upset, then to lie down. And if after that the anger remained, then make wudu to extinguish the internal fire with water. Though her heartbeat slows just from lowering to the ground, she senses where the conversation is headed and refuses to offer Zeba any indication of agreement.

"Really, the only time you'll be stuck together is at night, and yeah, it's not ideal, but don't you think sharing close quarters might offer some advantages?"

"Like what?"

"I don't know, you could have a chance to talk to her one-on-one. Like an actual conversation that doesn't involve you toppling over inventory and running away after two words."

Nadia is quiet.

"We've already gone over this." She hears Zeba's frustration rising. "The only way you can convince Lena to leave Aman is by getting her to trust you. Last time I checked, trust is hard to generate without at least a conversation. Rather than looking at this as an inconvenience, maybe consider it an unexpected blessing?"

"This whole thing is too much, Zeba," Nadia mutters. "Every time I look at her, I feel sad and angry and jealous and crazy. How is this ever going to work? What am I doing here?"

"What you're doing is fighting for your marriage. Listen to me, Nadi." Zeba speaks firmly into the phone. "You're going to walk back to your room, put on your sweetest smile, and do whatever you can to convince that woman to back the fuck off—even if it means having to play nice for a couple days. Take a deep breath and stay focused on the bigger picture."

Easier said than done, Nadia thinks, but despite her panic she knows Zeba is right. This might be her one and only chance. And with Lena completely oblivious to her identity, the situation is ripe with opportunity if she can just get her emotions under control. She ends the call, takes a few deep breaths, and goes back into the "hive" to grab her luggage.

"They'll take that to your room for you," one of the Garys explains, coming up behind her. "See, they've already marked them." He points to the yellow stickers taped to her bags, which read YURT 8.

"Oh," Nadia says. At least she won't have to lug her things through the mountains on her own. She pulls out the printed map given with her room key and charts out the best route to the room.

"You heading to the yoga session on the bluffs?" he asks, holding up the schedule.

"I'm not really dressed for yoga," she says. "Besides I didn't bring a mat or a towel with me . . ."

"And I didn't bring any goats, but that's not stopping me." He loops his arm into the crook of her elbow and leads her outside. "Don't worry, they'll give you everything you need. I don't know about you, but I've spent the past six months in soggy Seattle weather. A little sunshine and fresh air sounds like a perfect start to the weekend."

Though Nadia's weekend agenda differs from Gary's, she follows his lead nonetheless. If a few posed stretches will stall her from having to deal with Lena and the whole roommate situation, she'll twist herself into a pretzel.

THE "BLUFFS" ARE a small flat space about a quarter mile from the hive, offering unobstructed views of the canyons on all sides. While Gary joins the other Gary, Nadia removes her shoes and takes a seat on an empty mat near the back row. Most of the guests are already warming up. Near the front,

Steph and Stacey assist each other with partner squats while Iris pulls herself into a backbend beside them. Opposite them sits Patricia, cross-legged and Zen-like, resting both hands on her knees as she practices her breathing. To ease her intimidation, Nadia follows suit with the only warm-up she knows: ankle circles. She extends her legs in front of her and rotates her ankles in a clockwise movement. She tries leaning her torso forward, but the pull of fabric around her shoulder blades restricts her arms from reaching beyond her midthigh. Embarrassed, she returns to the ankles, hoping her position near the back will allow her to go unnoticed.

"This class is going to be a breeze for you," Brandon says, taking a mat beside her.

She's tempted to tell him this is her first yoga class, if only to shatter his illusion of her.

"I did some yoga training in Rishikesh, which—as you know—is where yoga originated."

Nadia knows as much about yoga as he does about social cues, but she refrains from responding. She checks her watch to see how soon the class will begin.

"It's a beautiful little town. The first place I visited was the Ganges River."

"The *Gan-jeez*?"

"The holy river. You know, the famous one?"

Nadia's never been to India, but she knows enough to know it's pronounced *"Gung-gah."*

"It's been on my bucket list ever since the sixth grade."

She feels a headache coming. As Brandon describes to her his "awakening" while swimming in the river, she questions whether dealing with Lena might be the less painful option.

"Hello, everyone!" Rick announces upon his arrival at the bluffs. "My name is Rick, and I'll be guiding us through our first yoga session." His green instructor tee from earlier has been swapped out for a neon tank top and fitted yoga shorts. He looks like a lean yet well-defined glow stick, the contrast striking against the neutral shades of canyon around him. He doesn't waste any time. "Let's begin in child's pose by bringing your knees to the mat. Make sure the tops of your big toes are touching."

Nadia looks around as everyone instinctively kneels, lowering their torsos to the space between their knees. Though she's never seen a child pose like this before, she bends her legs and tries to flatten her hips over her thighs.

"Now, stretch your fingers to the top of your mat and bring your forehead to the ground." Rick speaks in a clear, rhythmic voice. "Take a deep inhale"—he pauses for a breath—"and a cleansing open-mouth exhale."

Unable to touch her buttocks to her heels, Nadia releases a small groan on her exhale, a sound that Brandon imitates. Although it's the first pose, she can already feel a trickle of sweat running down her spine.

"Press your palms into the mat and spread your fingers wide. Slowly push up into downward-facing dog." Rick demonstrates, his body angling into a perfect triangle with the ground as his base. "As you press the heels of your feet into the ground, be sure to take a moment to find your stillness."

Nadia feels anything but still as she pulls herself into position. Rather than a sharp point, her body forms more of a rounded mound, her shoulders practically touching her ears.

"Swing your right knee toward your chin and then cradle it back. Straighten the leg and extend it to the sky . . ."

Perhaps it's the heat or the lack of blood flow to her brain that's making her dizzy. She breathes heavily, struggling to lift her leg behind her. She blows the loose curls from her forehead and looks up, watching in envy as the others swing their knees back and forth with ease. Even Patricia, who appears less than graceful, stretches her leg back in one lithe movement. Embarrassed by how hard it is, Nadia tries her best to not fall over. *Maybe hating yourself is part of the process*, she thinks.

By the time they get to the warrior sequence, a steady sweat drips from every crack and crevice of her body. As she stumbles through the lunges, straining to hold each pose, she tries to visualize Aman completing these same stretches. It's hard for her to picture.

"With a tall, long back, let your arms fall to the side as you prepare for tree pose." Rick walks around gently tweaking incorrect postures. "Take a deep inhale and slowly lift your right foot off the ground, aligning its sole with the inside of your left thigh."

Of course, the trickiest pose comes at the point when she is most exhausted. Nadia lifts her arms, shakily bringing the palms together in an inverted V.

"Point your toes downward, keeping your pelvis completely straight."

She can feel Brandon watching from the corner of her eye.

"Your balance is impeccable," he whispers. "I too have been gifted with a stable core."

Nadia looks ahead, focusing on her breathing.

Deep inhale.

She wonders how frequently Aman and Lena practice yoga together . . .

Open-mouth exhale.

She wonders if that's the thing that brought the two of them closer . . .

Deep inhale.

She imagines him and Lena in a sweaty room, finding their stillness together . . .

Her foot drops as she loses her balance.

"Good work! Now let your arms fall slowly to your sides." After the longest hour imaginable, Rick wraps up the class, instructing them all to return to child's pose. This time, Nadia forgoes the kneeling and lies all the way down, curling her knees into a fetal position. She rocks back and forth, trying to erase the image of Aman and Lena from her mind.

"What's that pose called?" she hears Brandon whisper.

The my-husband-is-cheating-on-me-and-I-can't-cope pose, she thinks. Squeezing her eyes, she drowns out the voices until all she can hear is the sound of her heart beating against her chest. When she opens them next, the others are rolling up their mats and discussing their plans for the next activity. Nadia gets up, drops her mat into the pile, and quietly slips away before anyone can notice.

23

It is quiet inside the yurt. This is the first thing Nadia notices upon entering. The second is her and Lena's bags lined up in a neat row. From the looks of it, Lena hasn't come in yet—the two full-size beds in the center of the room are perfectly made, the crisp white sheets and hand-crocheted bedding neatly tucked and folded at the foot of each. The surface of the shared nightstand is empty save for a white lamp and a glass vase holding bright, cheery sunflowers. Even the bathroom is untouched, with freshly stacked towels and pairs of plush white slippers on a wooden bench beside a claw-foot tub. The accommodations are much nicer than Nadia expected.

After the yoga session, she desperately needs a shower, but there's no way of knowing how long this solitude will last. She'd hate to be caught with her pants down, *literally*, the first time Lena arrives. So instead, she stakes her claim on the bed closest to the window. She did arrive first, after all. Dragging her bags to the far corner of the room, she shuts part of the drapes to block out the incoming light and plops down on the firm soft-top mattress. Across from her, the wall clock reads half past two. She pulls out the folded retreat schedule from her backpack to see what activities she plans to skip.

Breath Work and Mindful Meditation—2:30.

Digital Detox Healing Hike—4:00.

Plant-Based-Eating Workshop—5:30.

None sounds as appealing as an afternoon nap. Tossing the schedule aside, she sinks into the large goose-feathered pillows and closes her eyes. Within minutes she drifts off into a dreamlike state, conjuring up a memory even more distant than her present surroundings.

SHE IS ALONE in a long, brightly lit corridor. On either side are large wooden doors towering over her. She reaches out, grazing her fingertips across the textured wallpaper.

Where am I? she wonders as she passes each door, unsure of what she's looking for.

At the other end of the hallway, she hears voices. A conversation between a man and a woman. Walking faster, closer, she inches toward the door from behind which the voices seem to come. She cannot make out what they are saying. She leans forward, ear pressed against the wood.

The door cracks open. Unlocked. She peers inside, attempting to glimpse whom the voices belong to.

"Log kya kahenge? How can you be so reckless? Do you understand the situation you have put us in?" the woman pontificates. Although the tone of her voice is low, Nadia senses that she is upset. She leans farther in, hoping to get a better look inside the room.

"I'm not going to apologize, if that's what you're asking me to do, Ma," the man replies.

Nadia removes her hand from the door. His is a voice she recognizes.

"We cannot accept this in our family, Aman. How can you even ask this of us?"

Nadia steps back into the hallway; her heart pounds. She looks around, suddenly recognizing the Persian silk runner racing across the floor and the large Jamini Roy painting on the far end of the wall—she is inside Aman's parents' home in Atherton. She remembers this day well. It was the first and only visit they made in the months before they married.

"What are you asking me to do? I'm in love—*we're* in love, Ma. You want me to just ignore how I feel and continue living a lie?"

"You will have to, Aman. There is no other choice."

"And you think that's fair—*to her*?"

"Think about the shame it will bring on all of us if you

don't. No. We cannot bear it, Aman. Nor will we accept it. Ever."

"I don't believe this."

"Aman, listen—"

The door swings open, and Nadia slips into one of the adjacent rooms just as Aman storms into the hallway. His face is dark; the frustration in his eyes reflects with an intensity Nadia has not seen since. She holds her breath, waiting for the footsteps to fade before she emerges. Without another thought, she begins to run through the corridor—the dupatta of her salwar kameez billowing in waves as the lights flash above her. On and on, she continues to run, refusing to stop until she makes her way to the other side . . .

WHEN SHE AWAKENS, the room is dark except for a tiny sliver of light beneath the bathroom door. Nadia rubs her eyes, blinking through her disorientation. The vividness of her dream still lingers with her. It has been years since she thought about that visit, the conversation that took place, the shame she felt at hearing her mother-in-law's disapproval of her. Although she never confronted Aman about what she had overheard, remembering it brings back feelings she was certain had been buried.

Searching for the switch, she presses a button on the lamp base, allowing her vision to slowly adjust to the yellowish light. The sweet, earthy smell of sunflowers reiterates the foreignness of her surroundings, and it takes a moment for her brain to register where she is. As the rest of the room gradually comes into focus, fragments of the present piece themselves together.

The weekend retreat.

The shared yurt.

Lena Dewan.

She looks over to the next bed and notices a blue cotton sundress draped across the sheets. The sight of it, along with the open suitcases in the corner, causes a sudden rush of blood to her head. Lena must have come in while she was asleep. Her things are scattered around the room: A line of colorful sneakers against the wall. A rose-tinted cell phone on the floor with a white wire that feeds directly into the outlet behind the dresser. A lacy strap, from what appears to be a camisole, hanging limply from one of the partially opened drawers.

Nadia holds her breath as a squeaky faucet silences the sound of water from the bathroom. Her mind rattles with panic. In that moment, she is tempted to grab all her things and flee before Lena comes out, but her anxiety leaves her immobile. When the door of the bathroom finally opens, she hugs her knees to her chest, reminding herself that no one, including Lena, knows who she is. That thought alone calms her nerves.

"You're awake." Lena smiles as she walks into the room.

With just a towel wrapped around her tiny frame, she grabs the sundress from the bed. Her wet hair drips onto the floor as she heads back into the bathroom, this time not bothering to shut the door. "I just needed to take a quick shower before dinner," she says. "I hope I didn't wake you."

When she reemerges, she is fully dressed. The same towel that she was wrapped in is now balled in her hands, and she uses it to scrunch the moisture from her hair. As she leans forward, Nadia can't help but admire how defined Lena's shoulders look in the ruched bodice of her dress and how slender her waist is above the tiered ruffles. "Shaman Osiri is going to give a short lecture before dinner. You won't want to miss his talk on spiritual energies and altered states of consciousness." She drops the towel on the floor and uses her fingers to form her damp curls into perfect waves. "Do you want to walk over there together?"

"Oh, uh . . ." Nadia fumbles to find an excuse. It's the first time she's spoken aloud in hours, and her voice cracks as it clears the sleep from her throat. "I think I'm going to freshen up first."

"I don't mind waiting—"

"No," Nadia blurts more forcefully than intended. Her cheeks burn as Lena hesitates, the pale hue of her sundress reflecting the steely blue in her eyes. "I mean, it's not necessary. I'll need some time to get ready, and I wouldn't want you to miss the lecture."

"Okay." Lena's face falls. She smiles, but there is something forced in it. As if she is genuinely disappointed by Nadia's refusal.

"I'll head over when I'm done," Nadia says. She knows if Zeba were here, she'd be pushing Nadia to take advantage of every opportunity to get to know Lena; however, she needs to move at her own pace. It's hard enough adjusting to the shared room. Having to accompany the woman to group activities is more than she's willing to do. At least for now.

"Do you know where we're meeting—"

"Got everything right here." Nadia holds up the schedule. "Anything that's missing, I'll figure out."

"Okay." Lena grabs her bag. "I'll see you there."

When the door shuts behind her, Nadia releases a long exhale. At some point, she will need to separate Lena, her roommate, from Lena, Aman's mistress, if the plan is going to work. But that's not a task she needs to figure out tonight.

The group dinner begins at seven thirty, which means there's less than forty minutes to get ready. Sighing, she lifts the suitcase onto her bed. She has rolled her clothes into little cylinders to spot each item more easily while also leaving space for shoes, makeup, and other necessities. As she thumbs through the garments, most of which are hiking and workout clothes, she is careful to keep them neatly packed—unlike Lena, who has emptied her belongings into every available space. She wants to be prepared for a quick getaway in case things go awry. Judging from day one of this retreat so far, a sudden exit may not be the most surprising way to end the weekend.

24

When Nadia arrives at the hive, all the guests are already gathered around the dining table. Her shower left her with barely enough time to brush her hair, apply a coat of mascara, and change into a striped tunic with white linen pants. Though it's not as cutesy an ensemble as the flouncy sundress Lena donned, her choices were limited between this and a polyester track suit with mesh lining. Upon seeing the other guests, most of whom have come directly from the detox hike—fleece jackets and all—she wonders if the track suit would've been the more appropriate choice after all.

On the far right, she spots an empty chair wedged between Rick and the two Garys. Though she'd much prefer her meals delivered to her room, that option, unfortunately, was not offered in the schedule.

"Excuse me," she says, making her way to the open seat.

"Oh, there you are," Quinn remarks as Nadia passes by her. "How are the accommodations working out for you?"

"Splendid," she lies. Her focus remains on the empty seat for the simple reason that it's four chairs down and across the table from where Lena sits. Squeezing her body through the small gap between the table and the wall, she bangs her knee into the back of one of the Garys' chairs. "I'm so sorry," she apologizes.

"You're fine, honey," he says, scooting forward.

"I just need to get through . . ." She sucks in her stomach and maneuvers around the edge of the table. When Rick sees her approaching, he pulls out the chair just as she plops into it. "Thanks," she says, breathing heavily.

"You were in my yoga class earlier."

"Mm-hmm," she says, embarrassed by the amount of energy it has taken to sit down.

"And didn't you come into Purple Clover Studio?"

The color drains from Nadia's face. Rick stares back, brows arched with curiosity. Though she knew there was a chance of being recognized, his acknowledgment still catches her off guard. "Yeah, um, I . . ." she stammers as Rick's expression eases into a smile.

"I remember you." He leans back. His mien is open, friendly even, but still, she worries his recollection might somehow blow her cover. To her relief, Martha cuts in just then, interrupting the chatter with a brass bell.

"Welcome to our first family dinner," she announces, standing at the head of the table. "We hope everyone is feeling reinvigorated after our first day of activities." The other guests respond with enthusiasm. "We believe wellness begins with our inner health and the nutrients we introduce into our bodies. For that reason, all the meals prepared this weekend will be organic, vegetarian, and predominantly plant-based."

Nadia's stomach grumbles with disappointment. She sips from the glass of water in front of her, hoping the liquid will muffle her hunger pangs.

"Many of the ingredients served in tonight's dinner are seasonally grown in our very own garden, just a short walk from this dwelling. The garden is nurtured and cared for by our retreat leader, Quinn Perry, and it is truly a labor of love."

Quinn smiles, resting her palms over her heart in a show of gratitude. Nadia takes another sip, this time to drown out the cringe.

"We welcome each of you to stop by for a visit sometime this weekend. Quinn or one of the garden keepers will give you a tour, and if you're lucky, a sampling of succulent blackberries or crisp, juicy kohlrabi. Now that I have everyone's mouths watering"—Martha beams—"let's move on to the fun part of the evening."

Finally, Nadia thinks, bored by all the buildup. She just

wants to eat, head back to her room, and put the first day of the retreat behind her.

"I'll hand it over to Lena Dewan now, a certified yoga instructor as well as our resident nutritionist."

Nadia tenses.

"Lena's going to tell us all about the delicious meal that's been prepared for tonight's dinner."

Lena's face flushes beneath the halogen lights of the pendant chandelier above them. "Hi, everyone," she says, smiling. "Tonight's first course will be a fresh garden salad drizzled in a lemon-herb vinaigrette. All of the vegetables, as Martha mentioned, have been hand-picked from our very own garden . . ." As she launches into a comprehensive breakdown of the nutritional value in each ingredient, two members of the kitchen staff enter the dwelling. They balance large platters on their forearms with individual servings for each of the guests.

Nadia unfurls the cloth napkin, laying it smoothly across her lap, and sets out the silverware on the table in front of her.

"Our salad will be paired with a signature chickpea masala stew with braised red cabbage, house-made vegetable stock, and creamy coconut milk . . ."

Nadia stabs her fork into the arugula, chewing silently as its peppery taste fills her mouth. She thinks of how ecstatic Aman would be about these offerings, considering how perfectly they fit into his new diet. His obsession with clean eating suddenly makes a lot more sense. It wasn't just a midlife crisis that brought about the change. It was an impress-your-new-yogi-slash-nutritionist-girlfriend phase that commenced his transformation.

Completely oblivious to the damage wreaked by her involvement with Aman, Lena introduces the next course—a roasted beet risotto with truffle gremolata. Nadia's stomach growls. She is reminded of her hunger, but the irony of her situation reduces the desire to abate it.

"I take it you're not a fan of the plant-based cuisine?" Rick says, pointing his fork to her barely touched plate.

"As much a fan as you, it appears," Nadia replies, noticing that he has hardly made a dent in his risotto either. Her embarrassment from earlier has been overtaken by melancholy as she struggles to wrap her mind around Lena and Aman's relationship.

"Touché." Rick smiles, unbothered by Nadia's curtness. "I guess I prefer my roots in the ground versus on my plate."

"Isn't this whole raw, vegan, superfood thing kind of in your wheelhouse? I thought treating your body like a temple was part of your job description."

"I grew up bi-religious with a Hindu-practicing mom. If I believed in treating my body like a temple, I'd be cramming it with sweets right now." His eyes dance with amusement as he searches Nadia's face for a reaction. Her expression remains neutral, though his background catches her attention.

"You're half-Indian?"

Rick shakes his head. "Indonesian. But we always tell my mom that her obsession with Shah Rukh Khan should make her a nominal Indian at the very least."

If that's all it takes to earn an Indian pass, she thinks, glancing across the table at Brandon, who is eating his meal with his hands. "My mom loved SRK too," she admits. "But the nineties version. You know, *Baazigar, Karan Arjun . . .*"

"*Dilwale Dulhania Le Jayenge*," Rick finishes.

Nadia pauses. "I think it had something to do with the shaggy hair."

"I thought it was the dopey grin?"

"Likely the combination."

"Totally iconic."

She sits back, intrigued by the shared coincidence. After some thought, she makes another attempt at the beet risotto. Once she gets past the mushy texture, its delicate sweetness surprises her. She eats quietly until the dinner plates are eventually swapped out with the night's dessert—a carob avocado mousse with fresh strawberries and mint. Lifting her dessert cup, almost like a toast, Martha encourages them to savor the final course more comfortably by the fireplace. As the others stand, Nadia recognizes the invitation as her cue to leave.

"I'm going to head back," she tells Rick. "But you're welcome to help yourself to my mousse," she offers, pointing to the dessert cup. Rick scrunches his nose.

"Hard pass on the faux chocolate. But thanks."

"Too trendy?"

"Sacrilegious." Rick grins.

As she heads toward the exit, she sees Lena near the door with Martha and Iris. Lowering her head, she tries to sneak past.

"You're not leaving, are you?" Lena asks, catching her on the way out.

Nadia presses her lips together and nods. "I'm feeling a little wiped out from that yoga class earlier."

"You know, if you're in need of an energy boost—" Iris pulls a Sucker from one of her space buns.

"It's nothing sleep can't probably fix. But thanks," Nadia says.

"It's just . . . we typically end with a nightly gratitude circle," Lena explains. "It's kind of a family tradition around here."

Nadia glances back at the others around the fireplace. She's had her fill of "family" time for the day. "Maybe I could just share mine with you now?" She thinks for a moment. "I'm grateful for solitude, real chocolate, and the short walk back to the yurt. How's that?"

"Great," Lena says, shaping her mouth into a smile. "Thank you for sharing."

After an awkward goodbye, Nadia exits the hive. Outside, the tension from her shoulders finally releases. She looks up at the night sky, its luminous texture punctuated with a single shooting star. She closes her eyes, wishing for a sense of calm, of hope, but when she opens them again, all she feels is drained and depleted. At some point she'll need to be comfortable enough in Lena's presence to speak to her without panicking. What it will take for that to happen, she has no idea. All she knows is it won't be happening tonight.

As Nadia ponders ways to overcome her discomfort, her thoughts are interrupted by a sound behind her. In the bushes outside the dwelling, something rustles in the leaves.

"Hello?" she calls, turning around. Shadows cast by moonlight snake through the trees, obscuring her vision. She takes a few steps forward before the rustling sounds again.

"Who's there?" Her heart races as she imagines the night creatures lurking in these mountains. Despite her uneasiness, she remembers her promise to Zeba to check in at the end of the night. She pulls out her phone and presses the "call" button, hoping for a signal and an increase in the odds of her making it to her room alive. Just as the call connects, the door of the hive opens behind her.

"Hello? Nadi?" her sister's voice crackles through the speaker.

Nadia braces herself, expecting to see Lena bounding through the doors, but instead, she sees Rick leaning over the railing.

"Hey," he calls, flinging a baton-shaped object in her direction. Instinctively she steps forward to catch it.

"Nadi, can you hear me?"

"In case you wanted to fill your temple with something more substantive."

She unclasps her hand to find a Snickers bar resting in her palm.

"Is everything okay?" Zeba asks.

Nadia pauses, staring at the candy bar. "I think I'll survive," she responds, just as the call disconnects. She looks back at Rick, unable to hide the faint smile that hovers about her lips.

"G'night." He grins before stepping back inside.

25

The next morning, when the sky is still cloaked in a misty gray, the sound of Lena vomiting jolts Nadia from her sleep. She lies awake, listening to a dry heaving from the bathroom before the toilet lid slams shut and flushes. When Lena finally comes out, she is clutching her stomach as she hunkers down in bed.

"I'm so sorry; I didn't mean to wake you," she whispers when she sees Nadia up. As Lena swipes the corners of her mouth with the sleeve of her robe, Nadia realizes this is the first time she has seen Lena look human. Maybe it's the tangle of unkempt hair or the fatigue in her eyes, but it causes something inside her to soften.

"Are you okay?" she asks, the concern in her own voice surprising her.

"Yeah," Lena says, laying her head against the head-board. She closes her eyes and remains still, the sound of her exhales shaky and uneven. "It must've been something I ate earlier."

Nadia rolls over. Despite the hollowness in her own stomach, she has no regrets skipping most of that dinner. Though the candy bar was hardly sufficient to carry her through the night, hunger seems a more manageable discomfort than whatever bug Lena has caught. While Lena tosses around in the bed beside her, Nadia drifts back into a restless sleep.

When she awakens next, Lena's alarm is blaring atop the dresser. Nadia groans, burying her face into the pillow. She has no idea what time it is, but the darkness behind the windows lets her know it is way too early.

"Sorry, sorry, sorry." Lena rushes out of the bathroom to silence her phone. "I totally forgot to turn this off." She is already dressed in high-waisted leggings and a cropped sweatshirt, her hair pulled back into a bouncy ponytail and skin aglow with its natural dewiness. If Nadia hadn't heard her spewing chunks into the toilet earlier, she never would've guessed that Lena had been sick. "The group planned a hike this morning through Eagle's Nest. Have you done that trail before?" She stands in front of the mirror, securing the flyaway hairs from her face.

"No," Nadia replies. Why would she have? If it weren't for Lena, she never would have been on this retreat in the first place.

"We set out at sunrise, if you're feeling up to it?"

"I don't do a sunrise anything unless I've consumed copious amounts of coffee first."

"I'm sure we can arrange that." Lena smiles.

The way she boldly lumps herself into that *we* irks Nadia, but she bites her tongue. Instead, she unplugs her phone from the nightstand and glances at the screen. Zero bars. "Is there any place I can make a decent phone call around here?"

"None of the yurts have cellular service," Lena says, speaking to Nadia's reflection through the mirror. "The main dwelling has some, but it's hit-or-miss. Your best bet would be to try and catch a signal in one of the open clearings off the trail."

"Great," Nadia mutters. She had no plans of joining Lena for the hike, but after getting disconnected last night, she still owes Zeba a phone call. Reluctantly, she hauls her tired limbs from the bed and slips out of her pajamas and into her polyester track suit. She splashes cold water onto her face and twists her hair back into a messy bun. Despite her urging Lena to go on without her, Lena insists that the two of them walk to the trailhead together, refusing to let up until Nadia acquiesces. When ready, Nadia tucks her phone into her fanny pack, and they step out into the crisp air.

The eastern sky glows a rosy pink and is fretted with little golden clouds. Nadia is too tired to notice its beauty.

Still prickly about having been disturbed from her sleep not once but twice by Lena, she walks in silence. Her reticence, however, does not discourage Lena from rambling endlessly about the cognitive effects of early-morning hikes. As she drones on about her hopes of renewing an "appreciation for Mother Nature and her bounties," Nadia busies herself by pressing every button on her phone, hoping somehow to reconnect the signal. Each attempt is met with a grayed-out notification: **No Service.**

"Shit," she gripes, feeling flustered.

"Take it as a sign," Lena says. "Perhaps this is the universe's way of helping us break free from the confines of our atomistic society."

Nadia rolls her eyes. "It's a sign that I'm too far out in the middle of fucking nowhere."

"Once we get out there and you see the sun rise over that summit, you'll forget all about—"

"This isn't a Cheryl Strayed memoir, Lena," Nadia interrupts. "Doing five A.M. hikes may be the experience you're seeking from all of this"—she waves her hands—"but some of us just want to be back at the yurt still in bed with better-connected Wi-Fi." She rubs her temples, flustered by her lack of control over the situation.

The dry leaves crunching beneath their hiking boots are the only sounds that fill the silence. They continue walking. Nadia thinks of Zeba and how disappointed she'd be that

Nadia isn't seizing this opportunity to extract as much information from Lena as possible. Considering that was the goal for this weekend, Nadia admits she hasn't been doing a great job. Taking a deep breath, she starts again, this time speaking in a less irate tone. "Look, I've got a lot on my mind right now. I'll probably feel better once I get some caffeine in me."

"I understand." Lena smiles. She waits a few minutes before turning to Nadia again. "I know we don't know each other well, but if you need someone to talk to . . ." She shrugs. "I've been told I'm a pretty good problem-solver."

Nadia laughs. She can't help it. If Lena knew how directly related she was to every single one of Nadia's problems, she'd probably rephrase that statement.

Lena remains quiet.

"I'm sorry," Nadia says, dabbing the corners of her eyes. "I meant . . . *thank you*," she says, fighting back the urge to laugh again.

"I wasn't trying to overstep," Lena explains. "It's just . . . retreats like this oftentimes draw people looking for an escape, a break from whatever it is they're dealing with back home."

"If that's true, what is it you're taking a break from?" Nadia ventures. She's not sure if shifting the focus will steer the conversation in the direction she hopes but deems it worth a try. She waits as Lena chews her lip, discernibly deliberating how much to disclose. "I mean, sure it's your job, but certainly these weekends offer a convenient break from other aspects of your life as well?"

"I guess," Lena says. She opens her mouth, stops, and then sighs. "I'm not so much taking a break, but it'd be nice to gain some clarity on my current relationship."

Bingo.

"My boyfriend and I have been struggling with this on-again, off-again relationship for months now."

Nadia cringes at Lena's use of the term *boyfriend*, but she presses further. "So where do you stand now? Is it on or off?"

"We're back on for now."

"I see," Nadia says, disappointed.

"But . . . I don't know." Lena shrugs, her voice thinning. "The constant guessing game is starting to wear on me— where do we stand? What are we? Where is this going? Not that I need a label, but *some* reassurance would be nice."

"Mmm." Nadia times out a pause before proceeding. "As someone who's had her share of relationship issues, I could offer some advice." She waits, testing Lena's response.

"Please," Lena replies. "I'd love your advice."

"Well, in my experience, those on-again, off-again relation-ships rarely find the stability needed to work out long-term. It depends on whether you believe what you have is worth the emotional roller coaster. And for most couples, it's not."

"Yeah," Lena says, thinking it over. "I'm not saying we don't have our issues. We do. But . . . the problem is I love him. I'm hoping this weekend apart might push him to take the next step."

Next step? Nadia isn't sure what exactly that entails, but this time, she can't bring herself to ask. Not after what she's just heard: Lena loves Aman. *Loves?* Nadia was under the impression that it was purely superficial, a run-of-the-mill fling, a meaningless affair. She never expected it to be deeper than that.

"I'm sorry. I didn't mean to get all heavy so early in the morning." Lena laughs, looking embarrassed. "It's not as doomed as it sounds. I swear. We'll figure it out. We always do."

Nadia swallows the pit at the base of her throat, struggling to quell the jealousy she feels. Though she didn't foresee Lena breaking it off with Aman based on one conversation, the confidence with which she expresses their ability to "figure it out" reignites Nadia's insecurities. What if her efforts are all in vain? The only person capable of pulling her back from this downward spiral she feels herself tumbling toward is Zeba. Connecting with her suddenly feels more vital than ever.

WHEN THEY ARRIVE at the trailhead, the rest of the "family" is already warming up in their hiking gear. Lena hurries over to greet Martha and the hike leader, leaving Nadia alone. Off to the side, she spots Rick doling out granola bars and coffee.

"Rough morning?" he remarks, offering a cup as she walks over.

"You have no idea," Nadia says, readily accepting. Though she doubts it's strong enough to improve her mood, she takes a sip anyway. Her mouth fills with bitterness. "This is coffee?" she asks, wrinkling her nose.

"Don't tell me you were expecting something fancier?"

"I was expecting passable."

Rick laughs, unoffended. "You sound like my mom. She's very particular about her coffee."

"In that case, don't ever serve this shit to her. She'd be so disappointed."

"It wouldn't be the first time." Rick winks.

Nadia spoons a heap of sugar into the cup, following it with creamer. "Not how I usually take it, but desperate times."

Rick grins.

She stuffs a granola bar into the pocket of her windbreaker and lifts her cup in a gesture of thanks. Behind her, the others gather around Thom, the hike leader—a chiseled-faced outdoorsman with a slicked-back ponytail and legs as sturdy as the sycamore trees surrounding them. Nadia walks over in time to catch the middle of Thom's spiel.

"—the terrain itself is fairly moderate, but I suggest you mentally prepare yourselves for that incline. There's some pretty steep switchbacks about a quarter of the way in; however, once we get to the cairn, we'll be less than a mile from the waterfall and then it's just a little over two miles back."

"And if you're not feeling quite as adventurous," Martha adds, "not to worry. There are less strenuous routes you can take instead. Lena and I will happily guide you on any of those trails; the good news is they still lead to the waterfall but may require a slightly longer trek."

Nadia plans to avoid whichever route Lena is on. She needs some distance to process everything that Lena has shared.

"Is there someplace to meditate on the trail?" Brandon asks.

"Oh, yes, like we did at our breath work session yesterday." Gary nods.

"Can we also squeeze in time to take photos? I'm really in need of some new content," Iris explains.

Thom responds to the group questions, while Martha and Lena map out alternate routes with the other guests. Nadia remains close to Thom's group. Though she's not the most outdoorsy person, she has hiked before, so she's not a total newbie, as some (like Patricia-with-a-soft-*C*, who is already capering down the footpath) might assume. Unlike the others, she has no interest in meditation, taking selfies, or even seeing the waterfall. The only "must" on her agenda is to reach a higher elevation and hopefully secure that crucial bar of coverage.

As Thom leads the group down the trail, Nadia follows behind, straggling a few feet to create some space between her and the others. She hopes that sticking to this low-key, fly-under-the-radar method will work to her advantage—at least until she spots one of the open clearings Lena mentioned and can discreetly slip away.

Large trees angle inward on both sides of the trail, creating a canopy of shade overhead. Blinking pockets of light steal through the leaves, reminding her of the last hike she and Aman took, the morning of her birthday. Memories of the two of them atop Inspiration Point, side by side as they soaked in the sunrise, spill into her mind. She had no idea the contentment she felt that day would be so short-lived. That everything she believed about Aman and their marriage would change so drastically in the weeks that followed. It feels like a lifetime has passed since. A deep sadness covers her, weighing her down with every step. But she pushes herself to continue.

When they reach Solstice Canyon, the trail splits into two divergent paths, one going north and the other east. Collectively, they decide to take a short break. The trees along the path have visibly thinned, and with the sun nearing the horizon, Nadia wipes the sweat from her forehead, wishing she had remembered to put on a hat or visor before she left.

"Once we turn this bend, the trail will flatten out a bit," she hears Thom say.

As Nadia rehydrates near a thicket of chaparral plants, Patricia-with-a-soft-*C* walks up beside her. "I hike this route every year, but these views never get old."

Nadia pulls out the granola bar from her jacket. She is not too keen to engage in idle chat and hopes that Patricia might grow bored and move on to someone else.

"That little oatmeal bar isn't going to give you much energy," Patricia remarks. "Here, have some of these." She holds out her hand, and cupped in the palm are what looks like rabbit droppings. "They're raisins. Go on, take a few. Trust me, once we get to the switchbacks, you're going to need every source of energy you can get."

Nadia reaches out and pinches a few raisins between her index finger and thumb.

"I dried them in my dehydrator," Patricia says as Nadia places them into her mouth. "My secret is I douse them in my home-brewed chardonnay first."

"Mmm," Nadia says, waiting for Patricia to turn away before she spits out the alcohol-sodden raisins in the sage-brush behind her. To rid her tongue of the acidic taste, she takes a large bite of granola bar, absently listening to

Patricia describe the various creations she's concocted in her dehydrator—most of which involve a disproportionate amount of liquor. Nadia looks out toward the deviating trail, waiting for Patricia to take a pause. "What's that way?" she finally asks, pointing eastward.

"If I remember correctly, some remnants of a burned lodge at the end of an open field. But unless you've trekked through overgrown brush before, it's quite a hassle compared to these paved, more shaded trails."

Her opinion, however, is lost on Nadia, who stops listening the moment she hears *open field*. Certain she'll be able to acquire a stronger signal from there, she decides to take her chances on the "hassles" Patricia warns against. If she can just steal away for a quick minute, check in with Zeba, and catch back up with the others, she doubts anyone will even notice her absence.

"All right, hikers. Let's keep it moving," Thom says, pulling his ponytail through the neck strap attached to his GPS tracker. "Patricia, why don't you lead the way to the switchbacks."

"Looks like my expertise is needed," Patricia says, wiping her wine-moistened palms against her bike shorts. She struts toward the front, using both arms to clear away any foliage or people in her path. "Coming through," she calls.

While they map out the route, Nadia finishes her granola bar. When the rest of the group starts moving north, she stuffs the wrapper into her pocket and stoops down, pretending to tie her shoelaces. Once the final hiker circles around the bend, she pulls her phone from her fanny pack and heads east, toward the opposite trail.

"NADI! I'M SO glad you called! I kept trying your phone last night, but it wasn't going through."

Even without clear audio, Nadia feels emotional at the sound of Zeba's voice. "Zeba, there's no reception anywhere in this whole damn place!" Her words come out rushed as she tries to catch her sister up on everything that's happened so far. "Everybody's eating sticks and leaves and discussing auras and shit. This morning I got woken up at five to go on a sunrise hike in the middle of these fucking mountains—"

"A sunrise hike . . . that sounds lovely!"

Lovely is not how Nadia would describe her morning, but there's no time to get into it. There's so much she and Zeba need to discuss, and she has no idea how long their connection will last.

"Tell me, what's going on with L?" Zeba asks. "How is the room situation working out?"

"Well, for one, she walks around in a towel. Her hair is always perfect; her skin is flawless up close. The woman literally has no pore. She probably doesn't even have stretch marks . . . not even on her *ass*!"

"Oh geez," Zeba mutters. "Has she said anything about Aman? Were you able to get any intel on their relationship?"

"She mentioned they've been struggling, and that she's still waiting for him to give her some reassurance."

Zeba is quiet for a moment. "It sounds like he hasn't fully committed to her yet . . . that's good news, right?"

"I suppose. But . . ." Nadia hesitates. "She also said that she loves him. I don't know. I got the impression that it's serious . . . at least from her end." When Zeba doesn't respond, she asks, "What if it's more than just a fling like we thought?"

"That would definitely complicate things," Zeba admits with a tone of disappointment. "Speaking of complicated, I wasn't going to say anything, but Aman called me last night after we got disconnected."

"What did he say?"

"Just that he's been trying to reach you but none of his messages have been going through. He kept asking if I knew where you were."

Although there's something satisfying about Aman possibly worrying about her, Nadia holds back from reading much into it, especially now that she knows more about his and Lena's relationship.

"To be honest, I didn't really know what to say."

"Did you tell him that I'm *here*? At this retreat?"

"No, of course not."

Nadia exhales. Across the field, a gulp of swallows take wing through the trees. As they scatter and speckle across the blue sky, a strange hush surrounds her. She presses the phone against her ear.

"I basically told him it wasn't my place to disclose that information. And if you had wanted him to know where you were, you would've said something to him in your text."

"Thank you for not saying anything," Nadia says. A faint rustle of leaves sounds behind her. The same uneasiness from last night returns. She turns to get a broader view of the field.

"I'm not sure it made any difference, though, because I had another missed call from him this morning . . ."

Nadia sucks in her breath, no longer listening. As her sister continues about Aman, a sudden movement flashes among the trees. Her voice catches in her throat. "Zeba," she murmurs.

"But now if you're saying his relationship with Lena is more serious than we thought, maybe I shouldn't pick up his calls at all—"

"*Zeba*," Nadia whispers again, keeping her voice low.

"—at least until you find out more. What do you think?"

"There's a *bear*."

"Nadi, I can barely hear you." Zeba's voice breaks up. "Do you think I should respond?"

Nadia takes a deep breath, trying to steady her voice. "Zeba. A bear. He's big. Standing right across from me." Her sentences are fragmented as she struggles to speak.

"What? Did you say *a bear*?! Where are you right now?" Zeba's panicked voice screeches through the phone. "Nadi, you have to get away! No. Wait. I think you're supposed to freeze. Or is that for a snake? Shit, I'm all mixed up! Listen, Nadi, don't do anything. Let me Google it first."

As Zeba rattles off random instructions from her search, Nadia's breathing becomes labored and uneven; she is unable to comprehend anything spoken on the other end. Zeba's words bleed together, forming a garbled, indecipherable noise muffled under the pounding of an elevated heartbeat. Her sister's voice fades into a hum. She stares across the field, her pulse drumming in her ears. Amid the bordering trees, not more than twenty yards from where she stands, a large bear with matted black fur and piercing dark eyes stares back at her. Anchored in place, she is unable to move.

It is not uncommon for an entire life to flash before one's eyes in the moments before a precarious situation. For Nadia, however, it is a rapid succession of carefully stowed memories. The smile flickering across Aman's face when she enters the reception hall in her carmine bridal lehenga. The warmth of his palm against her back as the real estate agent hands them keys to their "forever" home. His troubled expression when he sees the dark splotches on the inside of her panties. His listless body as she cries into his shoulders and the blankness in his eyes as the doctor explains why it didn't stick . . . again. As each memory flutters across her lids, the bear lifts its front leg and inches a step closer, shoulder blades jutting upward. Every muscle in Nadia's limbs goes numb at the sight. She squeezes her eyes shut, the cell phone in her hand dropping into the loose dirt beneath her feet.

A short distance away, a din of shouts ricochet across the field, the bellows disrupting the stillness in the air.

"Hey! Get out of here!

"Scram!

"I said leave! Shoo!"

Nadia opens her eyes just as the bear pauses midstep and turns its head in the direction of the racket.

"Get out of here! GO!" She sees Lena standing on the other side of the overgrown trail, arms flailing wildly as she shouts at the bear at the top of her lungs. *"Go away! Scram!"*

A few steps behind is Martha, along with Steph and Stacey, their eyes rounded into oversize disks. She sees Steph grab her daughter and cover her face. The bear lifts onto its hind legs, releasing a low growl from the bottom of its gut. For a moment, everything halts, time itself holding its breath. The bear drops gently to the ground. Almost as suddenly as it appeared, it scarpers through the field and vanishes into the trees.

Nadia, too shocked to move, remains still as Martha and the others rush to surround her. All she can do is blink as the questions come darting her way. *Are you hurt? Where is the rest of your group? Did you get lost? Are you okay?*

From the corner of her eyes, she sees Lena bent into the tall grass. Her tiny frame convulses violently as she vomits into the field. When she finally stands, her face is sallow, her dewy complexion hidden beneath a more pallid hue. The moment her eyes lock with Nadia's, the fatigue in her face is immediately supplanted by a genuine concern. *Are you okay?* she mouths.

Nadia nods, blinking back tears as the gravity of what Lena has just done suddenly dawns on her.

26

———————

"How is she?" she hears Rick ask at the door of their yurt as Lena ushers him inside. In his hands he balances two covered plates, a large bottle of water under his arm. "I brought some sustenance," he announces, setting both plates on the nightstand beside Nadia.

Nadia remains in bed, where she's been for the greater part of the day. Since returning from the hike, Lena has taken on the role of her caretaker, periodically checking in while she drifts in and out of sleep. Somehow, she even managed to borrow Quinn's external antenna to boost the cell reception in their room so Nadia could call Zeba back and let her know she's okay. Explaining to her sister that the woman responsible for destroying her life was the same one who ended up saving it was a conversation for which she had not been ready. Nor was she prepared for the kindness Lena has bestowed upon her since—all this to say, the resentment and anger she'd been harboring toward her was slowly chipping away and being replaced by something less hostile.

"I know you're not a fan of this food, but you still need to eat something," Rick says, uncovering a plate of brown rice nori rolls with a watermelon-radish and kale salad. Garnishing the salad are goat cheese and edible wildflowers. Nadia makes a face as she picks them off one at a time.

Across from her sits Lena, balancing the second plate of food on her crossed legs. She chews slowly, careful not to upset her fragile stomach.

"You've had quite the day, haven't you?" Rick says, peering at Nadia.

"Is it all anyone is talking about?" she asks, imagining the conversations happening back at the hive. Everyone, she assumes, has heard about her bear encounter at least a half dozen times. Embarrassed by the thought, she's thankful to be in the privacy of her room, away from the unending questions that await.

"Girl, soak it in. What happened to you is the most eventful thing that's come from this retreat since 2016."

"What happened in 2016?"

"The question is, what *didn't* happen in 2016?" Rick remarks, drawing out his response for added suspense. "But since you ask, one of the guests—a Ms. Sophie Willis—

made a huge brouhaha over what she believed was a Sasquatch sighting outside of yurt four."

"I heard about that!" Lena says. "It was a few years before I started at Purple Clover. Didn't they shut down the retreat because of how spooked everyone was?"

"Mm-hmm. Trust me, that's a story that'll outlive us all . . . in addition to yours now."

Nadia sighs, not exactly thrilled about her terrifying experience being casually shared and circulated among future retreat-goers.

"What's crazy is, I didn't even know these mountains had bears," Rick says. "We've been coming out here for years; I always assumed this location was free and clear of that kind of wildlife."

"I was talking to Thom earlier, and he said the grizzly population was eradicated decades ago; however, black bears are known to live in nearby mountain ranges, so the latter is likely what we encountered," Lena explains. "Even so, they're rarely, if ever, sighted, which means this morning was a total chance occurrence. Lucky us, huh?"

Nadia's not sure about that, but she does feel lucky that Lena was there. "I keep thinking of what might've happened if you hadn't shown up."

"I'm just glad that *that* was the alternate route we decided to take. It was the only reason we were able to get to you when we did."

"Hear, hear," Rick says, raising the water bottle. "I would've felt awful if the last thing I served you was that terrible coffee. Can you imagine having to live with that guilt?"

Nadia laughs. "My mom used to say the only thing worse than death is a bad cup of coffee . . . or chai, in her case. Sometimes these lessons just have to be learned the hard way."

"No kidding." Rick shakes his head.

While he and Lena chat, Nadia finds herself thinking about those final moments before she was rescued. There was a sense of recognition when she locked eyes with the bear. It lasted only a fleeting second, but she remembers it nonetheless—like the creature had appeared just for her. To convey a message of some sort. Irrational as it sounds, she can't shake the feeling that there might be a connection to her mom . . . She falls quiet, lost in thought as she considers the possibility.

"Hey," Lena says softly. "Are you okay?"

"Yeah." Nadia shakes her head, trying to rid herself of the emotions she's feeling.

"Are you sure?"

"It's just weird," she explains, still tucked deep into her thoughts. "I always believed that if I was ever in a life-and-death situation, my whole life would flash before my eyes.

But right before you showed up"—she looks at Lena—"the only memories I saw were of my husband. His was the only face I remembered."

"Is he . . . *dead*?" Rick asks, his expression so serious that Nadia can't help but smile.

"No," she says. "Although our marriage might be." She catches herself before divulging too much as her audience of two listens attentively.

"Is it something that can be fixed?"

Nadia turns to Lena, whose face is filled with such earnestness, with such an undeniable oblivion to any role she plays in her and Aman's failing marriage. She sighs. The more she thinks about it, the more difficult it is to maintain this image of Lena as some unscrupulous home-wrecker, when in truth, she's likely as unsuspecting of Aman's infidelity as Nadia herself had been just weeks ago. "Whether it can be fixed is beyond my control." Nadia pauses. "But I think the possibility of leaving things unresolved, without a chance to even work through our issues, is a fear I hadn't considered until today." She rubs the space between her temple and brows, unsure if her words make any sense. "It's complicated," she admits. "I guess I'm still in the midst of processing it all."

"I doubt I'm in a position to offer much advice, given my current relationship is the first serious one I've been in," Rick says, "but just the fact that you're feeling these things, maybe it's a sign that there still might be hope for you two."

"I agree," Lena says. "I feel like anything is worth fighting for as long as there's love. And it sounds like you still love him. A great deal."

Nadia falls quiet. Fixing her relationship with Aman requires that he end his with Lena. But how can she explain this? It was so much easier when she just hated her. "Maybe," she replies, hesitation in her voice. "But I think that's what makes it so hard. Even after everything, I still love him. I never stopped. And I probably always will."

27

After they eat, Rick and Lena invite Nadia to walk back with them for Shaman Osiri's evening lecture in the meditation dome. Feeling like she's experienced more than her fair share of retreat life, Nadia demurs. But they insist that fresh air will do her some good.

The geodesic dome sits on a hill above the hive. Its top half is covered entirely in triangular windows offering panoramic views of the constellations that light up the night sky. When they enter, Nadia is immediately besieged by the other guests. Each of them worried. Each of them wearing the same cloying smile.

"We're so glad you're okay!"

"How are you feeling?"

"Better," Nadia says.

"Imagine if you had been live," Iris muses. "You could've doubled . . . maybe even tripled your follower count."

"How close to the bear were you?" one of the Garys asks.

"Closer than us," Lena says. "And we couldn't have been more than fifty feet away."

"Could we lower our voices?" Steph asks, still visibly shaken by the experience. "I don't want to expose Stacey to any more emotional distress." She turns to her daughter, who is off in the corner meditating on her own. "Sweetie?" she calls. "Sweetie, how're you holding up?"

"Great!" Stacey smiles, her upper lip disappearing above her braces. "Everything's great, Mom."

"That's my girl."

"Whenever something out of the ordinary happens, I always ask two questions: Why me? And why now?" Brandon muses. He rubs his chin, deep in thought. "Do you think it might've sensed some deeper connection with you?"

"What do you mean?" Nadia says. Her earlier thought connecting the bear to her mom resurfaces, and she wonders if there might be something to it after all.

"You know, since bears are native to the Himalayan region, maybe the two of you share some kind of ancestral bond . . ."

Nadia shakes her head. Though she sincerely appreciates their concern—however misguided it may be—she's starting to feel embarrassed by their fixation on it. "It was a close call, but I'm fine now. Really."

"We're glad to hear that." The other Gary squeezes her shoulder, his relief apparent.

"Let's go say hello to Shaman Osiri," Rick whispers. He pulls her away, leading her to the center of the dome. Under the stars sits the shaman: a fragile-looking man with a gentle smile and dark, placid eyes encased in a nest of fine lines. His hair is long and parted, and he wears a robe-like garment over wide pants. Nadia is immediately drawn to his presence. Though he's been at the retreat all weekend, this is the first time she recalls seeing him. She's certain he has one of the rare private rooms, which explains why he hasn't been floating around like the others. Although she doesn't believe in these New Age–type practices, there is an air of serenity surrounding Osiri as she nears him. Following Rick's lead, she bows slightly as he clasps her hands in his.

"How wonderful of you to join us," he greets her. His voice is warm, rounded and comforting. Nadia smiles, feeling awkward. She waits as Rick and the shaman exchange a few words before taking a seat on one of the bamboo mats arranged around the center space. As the others quietly meditate, Nadia looks up at the stars. She can't remember ever seeing them so bright.

Osiri's lecture is reminiscent of her conversation with Lena that morning. No time is wasted: he delves deep into a discussion of different forms of stimuli and how overexposure may lead to internal stress. As he speaks of the importance of reconnecting with the natural world, it becomes clear these talks have had a profound impact on Lena's worldview. Nadia, however, is not quite as taken by the sentiments. Promising herself to look into it more, she glances around the dome.

"Where's Lena?" she whispers.

Rick shrugs, his attention on Osiri.

Unable to focus, Nadia waits for her to return. When she doesn't, she wonders if Lena has left early. Not wanting to cause a disruption, she waits until the group begins chanting before quietly excusing herself. She exits the dome and walks back to the yurt. Inside, it is quiet, but she notices the bathroom door is locked.

"Lena?" She knocks gently. "Are you in there?"

Apart from the sound of the toilet flushing, no answer comes from inside.

"I didn't see you at the dome, so I came back to check on you. Is everything okay?" She sits on the edge of Lena's bed, waiting for her to come out. When she finally does, it only takes a moment to recognize the greenish tint in her face. "You're pregnant." The words fly out of her mouth so matter-of-factly that she is almost surprised she didn't notice the signs sooner.

Lena sits down beside her, shoulders drooped forward.

"They said the morning sickness doesn't usually kick in until about six weeks—"

Nadia is stunned. *So, it's true.* "How long have you known?"

"About two weeks." The tremor in Lena's voice reveals that the news hasn't been any easier for her to digest.

"Have you told Am—your boyfriend?"

Lena shakes her head, looking directly at Nadia. "I haven't told anyone."

Nadia feels ill; she stands, her mind flashing to Aman. The back of her throat goes dry. "Why haven't you told him yet?" she asks, blinking. Though she hears herself talking, speaking the words, it feels as if they belong to someone else. Every part of her is someplace else, mentally and physically detached from her body, hovering somewhere in the ether above.

"I don't know," Lena says, straightening her back as the tension returns to her shoulders. "We just got back together, and I'm afraid of how he'll respond . . ." Her voice trails off. "If he doesn't take it well, I'll be devastated."

Nadia clears her throat. Unlike Lena, she can predict with certainty Aman's response. Being a father is the one thing he has always wanted, the one thing she could never give him . . . Painful as it is, she forces the words out. "I think you should tell him."

"But what if he isn't—"

"He still has a right to know. He's the father . . . and for what it's worth, he will be."

Lena thinks, her face filling with so much hope that Nadia looks away. "I guess I should do it while we still have this thing." She points to Quinn's external antenna sitting atop the dresser. But before she stands, she wraps her arms around Nadia first. "Thank you," she whispers.

Nadia squeezes her eyes, trying not to crumple. She watches Lena pick up her phone, listening for a voice on the other end. "I missed you too, babe," Nadia hears her say. Nadia steps into the bathroom and shuts the door. She turns the faucet all the way, feeling the pressure intensify at the base of her diaphragm. Leaning over the sink, she takes a deep breath. In then out. Her stomach contracts in short, rapid pulses as she tries not to hurl. She has yet to sort through her feelings about Lena's relationship with Aman. But to learn that she's pregnant too—with *his* child—it's more than she can bear. "Allahumma barik," she whispers. She covers her mouth and cries without restraint, her tears washing away any shred of hope she might've been carrying. Nadia grieves. She grieves for her and Aman. She grieves for what was lost. She grieves for what they once had, but mostly for what she knows for certain they'll never have again.

AFTER A NIGHT of staring into the darkness, lost in her thoughts, Nadia climbs out of bed and readies herself for a walk. No intentions were set. No expectations were levied. Yet somehow, she ends up back at the trailhead of Eagle's Nest, where only twenty-four hours prior she faced what she thought at the time was her greatest challenge. Now, as her mind replays everything that has occurred since, she contemplates how her plans for the weekend ended up so muddled. She came in hoping this retreat would lead her to the answers needed to save her marriage. Answers were given. But they were lent in such a way that makes a future for her and Aman almost impossible. Never had she expected such an irreversible blow. Never had she foreseen such a definite end to the relationship she cherished most.

More than sad, she is angry. Angry at her kismet, at Aman for making this decision without her, and at her mom for being right in her initial prediction. Though she questioned it before, she feels more certain than ever that the bear was a final attempt by her mom to rub her righteousness in her face. Before the rational part of her brain can kick in, Nadia heads down the trail.

It's the same route as yesterday, but it somehow feels different hiking it alone. The trees are denser. The chaparral is more overgrown. Perhaps it's the lack of sunlight or the murkiness of her internal state, but Nadia questions every turn and bend she passes. Relying on small markers—like an exposed tree root twisted across the footpath, or clusters of scarlet larkspurs sprouting along the trail, she hopes her memory is potent enough to keep her on track.

When she finally reaches Solstice Canyon, she pauses to catch her breath. Her anxiety returns the moment she glances eastward, reminded of where the trail in that direction leads. She forges ahead, however, ignoring the small knot that's formed in her chest. Goaded by rage, she makes her way to the open field, though her senses remain on high alert—every cracked twig, every sway of the distant trees causing her to jump with anticipation. She yearns to see the bear, to give it a piece of her mind, but she hopes the fear that might arise at its sight won't paralyze her from doing what she came to do.

Nadia peers across the field. As she silences her thoughts, subtle sounds of activity rise around her. The buzz of small insects. The distant chirps of birds flitting from branch to branch. The cool breeze licking through the leaves. But she hears something else: a rustling not far from where she stands.

"Who's there?" she calls, her voice small in the expansive space. But when she scans the perimeter of her surroundings, she detects no movement attached to the sound.

"I know you're here!"

The rustling sounds again, this time more distinct, but still she sees no signs of anything or anyone.

"You win, Ammi. You were right." Nadia waits, listening for a response. "Isn't that why you're here?"

From the trees, a group of birds take flight all at once, the branches on which they perched momentarily swaying before stilling. She holds her breath, but whatever she heard just moments ago seems to have vanished. A heaviness presses down on her.

"I said, you win! *You win!*" She closes her eyes and screams, her frustration echoing through the field. As its reverberation encloses the space around her, she drops to the ground, tears streaming down her face. "What more do you want from me?" A great hopelessness takes hold of her, grasping her in its clutches.

"It's over. Me and Aman. Just like you said," she chokes out between the sobs. "I failed. But you already expected that, didn't you?" Her forehead touches the ground as her body leans forward into sajdah. She realizes how long it has been since she last prayed. Her mom used to say the best time for dua was while prostrating since this was when one was closest to Allah. She squeezes her eyes. There is so much she wishes to say, to release from the depths of her heart, but she struggles to find the words. What dua can she make when what she wants no longer exists? As she contends with this reality, her thoughts are disrupted by another sound. From the fanny pack around her waist, her cell phone vibrates. She forgot that the signal was stronger near the field. Sitting up, she wipes her cheeks with the back of her hand

and unzips the pouch. Glowing on the phone screen, a text message flashes from Zeba.

> Nadi, where are you? I went to your yurt, and no one was there.

Nadia reads the message again. Zeba went to her yurt? Her sister isn't scheduled to pick her up for at least a few more hours. Why is she here so early? Standing up, Nadia brushes the dirt off her knees and glances around one final time. Everything within her view remains perfectly still. She feels foolish for coming out this way. How stupid it was of her to think it would make a difference. The bear is gone. And so is her mom. Neither is coming back. The only relief is in knowing that she'll soon be leaving this place. She's ready to go—even more now than at the start of the weekend.

WHEN SHE ARRIVES at her yurt, Nadia searches around. She finds a damp towel crumpled on Lena's bed next to a heap of clothes. No one is there. It appears Lena has already headed out for the final day's activities. The tension from her shoulders releases. Though she doesn't blame Lena for the bombshell that was dropped last night, she cannot bring herself to face her, given that the outcome of her news will undoubtedly upend everything in her own life. Not wanting to waste another minute, she grabs her things, wondering if Zeba might be waiting for her at the hive. She quickly zips her suitcase, which she never bothered fully unpacking, and does a final scan of the room before stepping out. A few feet from the yurt, she hears her name being called.

"Nadia! Over here!"

Rick walks toward her holding two cups. Despite how early it is, he looks energized and well rested as he struts forward with bright, eager eyes.

"I thought we could commemorate our final day with some coffee. Don't worry, I didn't make it this time."

"Thanks," Nadia says, taking one of the cups.

"Where are you off to so early?" he asks, glancing at her suitcase.

"I was headed to the hive."

"Great!" Rick grabs the luggage from her hand. "I'm going that way too." As they walk side by side, he chatters away like a songbird. "I ran into Lena before her morning session, and she said you weren't in the room when she left."

"I went for a walk."

His brows rise in surprise.

"I couldn't sleep," she explains. "I thought the fresh air might help clear my head."

"I'm impressed. After yesterday's scare, most people, I assume, would want to stay as far from nature as possible—but *you* are a lot more badass than I thought."

Nadia manages a smile, though she feels much less impressed with herself than Rick seems to be. If he knew her reasons for going out there, his assessment of her would shift.

"It's like Shaman Osiri said last night: nature is exponentially more powerful than we will ever be, but we can't allow our fear of it—both real and imagined—to keep us from reaping enjoyment from our surroundings . . ."

As Rick philosophizes, Nadia walks quietly, letting him believe that she's somehow been transformed by the shaman's words. It's far easier than expecting him—or anyone, really—to understand what she's feeling. All she knows is that after everything she's been forced to reckon with this weekend, the bear is the least of her concerns. When the hive finally comes into sight, she spots Zeba pacing in front of it.

"Zeba!" she calls, waving her arms. "That's my sister," she tells Rick as she takes her luggage from him and rushes ahead.

"I'll meet you back here in a few minutes," Rick calls as he heads toward the meditation dome.

When she reaches Zeba, Nadia immediately notices her agitation. Zeba's eyes flicker frantically, and the edges of her mouth are set in a hard line. "Nadi, where have you been? I've been looking all over for you." A deep frown creases between her brows.

"What's wrong? Is everything okay?"

"Everything is *not okay*." Zeba lowers her voice. "I needed to tell you—"

"Nadia?" The door of the dwelling opens. Aman steps outside.

Nadia's breath catches in her throat.

"What are you doing here?" She turns to Zeba; her heart races as she tries to make sense of what is happening. "Why is he here?"

"Let me explain," Aman says. "I've been trying to reach you. I know I shouldn't be here, Nadia, but we really need to talk."

"He showed up at my house this morning, refusing to leave unless I brought him to you," Zeba explains, the words spilling out faster than Nadia can process them. "I'm so sorry. Please don't be upset. I didn't know what else to do."

"Nadia, can you please hear me out?" Aman says, walking toward her. "Just give me a chance to explain—"

"I know she's pregnant."

"Who?" He draws to a halt.

"*L!* The woman you're cheating on me with. *Lena,*" she blurts, frustrated by Aman's continued charade. From beside her, she hears Zeba gasp. "You probably thought I wouldn't find out, but I already know. She's at this retreat too. In fact, we've been sharing a room all weekend, so whatever it is you came here to tell me, don't bother. There's nothing left to explain."

"I-I don't understand." Aman shakes his head. "Who's Lena? Nadia, what are you talking about?"

"Just stop it already!" Nadia cries. "Stop lying to me, Aman! The truth is out."

Aman gently takes her elbows, attempting to console her. "I don't want to lie to you, Nadia." His eyes sag downward. He looks as if he hasn't slept in weeks. "I'm tired of hiding the truth too. That's why I came here. To tell you everything—"

"Aman?"

Startled by the sound of another voice, the three of them turn.

"Hey . . ." Rick clears his throat. "Mind telling me why you're here?" He looks at Aman and then to Nadia, his face expressing the same confusion that bears on everyone else's.

"Eldrick?" Aman steps back. For a moment, no one says anything.

"I don't mean to interrupt whatever is happening here, but . . . how do you two know each other?" Rick asks, looking to Nadia for answers.

"Aman is my husband."

"Oh . . ." Rick sucks in a breath. His forehead puckers; a knowing regret washes over his face.

"But . . . how do you two . . . ?" Nadia's voice trails off, confounded, as Aman walks over to Rick and weaves his fingers into his. The two of them take a quick glance at each other before turning back to Nadia. "I don't understand." This time it's Nadia who stammers, her mouth twisting as she struggles to speak. "How do you and Rick . . . or *Eldrick*—" She stumbles on the first syllable of his name, her jaw dropping in recognition. "*EL*-drick . . . *EL* . . . you're L?" She draws back as the image of what is right in front of her finally sinks in.

"Nadi," Aman says softly, the inner corners of his brows pulling up with his sadness. He lifts the hand still intertwined with Rick's. "I never expected you to find out this way. I don't know what you must be thinking right now, but—"

"No. This can't. I-I . . ." Fragments drop from her mouth as she clutches the front of her body and backs away. "This can't be." Her eye catches Zeba's; devastation is written all over her sister's face. "I have to go . . . I have to go."

"Nadi," Zeba whispers, reaching out for her, but Nadia moves away. She brushes past Aman and Rick, tearing in the opposite direction toward the hills.

Despite the breeze that sweeps through the air, she feels as if she is suffocating. Her mom's words after that first meeting with Aman ring in her ears: *Think of me what you will. But I stand by what I said.* Did she know? Is this what she was trying to tell Nadia all those years ago? Is this the message she came back to convey?

Deeper and deeper, Nadia continues past the sharp spindly branches nicking her arms, pushing them aside until everything she once loved is far, far behind her.

28

"Can I join you?"

The spinning in Nadia's head has finally subsided when she turns around to see Aman standing behind her. Unsure how to respond, she waits as he lingers for a moment before taking a seat on an adjacent rock formation. Neither of them speaks; Nadia struggles to even meet his gaze. They stare straight ahead, quietly overlooking the vista.

"Nadia, I—" Aman's voice cracks. "I never wanted for any of this to unfold this way." He falters through his words, trying his best to articulate the remorse he feels. "I thought if I came here, I could try and explain . . . but there's nothing I can say to justify the hurt and pain and confusion you must feel."

Nadia wipes her cheek, his words causing her insides to ache.

"If you're not ready to speak to me—now or for a while—I understand. You have every reason to be disappointed by me. I just . . . I want you to know how sorry I am. *For everything.*"

Nadia turns away, shading herself from the sunlight overhead. The golden rays blend into the greenery contouring the hills in its soft haze. For a moment she wishes it were all a dream, one she could wake up from by simply snapping her eyes open. But it's not. Nothing can pull her from this reality or the tangle of questions surrounding their situation.

"How long have you and Rick . . ."

"We met last year," Aman explains. "It started off as just a friendship."

Nadia recalls the anniversary card, the photos of their celebration. She wonders when things changed for them and how it turned from a friendship to . . . something more.

"On a whim, I signed up for his class and we somehow struck up a conversation afterward. He knew I was married. He mentioned he had just gotten out of a relationship. We never planned for it to turn into anything . . . and for a long time it didn't." Aman pauses, visibly grieved by the hurt that has been caused. "Nadi, please believe me when I say I never wanted to hurt you."

"Were there others?"

"No," Aman says, looking firmly into her face. "In all the years we've been married, there was no one else."

"But before we married?"

He hesitates, grappling with the truth. "In med school," he finally says. "There was one other relationship. It ended right before we met."

It's the first time she's heard him speak of a former relationship, and in that moment, it dawns on her why. The past suddenly unravels as splinters of the dream she had the other night rush back to her. "Your parents knew, didn't they?" she says—the reason behind their sudden change of heart finally making sense.

Aman is quiet, his face gray.

As the words claw at the back of her throat, she forces herself to ask the one question she needs to know. "Is that the only reason you married me?"

Aman looks at her, his eyes full. "I married you because I loved you. I still do."

The sincerity in his voice pierces through her, but she questions its truth. How can he love both her and Rick? As much as she wants it to make sense, she can't reconcile two seemingly opposed things.

Sensing her doubt, Aman continues. "I won't pretend like these feelings just appeared out of nowhere. They've always been there somewhere underneath. But you and

I . . . everything we've shared over the years . . . it *was real.* All of it." He reaches out, clasping her hands tightly in his. She can feel his pulse palpitating through his palms. "We created a life together, and for a long time, Nadi, you were everything I needed. The two of us—we were happy. We really were." He drops his head, the warmth of his forehead radiating against the back of her hand. "I know it was unfair of me to not tell you, but part of me believed it was something I might be able to leave in the past . . ." He looks up, staring into her eyes. "But then I met Eldrick, and everything changed. He was never meant to be part of the plan, but he just showed up, and no matter how hard I tried to fight it, I couldn't prevent the past from reemerging as strongly as it did."

"Why didn't you just tell me?" Nadia whispers, overcome with emotion.

"I wanted to, but I was afraid," Aman explains. "I was afraid you wouldn't understand. I was afraid you'd think our whole marriage was a sham. I was afraid if you knew . . . you might stop loving me." His voice breaks as he turns away.

Nadia closes her eyes. Though Aman's fears are not unwarranted, she cannot imagine her love for him ceasing. Not then. Not now. Not even after everything that's come to light. As they sit in silence, listening to the wind stirring through the hills, the knot in her chest begins to loosen.

While there are still layers of pain and heartbreak to work through, the hope that's been driving her for the past few weeks finally begins to wane, releasing her from its burden by replacing itself with something less heavy.

From under Aman's grasp, she feels him squeeze her hand. Once. Twice. Although she's not sure where they go from here, there's a glimmer of clarity that she didn't have before. Perhaps it was possible for Aman to care for Rick while still cherishing the life they shared together. Just as it was possible for her mom to resent their father for leaving while continuing to long for him. One truth did not always cancel out another, and though it might not make perfect sense, things that mattered rarely did.

Nadia resists pulling her hand away. Instead, she takes a deep breath and squeezes Aman's hand back—once, twice, three times, each firmer than the last, just enough to let him know, in case he still doubted, that she loves him too.

29

Back at Zeba's house, Nadia shuts herself off in the spare bedroom at the end of the hall. The same space that she struggled to enter just one week prior is now where she feels herself most drawn. Curled up on the bed, Nadia breathes in the scents surrounding her, wishing more than anything she could summon them to life. Although her last attempt to connect with her mom fell short, the message she sent was received nonetheless.

Seeing Aman was not something Nadia was prepared for. Seeing him with Eldrick—even less so. The pain and grief of her loss is weightier than she imagined, but there is also a relief in the truth being out.

"How are you holding up?" Zeba asks, knocking at the door before opening it.

Nadia shrugs. "I've been better," she replies honestly.

Aside from the hurt and confusion, what she feels more than anything is an overwhelming sadness. Zeba climbs into bed beside her, wrapping her arms around Nadia's frame. For a moment, they hold each other, comforted by the reminder that neither is alone.

"Do you remember my nikkah?" Nadia asks.

"Like it was yesterday," Zeba replies. Though she cannot see her sister's face, Nadia feels her smile.

"I keep going back to that day—the flowers; the light from the masjid windows; Aman's voice when he repeated 'Qubool hai.'"

"It was a beautiful ceremony," Zeba says, but Nadia is lost in her own memories. She looks at her hands. The dent from her wedding band encircles her finger, and she runs her thumb over the empty space.

"Do you remember how swollen Ammi's face was the morning of? How red her eyes . . . like she had been crying all night." Nadia reflects on that day, struggling to verbalize her thoughts. "I didn't ask her what was wrong because I thought I knew." At the time, she assumed her mom's sadness had to do with their father. That Nadia's getting married to Aman reminded her of all she had lost. It grieved Nadia to witness this, but she pretended not to notice. Selfishly, she didn't want her day to be about *that*.

She turns around, facing her sister. "It wasn't about our

father, was it? She knew, Zeba. Maybe not everything, not the whole truth, but she knew he wasn't right for me. She knew we wouldn't last, didn't she?"

"Would it have made any difference?"

Nadia is silent. Their mom's hesitation only strengthened her decision. She was resolved to marry Aman in spite of her mom's disapproval. She loved Aman, yes. But it was also a chance to prove herself worthy—of Aman; of love. Nothing spoken, she knows deep down, could have changed her mind. Of that she is certain.

Zeba sits up, pressing her back against the headboard. "You and Ammi were alike in more ways than you knew."

"Both rejected by the men we married?" Nadia scoffs.

"You both *loved love.* And anyone who was lucky enough to be the object of that love received it in its purest form. Unconditionally."

Nadia's throat closes. She swallows back a lump.

"I think that's why she worried so much about you. She didn't want you to make the same mistakes she did."

"Too late for that." Nadia looks away, her eyes full. "But I guess she was used to being disappointed by me."

"Nadi, you were all she ever talked about. She asked about you constantly. It used to drive me crazy," Zeba admits, her brows pinched with sadness. "Sometimes it felt like nothing I did was ever enough . . . it was impossible to compete."

"With *me*?" Nadia can't imagine her sister vying for their mom's attention. How could that be? "Zeba, *you* were the favorite. The perfect daughter. If anyone was lacking, it was me. Especially after she got sick."

"Is that why you stopped coming over?"

It seems foolish, but she was jealous of Zeba, of the relationship she thought her sister and their mom had. Zeba was the one who made Ammi a grandmother. She gave her a son-in-law whom she adored. If anyone couldn't compete, it was Nadia. "I could never get it right when it came to her. But you . . . you always had everything under control. I just thought it was better if I didn't interfere."

Zeba's silence conveys how mistaken Nadia was.

"It was unfair to dump it all on you," Nadia admits. "I should've stepped up. I should've visited more. Especially in that final year when she was here with you." Nadia looks around, the memory of her mom so potent that it emanates from every corner. "I should've taken some of that load off you. But I was so caught up in my own insecurities, in my own visions of 'family' and my obsession to prove something, that I couldn't see beyond myself."

"It's okay, Nadi—"

"But it's not," she says. "I know I never said this to you, but thank you, Zeba, for everything you did. You sacrificed a lot to take care of her. It couldn't have been easy."

"No, it wasn't," Zeba says quietly. "But she was a good

grandmother. Noman and Alim loved having their nani around. And fortunately, Shoaib didn't mind."

"Either way, I should've been there for her—for you—like you've always been there for me." She reaches out, taking her sister's hand. "I'm sorry."

"I'm sorry, too."

"For what?"

"This whole situation with Aman. I know how badly you wanted to fix things . . ." Zeba's voice tapers off, her face expressing her disappointment. "I know how scared you were to end up like her."

"There are worse places to end up, remember?" Nadia says, wiping her cheek. She lays her head on her sister's lap as Zeba rubs small circles into her back. The loss of her partner, of her marriage, feels profound; however, Aman's willingness to share his truth gives her permission to unburden herself from the expectations she's been carrying as well. She and her mom might've been similar in many ways, but there was one difference that Zeba didn't account for. Unlike her mom, Nadia refuses to let this become her end. Unlike her mom, she recognizes this moment for what it is: an opportunity to let go.

30

Nadia stands at the kitchen counter, box of chocolates in hand, and looks out the window. From her vantage point, she sees a small hummingbird hovering over a potted petunia; its iridescent wings flicker rapidly as its thin beak osculates the brightly colored bloom. Almost a year has passed since the retreat—since the weekend that changed the trajectory of her life. In the time it took to heal her broken heart, the world has moved on, as it does.

She settles on a dark chocolate truffle sprinkled with toasted coconut, letting it melt into her mouth. Eyes closed, she savors its taste, grateful to be able to enjoy small pleasures again. After Aman moved out, she found herself in a dark fog, floating from room to empty room. She granted herself time to go through the various stages of grief, some lasting longer than others, before finally arriving at a place resembling acceptance. There is still much she needs to work through, but she no longer feels tethered to the past. Life, they say, is a balance of holding on and letting go. But the same applies to love, she has come to understand. Despite what others may think or say about her and Aman's divorce, she knows that her choice to let go does not make her weak. Nor does it mean she has failed or that her life is over. Sometimes things have to come undone in order to be put back together again; it's in the process of mending that one discovers what it means to be whole.

Stepping over a few half-packed boxes, Nadia stows the remaining chocolates in the fridge for later. As she shuts the door, her eyes fall upon a pair of photographs stuck onto the stainless exterior. The first is of Aman and Rick, barefoot, smiling on some beach in Bali. The second is from their wedding, moments before they proclaimed their commitment to each other. The joy in their expressions—encumbered by nothing other than a vow to live their lives in unabashed truth—brings a smile to Nadia's face each time she sees it.

She couldn't bring herself to attend the wedding, but she mailed them a gift with a personalized note in lieu of her presence. In the note, she offered her congratulations as well as some advice to Aman on gift-giving—namely staying away from Roombas until at least year five. She also packed in a few Snickers bars for Rick, knowing they'd be well appreciated. The finality of mailing this package offered her that last bit of closure. By extending her sincere wishes for their long and happy union, she made room for herself to take the steps needed to finally move forward, which is precisely what she's been doing since.

Her cell phone buzzes from the countertop. She reaches out to grab it.

"Hey, salaams," Zeba says on the other end. "Dinner will be ready at eight. Does that give you enough time?"

"Yeah," Nadia says, looking around the kitchen. "I'll just pack up a few more things before I head over."

"What time are the movers coming this weekend?"

"Saturday at noon. I should have everything done by then."

Zeba pauses. "How do you feel?"

"The same as the last one hundred times you've asked," Nadia teases. Despite her complaints, she is grateful for the check-ins. Selling the house was not an easy decision. Moving required her to come to terms with the reality of her situation: the life she had planned with Aman was over. Difficult as that was to swallow, now that she's arrived on the other side, the future doesn't feel quite as doomed.

"I know how special that place was to you," Zeba says.

"It was at one time. But I'm ready to start fresh. And the condo is much closer to you and the boys, which means I can come over more frequently."

"More frequently than now?"

Nadia smiles. "The bonus is I won't have to pretend to be in the neighborhood since I'll *already be in* the neighborhood."

"You were never good at pretending anyway."

Nadia laughs. "But to answer your question, I feel okay. In fact, I feel more than okay. I feel good. I feel really, *really good*." She stresses it because this time, she actually means it.

AS IT NEARS eight, the familiar roar of an engine sounds outside. Nadia locks up and ambles down the driveway, opening the door to the passenger side.

"Hi," Ali greets her from behind the wheel. His beard has grown in fully, sharpening the angles of his jaw.

"Hi." Nadia smiles, sliding into the seat. When she decided to list the house, her sister suggested she call Ali for advice on getting her finances in order. He was eager to help, patiently walking her through the process, making sure she felt neither rushed nor pressured. Nadia was surprised by his generosity, by how much she enjoyed the time they spent together. As their friendship evolved, so did their feelings for each other.

"Do Zeba and Shoaib know that I'm coming?"

Nadia shakes her head. "I thought we'd surprise them."

"What do you think they'll say?"

"I think it's safe to assume we'll get their seal of approval."

Ali smiles. He reaches over and takes her hand, his thumb brushing over her knuckles gently. As they pull out of the driveway, Nadia leans back, feeling lighter than she has in a very long time. Curving past the end of the street, she looks out just as they pass the sign for Cedar Heights, its bright, ornate welcome shrinking in the rearview mirror.

About the Author

Zara Raheem, author of the acclaimed novel *The Marriage Clock*, received her MFA from California State University, Long Beach. She is the recipient of the James I. Murashige Jr. Memorial Award in fiction and was selected as one of 2019's Harriet Williams Emerging Writers. She resides in Southern California where she teaches English and creative writing.